# Deep Deception 2

# Deep Deception 2

*Tina Brooks McKinney*

www.urbanbooks.net

Urban Books, LLC
78 East Industry Court
Deer Park, NY 11729

ISBN 13: 978-1-60162-322-5
ISBN 10: 1-60162-322-4

First Trade Paperback Printing November 2011
Printed in the United States of America

10 9 8 7 6

This is a u... ...ences or si...ilarities to actual e...ents real people, living, or dead, ...r to real locales ar...intended to give the novel a sens... of reality. Any si...larities ...aracters, places, and incide...ts is entirely coincidental.

Distributed by Kensington Publishing Corp.
Submit Wholesale Orders to:
Kensington Publishing Corp.
C/O Penguin Group (USA) Inc.
Attention: Order Processing
405 Murray Hill Parkway
East Rutherford, NJ 07073-2316
Phone: 1-800-526-0275
Fax: 1-800-227-9604

# ACKNOWLEDGMENTS

It's been an incredible year and I have so many people to thank for it. First and foremost is God. I thank Him for giving me the talent and courage to pursue my dreams. Second, I must thank my family. My husband, William, for his undying support. I could not do anything without his strong arms around me. When I told him I wanted to quit work, he took a deep breath and told me it was okay. That's love. If I had one wish, it would be that everyone so inclined could experience the love and support of a good man. He has enriched my life and I appreciate him. My parents, Ivor and Judy, my children, Shannan and Estrell, and my sister, Theresa, are also a part of my support system. Without their help, I wouldn't be here today. My wonderful in-laws—Nana, Mac, Meredith, Barry, Chelsea, thanks for a great Xmas!

As I've said before, the road to writing is rough. It's solitary and I miss my friends. Big shout out to my lifetime friends Angela Simpson, Valerie Chapman, Andrea Tanner. You ladies knew me FOREVER and even though we don't talk every week, I know if I call you will be there to listen. My Keough crew—Launa, Tami, Wanda, Lessia, Lilly, Muriel, Marie, Lois, April, and Cheryl. Thanks for the memories and the fun.

My editor, Oasis, and Jay much love to both of you as well. Oasis, you've been my ride or die and I love you, boo.

# Acknowledgments

My other brother from another mother, Ricardo Mosby. Thanks for believing in me and giving me your hand in friendship. Talisa Clark, my sister from another mother, who has more love in her pinky than most have in their entire body. Kelvin, I promised I'd never mention you in another book but what you did was low-down and dirty! Can't believe I called you a friend, silly me. God protects idiots and fools so I suspect you and the dingbat will be all right. Maceo Haywood and Marvin Meadows—my knights in shining armor still standing and showing me love after all this time. Dee Ford, Kim Floyd (sis, you know I love you to death), Patrice Harlson, Muriel Broomfield Murray, Lynel, Shontel, Monique Brewer, Barbara Morgan, my cousins, Donna, Laura, Tarcia, Michael, David, Kevin, Stevie, Crystal, Kim & Candi, Brenda, Denise, and Earl. I love you all. Okay, I've got to end this.

My writer friends, Nane Quartay, Sydney Malore, Peron Long, M.T. Pope, Dwyanne Birch, Lee Hayes, Terra Little, Shelly Halima, Jaize Brown, VJ Alexander, Gregory Townes, Dwayne Joseph, Darrien Lee, all of you continue to touch my soul and I thank you because this life is tough and we've survived the true test.

My Urban family, thank you Carl, Natalie, Brenda, Karen, and everyone else I forgot to mention. Here's to another successful year!

Last but certainly not least, the book clubs and some special presidents, Tina Hayes (Between Friends), Carla Walker (Queens Book Club), Sonya Ward, Books and Beignets BookClub, Rose Wright (Savvy Book Club), TC Royal and my RAWSISTAZ (special shout out to Tee for the love she's given all of us), Press & Curl, BMore Readers, and Lawd if I didn't name you, please charge it to my head and not my heart. I hope

# Acknowledgments

I can continue to entertain you. And to all the readers who e-mailed me and gave me the strength to continue. Thanks so much!

# CHAPTER ONE

## TILO ADAMS

I pointed my gun at Ramón, my lover's brother. His head blew apart when I pulled the trigger. The gunshot seemed to reverberate throughout the house even though I used a silencer. I didn't blink. It didn't bother me that he was only seventeen and hadn't had a chance to experience life. It didn't bother me that he hadn't even had a chance to experience busting a good nut let alone fish dive between some thighs. All that was irrelevant now. It didn't even bother me that he never had a chance to experience love. He knew too much about me so he had to die. He didn't even get the chance to question what was happening before I shot and killed him. Turning the gun on Victória, my lover, was harder than I thought it would be, but there was no way I could let her live. She knew too much.

Shock and fear paralyzed Victória but none of it mattered. Sadly, her fate was sealed the day she had met me. What she believed to be a chance meeting was actually contrived and part of a plan to get close to her family's fortune. Her feet appeared to be rooted to the floor as fear infused her body. I was good until I gazed into her eyes. These were the same eyes that looked at me as we lay naked in bed, face to face. Our lips locked in a passionate kiss. I pulled the trigger again. One bullet. Point-blank range. Her body folded onto the floor.

Warm droplets of blood sprinkled my face, searing my skin, and pierced my heart with finality. I could not bear to look so I averted my eyes and stepped over her. Part of me died when I did it—not because of love—but because this was the most heinous thing I'd ever done, and somehow I knew I'd never be the same as a result of it.

"Sorry, babe," I whispered. I felt like shit as I prepared to leave the house. Victória was the only person I'd allowed close to my heart. Part of me wanted to sneak down to the basement and take care of Moses, but I wasn't willing to risk it. The potential for it to backfire on me could ruin all of my carefully laid out plans. I would have to deal with Moses on an entirely different level. He would be on the lookout for me and wouldn't hesitate to pull the trigger if he saw me coming. I'd originally planned on splitting the money with him, but he showed me that he wasn't trustworthy and wasn't worth the risk.

Tucking the gun back into the waistband of my jeans, I quickly gathered the money-stuffed envelopes Ramón and Victória had been holding. My fingers shook as I pulled them free, and I felt like I was about to be sick. I was almost out the front door before I realized I hadn't wiped the place clean of my fingerprints. Inwardly, I wished things could have ended differently. But as I've always said: two tears in a bucket, fuck it. After thoroughly wiping everything I had touched, I quietly closed the door behind me.

Victória and Ramón had known where I lived and I wasn't sure if they'd shared this with Moses. Every time I met with him, I'd always meet him at his office or in his home. So it was essential to take them out of the equation before I could move on to the next step, which was getting far, far away. Deception had a way of unraveling at the most unlikely times.

# CHAPTER TWO

## TILO ADAMS

I looked back once more at the carnage I'd created then casually walked to my car. Fortunately for me, I didn't see anyone lurking on the street or peering out the window as I backed my car out into the street. Something, however, was wrong. The car was driving like a piece of shit.

"Fuck." I slammed my hand on the steering wheel in frustration. I pushed the car as far as I could and got out at a corner to take a look.

My front tire was flat. Not in need of a little air; it was flat as if someone had slashed it. "Ain't this a bitch," I groaned. The car was not drivable. Even if I tried to drive it, it would draw too much attention because it made this loud thumping sound every time the tire buckled. I looked around to see if anyone was watching me. Conspiracy theories bounced around in my head because I didn't believe the tire could have magically gone flat on its own. Moses, I knew he wasn't to be trusted.

I looked around again. If anyone was there, they were well hidden. I started sweating. I needed to get as far away from my car as possible.

"Think, bitch." I was mad because I hadn't thought about a contingency plan. "Fuck. What the hell am I gonna do?" I kept staring at the tire like it was going to fix itself. I looked back down the street to the Mendoza house for any signs of life. Time was not on my side. I had to get moving before Moses came out with Mr. Mendoza. My heart was racing. I ran back down the street and tossed the gun I took from Moses' office on the front lawn, under the bushes. I turned and raced back to my car.

I opened the car door and retrieved the envelopes and my duffel bag. I left my purse on the front seat and the keys in the ignition. I pulled out my switchblade, cut my palm, and smeared blood throughout the car. If everyone thought I was dead, they wouldn't put so much effort into finding me. I lowered the window all the way down and left the door open. I walked away from the car without looking back. Fleeing a crime scene on foot was not in my plans but I didn't have a choice. I stuffed the envelopes in my bag then pulled out a disposable phone.

"You've reached Nine-one-one, please hold."

I expected to be put on hold so it did not upset me when I heard that awful music most organizations used. People were so stupid, they dialed 911 for directions or because their cat was up a tree and wondered why they couldn't get a real person on the phone when they really needed it. I thought the music was chosen simply to irritate the fuck out of folks so they'd hang up and save their resources. I used the time to get farther away from the house and to get my story straight. Once I cleared a few more blocks, I stopped walking so I wouldn't be winded when the phone was finally answered.

"Nine-one-one. Is this an emergency?"

"I heard shots being fired. It sounded like it was right next door. Please hurry . . . Someone may have been hurt." My voice was shaky and my shoulder hurt like hell from carrying the heavy duffel bag, but I hoped it added credibility to my call.

"Your name and address?" The dispatcher sounded as if she was reading from a script.

"Do I have to give my name? I don't want to get involved."

"Address?"

It was a trick question but it didn't matter. I gave them the address of the house next door to the Mendozas.

"Good luck with that," I said to myself after I ended the call and flipped the phone in the gutter. Even if I hadn't thrown the phone into the gutter, there was no way it could have been traced back to me unless I fucked up and got caught holding it. Whoever invented the disposable phone was a genius. Every crook in the country should've been on their knees thanking them.

"Adios, motherfucker!" I was about to get ghost.

# CHAPTER THREE

## GREG CARTER

Two Atlanta police officers stood outside of a Tudor house with their Glocks drawn.

"What are you waiting for? Kick the bitch in." Rome Watson was eager to get into some shit.

I said, "I'm waiting for the shift commander to give the okay."

"Fuck that. The call said shots were fired. Do you want a death on your hands?"

Rome could tell I was getting antsy, but I liked to err on the side of caution. He had no idea what was on the other side of the door waiting for us.

"Let's wait for backup," I nervously replied.

"While you're playing with your dick, I'm going in." Rome took two steps back and kicked the wooden door squarely in the middle.

"Son of a bitch," I mumbled. His actions left me no choice but to crouch down in a defensive posture and hope for the best. "Shit!" I exhaled the breath I'd been holding. I was convinced that Rome was one crazy motherfucker as I followed him into the darkened foyer.

"Police," Rome yelled.

"You're supposed to yell 'police' before you kick in the fucking door, you dickhead." We were committing all types of violations in protocol as we proceeded through the house; however, we were in now and had no choice but to proceed. "You better be right, nigga, 'cause if you're wrong, I'm singing like Jaheim on your ass."

"Aren't you sick of being the little puppy that sits on the porch? Come on out and play with the big dogs, nigga!" Rome laughed.

He was riding on an adrenaline high, but I did not share his rush. I was scared as all outdoors and wanted nothing more than to get in my squad car and wait for backup. I followed Rome while sweeping the room with my keen eyes for signs of danger. Anticipation caused my heart to beat faster. We cleared the small foyer and Rome motioned for me to go upstairs while he entered the living room.

Upstairs? Why the hell did I have to go upstairs? Shit! I didn't want to be in the damn house in the first place, so I damn sure didn't want to check out the upstairs. Part of me resented the fact that he took the lead, but the other half of me was relieved. I was a stickler for rules; we were breaking all of them. We should have been back at the station clocking out but Rome wanted to play super cop.

We were rookies, straight out of the police academy and ill prepared to be handling anything other than routine traffic stops, but Rome was eager to get his feet wet and my dumb ass was following him. I took the stairs slowly, dreading each step.

"Focus, Greg," Rome hissed and pointed at me as I mounted the stairs. He was right; my mind was all over the place. That could put both of us in jeopardy. We were knee-deep in shit and there was no turning back. I crouched down even lower as I edged my way up the stairs, constantly looking back. Rome had entered the living room and was soon out of sight.

Rome's deep voice said, "Get on your knees and make like you're touching the ceiling with your hands."

I had no clue who he was talking to. I was tempted to rush back down the stairs but that could also prove to be dangerous since I had no clue what I was going to find in the bedrooms above. My senses were heightened as I stepped onto the landing. Moving as quickly as I could under the circumstances, I was relieved to find the landing empty. I desperately wanted to call for backup, but I was afraid to take my attention away from the bedrooms. I searched each of the three rooms and was happy to find them empty.

"Clear," I shouted as I made my way down the stairs. I waited to hear Rome give the all clear shout but it never came. I moved a tad bit faster just to make sure he didn't need any assistance. I stepped over the dead body of a teenage boy, and a beautiful woman lay beside him. They were both covered in blood.

Rome said, "She's got a pulse. Call it in while I check the basement." He quickly moved toward the basement door. His face was flushed red and sweat was rolling down in his eyes.

"Don't you want to wait for backup?" My voice was a little higher than its normal baritone. I coughed, hoping Rome didn't notice the nervousness that was evident in my voice. My hands trembled. I'd never been around a dead body before.

"Why? If the perp is still in the house, we have to catch him. Get an ambulance before the bitch dies," he shouted as he opened the door and started down the basement stairs. If he noticed my hesitation to move, he didn't mention it. It was too much; I couldn't take it anymore. Blood was all over. I stumbled back. There was no way I could stay in this room. I didn't care if Jesus Christ Himself was in here. I rushed out the front door to keep from vomiting all over the floor and contaminating the crime scene. For the first time since graduating at the top of my class, I had second thoughts about my career choice.

I made the call but I didn't bother going back in the house. I was done. I waited outside for the paramedics to arrive. I was standing next to the squad car when Rome came out the front door.

He gave me a hard look. "Damn, you just left a brother hanging and shit."

I couldn't tell whether Rome was joking or if he was actually angry. Truth be told, I couldn't give a hairy tit if he was. I didn't tell his ass to rush down those stairs, and I damn sure didn't tell him to kick down the fucking door. "We'll be lucky if they don't kick our black asses out of the department or worse yet, turn us into meter maids." I was angry, but not necessarily at Rome. I was pissed off at myself for wasting the last six months of my life.

"Negro, please. We responded to a call and we were the closest unit to the scene. The way I see it, we should get a promotion for it."

I could tell he was feeling particularly proud of himself—that only made me madder. "Yeah, whatever." I wanted to get away from the scene before our sergeant arrived and read us the riot act. The sergeant hated cockiness, and he would've burst a blood vessel if he got one look at Rome strutting around like the only rooster in the barnyard.

"Did the chick make it?" Rome asked.

"Uh . . . I don't know. I couldn't get close to her."

Rome's look told me he was disgusted with me. I was glad that he didn't use the moment to make fun of me. I was beating on myself badly enough without any help from him.

"Let's get back to the station. I got a shell casing from the living room floor. I want to get the guys in the lab to run ballistics on it to see what we can find out."

"Rome, this is a crime scene. You should have left the casing for the detectives." I thought for a moment. "The paramedics haven't even gotten here yet."

"Oh, now you want to remember our training?" His look of contempt said it all. He stood in front of the car as if he was about to let the whole world know what a coward I was.

"What the fuck is that supposed to mean?" I bluffed, hoping he would leave me alone.

"It means your punk ass choked the fuck up as soon as we got in that bitch." Rome was a bigmouth fucker and I couldn't stand his ass.

"Fuck you. If your ass winds up in the unemployment line, I won't be standing behind you." I got into the car and slammed the door. As far as I was concerned, he could do whatever the fuck he wanted. I just wanted to get away from the house, which was sure to be the source of many bad dreams for me.

# CHAPTER FOUR

## CARLOS MENDOZA

It had been a long time since I'd visited the United States, so quite naturally I was feeling a little uneasy about it. It seemed like I walked into a different world. I got off the plane in Atlanta and wandered through the maze of Hartsfield-Jackson Airport to the baggage claim with one thought on my mind: revenge.

I had received a letter from a woman named Tilo Adams. She claimed that my brother, Monte, was responsible for the death of my wife. I did what needed to be done and headed for the States. When I boarded the plane in Bogotá, Colombia, I had no idea what I would be walking into, but I intended to get to the bottom of it.

During the plane ride, I had plenty of time to reflect on where I had gone wrong. I thought Monte was my confidant but turns out he was a snake. Every time I wanted to quit the business and go to Atlanta to be with my family, he persuaded me to stay. In fact, Monte volunteered to leave our home in Colombia and move to Atlanta so he could keep an eye on my family for me while I continued the business. To me, short of being there myself, he was the perfect surrogate. He was the last living member of my immediate family, and I told him everything and he used it against me.

Unlike me, Monte embraced the American ways of dress and was more flashy than I. Although we were brought up with the same set of values, while I was making money, he'd obviously made a deal with the devil and ultimately put my family in danger.

My heart was heavy. I could not believe my own brother had betrayed me in such a fashion. But what surprised me the most was that he'd done it right under my nose. I had no idea he was wheeling and dealing and using me and my family to do it.

I gathered my luggage and went to find the driver I had hired to chauffeur me around the city. In all my years I never learned to drive. To me it didn't make sense because everywhere I ever needed to go was within walking distance. However, this was going to have to change if I intended to make Atlanta my home.

Verónica looked like a beautiful angel. She slept soundly in her hospital bed, almost like she had been drugged. When they had directed me to the maternity ward I thought it was a mistake. I knew I had messed up and missed out on my children's lives but I never imagined how much. Even if I wanted to get mad, I could only get mad at myself. There were so many times when I could have come to visit, but, over time, it became easier for me to stay in Colombia. But that was going to change. I leaned over her bed and kissed Verónica's forehead. I never knew it would feel so good to touch my oldest daughter after so long. I whispered in her ear, "I love you, my child, I hope you know it. Please forgive me for being away. I will never leave you again. And, I will rebuild our family, starting by avenging your mother's death." I left her room on a mission.

It took less than twenty minutes for my driver to drive me across town to Private Investigator Moses Ramsey's office. It was an elegant brick building on Peachtree Street. I took a deep breath and knocked on the door.

"Who is it?" a man's voice yelled from inside, then he snatched the door open like he was pissed about something. "What!"

I stepped back some and prepared myself to fight if it came to that. His unprofessional manner caught me by surprise and put me on guard. "Are you Mr. Ramsey?"

"Son of a bitch—"

"I beg your pardon." I frowned at him over my horn-rimmed glasses.

"Uh . . . I'm sorry. Are you Mr. Mendoza?"

"How did you know?"

He just stared at me.

I said, "I received a letter from this woman named Tilo. She said my children were in danger. She told me Verónica was in the hospital so I stopped by to see her before I came."

"Verónica?" He sounded like he'd just called a dead person's name. For some reason, he all of a sudden looked worse. He got his bearings and said, "So what can I do for you?"

"I want you to find that woman Tilo. She obviously knows what happened to my family and I need to know what has been going on." I paused. "If I find out that she was involved, she will have to pay," I vehemently declared.

# CHAPTER FIVE

## MOSES RAMSEY

He sat back in the chair, adjusting his thick glasses on his face. For a Latino, he was pale. And with his glasses he almost looked Asian. I searched his face, but he bore little resemblance to his daughters. He did not even look like Ramón, as far as I could tell.

"I know how you must be feeling but I'm not sure that going after Tilo is a wise idea."

"If she was involved, that woman has to be punished. If you're not going to help me, I'll find someone else who will."

We sat in silence for a few seconds as I contemplated his request. Mr. Mendoza scared me when he mentioned Verónica. I needed to find out how much he knew. His offer had its pros and cons. On the pro side, Mr. Mendoza's job offer would provide me with a valid excuse for pursuing Tilo. On the flip side, Mr. Mendoza would expect progress reports, and I wasn't inclined to share much information with him until I knew which side he was playing for. The other con was if I didn't accept his offer, he may hire someone else who would unravel the mystery of Tilo's disappearance and my involvement with her. Accepting Mr. Mendoza's offer became a no-brainer.

I said, "Mr. Mendoza, the letter you showed me was postmarked before the death of your brother, Monte.

This makes me think she might be involved in his death. Your brother came to me posing as you and since we'd never met, I believed him." If he was surprised by what I'd said he did not show it. "He told me about some missing bonds and money that was never found. Chances are if you find Tilo she will have it, but you will probably have to turn that money over to the Feds. Are you okay with that?"

"That's bullshit and you know it. The Feds know nothing about it, and I don't care about the money. I want the bitch to pay for whatever her involvement was in my family's discomfort. If you recover any of the money or the bonds, keep it. Consider it a bonus, in addition to your fee for finding a missing person."

"Mr. Mendoza, finding Tilo is not going to be easy. Nine times out of ten she has already fled the States, so I may be required to travel out of the country."

"I'm well aware of that. Just draw up the agreement so you can get started." He pushed his glasses back up on his nose. He stood up, indicating that our meeting was over.

# CHAPTER SIX

## CARLOS MENDOZA

*Two Weeks Later*

I was nervous as I rang the bell. I didn't know what I would do if the door was slammed in my face. My heart was leaping around in my chest as if it were trying to get out. I wasn't prepared for the woman who answered the door. Stunned. I stepped back. For some stupid reason, I wasn't expecting an adult to answer, I expected to see the little girl I remembered. I knew she was grown, I saw it for myself at the hospital, but to me, she would always be my little girl.

"Hello, Padre," Verónica said.

There was little warmth in her voice. Given the circumstances, it wasn't a surprise. Tears welled up in my eyes. However, I brought this situation on myself and there was no one left to blame. How was I ever going to make them understand that I never meant to hurt them? That was the question I'd been contemplating for the last two weeks, the one I tried to answer before I showed up on her doorstep.

"Verónica. It's been a long time." What a lame-ass thing to say. If I could kick myself in the ass, I would have. My hands trembled and I almost dropped my suitcase. I scanned her face, and I could not help but to admire how beautiful she was. With the exception of her eyes, she was the spitting image of her mother, Alelina.

"Yes, it has been. Are you going to come in?" She opened her door wider and I walked into her home, humbled.

I was ashamed of myself for staying away so long. I stood in her living room clutching my bag and feeling like a complete jerk. My suitcase became a lifeline of sorts. It was the only familiar thing in the room, although I really wanted to hug my oldest child. She was no longer a child; she was a woman with enough reasons to hate me for the rest of my life, for all the lies.

"You can put your bag down over there." She pointed to a corner that I wanted to stand in myself.

I couldn't think of anything to say, so I continued to stand there with my head down.

"Can I get you something to eat or drink?" To her credit, she was trying to make it easier than it should have been. If her nerves were fucking with her like mine were, she didn't show it.

"No, I'm fine. I'm glad to be here. You are so beautiful." All my sentiments ran together. She jumped as if startled by my compliment.

"Uh, thank you. You, you look the same, except maybe for a little gray in your hair."

I smiled. At least she remembered me. She sat down on the sofa, and I finally relinquished the death grip on my suitcase and sat down beside her. She patted my hand. It wasn't the hug I craved, but at least she didn't smack the hell out of me. Freely, I cried. It was a start.

"Padre, don't. It is what it is. There is no way to change it; we just have to figure out where we go from here."

When did she become the grown-up and I the child?

"It's so much that I don't understand," I said, feeling like I had broken my children's hearts.

"Well, Victória and I have a bunch of questions for you as well, but why don't we wait to talk about them when we are all together?"

"What of Ramón, where is he?" I looked around the room, hoping to see him peering at me from around a corner or something.

Her cool veneer slipped. I should've known it was bad when Verónica started to cry. I wiped my own eyes and moved to hug her. Finally an opportunity to be supportive.

"Padre, I couldn't tell you this over the phone because I'm still trying to deal with it myself . . . Ramón is dead. The same woman who sent you a letter killed him in cold blood."

I pushed her away from me and jumped off the sofa. "I . . . uh . . . wait . . . oh Jesus." I fell to my knees. My heart felt like it was being ripped from my chest. My stomach hurt and I couldn't seem to get enough air in my lungs. I gasped as I tried to get words out of my mouth. "She killed my son? Oh God no!" It was a punishment. I knew in my heart that God was finally making me pay for all the deception and the lies.

"I'm sorry, Padre." Verónica lifted me off the floor.

I was trembling and I couldn't stop. So much . . . so fast. First my wife, my brother, and now this. Ramón shouldn't have had to pay for my sins. She allowed me the time I needed to get myself together.

"Cold blood, what does it mean?"

"It means there was no reason to kill him. The police said she shot him at close range. Since there was no apparent sign of struggle, I can only assume she shocked both of them."

"But why?" I paused. What did she mean? Both of them? Ramón was the third son I'd lost. It felt as if my heart were breaking into a million pieces. I loved my daughters with all my heart, but my sons held a sacred place in my heart. They were in charge of continuing the family bloodline.

"She also tried to kill Victória."

Both of my children? I was too distraught to put the pieces of the puzzle together. I noticed Victória's absence, but I assumed she didn't want to see me or she was otherwise busy.

"What? Where is she?" I looked around the house, expecting her to walk into the room from the kitchen. This was further confirmation that I had fucked up as a parent and as a husband. It was my job to keep my family safe and I failed. My head felt like it was going to explode; it was so heavy I could barely lift it.

"She's in the hospital but she's in a coma. We are hopeful she'll pull through," Verónica said.

"We? Who is we?" Either she was not making sense or I'd missed some of the conversation.

"My husband and I."

I did a double take. My eldest daughter married? How could I have been so far out of the loop? "You're married? When did this happen?" I was too confused and hurt to get mad. Tilo's letter told me Verónica was in the hospital but it obviously left out many other details. I was getting exactly what I deserved for not having an active part in their lives. I stood up; the walls felt like they were closing in on me.

Verónica wore a look of compassion and understanding on her face.

"I can't do this right now. It's too much." I paced back and forth while she silently watched me. "I'm sorry. I can't do this." I walked toward the door.

"Padre, if you leave now, don't come back."

It wasn't a threat. I heard it in her voice. She was forcing me to deal with too many emotions at one time.

I'd spent the last twenty years trying to block them out in order to keep them safe. Now she was basically telling me all my efforts were in vain because at the end of the day, I failed them.

I screamed at her, "What do you expect me to do?" I didn't mean to yell, I just felt so helpless. I didn't know this woman who stood behind me, but I could tell she wasn't kidding.

"I expect you to sit down and have a real dialogue with me. It's time to put the deception and lies behind us so we can move forward. It's too late for the past, but we can definitely work on the future."

I was torn. I didn't want to admit to the past. But unless I wanted to go through the rest of my life alone, I had no choice but to come back and take my punishment like a man. I was defeated. "Where do we begin?"

"Padre, before we go into all that, there are a lot of things I need to know. For example, is it true you and Madre both speak fluently in several languages? If so, how come we never knew this?"

Shamed again. I felt like she was beating me about the head for all my transgressions. We kept a lot of secrets when we lived in Colombia and things didn't get better when the family moved to Atlanta. I wanted to tell her everything but there were still some things that they didn't need to know, even after all this time had passed. I was only going to tell her as much as she needed to know. The rest I would take to my grave.

"I know I owe you some answers, but can we go see Victória first? I'd rather explain everything to both of you so I only have to go through this once."

"I can respect that. But she's still in a coma. The hospital said they would call if her situation changed." Verónica stopped talking and cocked her head.

I heard my grandchild crying somewhere in the house. Her eyes were trained on the ceiling, and I followed her gaze and smiled.

"I'll be right back." She rushed up the stairs before I could say anything. I found out about the baby when I went to the hospital but I didn't let her know I was there.

Verónica came down the stairs carrying a small baby wrapped in a blue blanket. She might have forgotten all about me as she went about caring for her child. I could hear her moving about the kitchen. I assumed she was fixing the baby's bottle. She was gone for a long time but she finally rejoined me.

"Sorry about that, your grandson is very demanding." She was beaming with pride, but she also looked nervous.

I, on the other hand, was trying to act surprised, but my emotions were raw. "How old is he?" It seemed like the appropriate question to ask.

"Four weeks, he was such a tiny baby he had to stay in the hospital until he got his weight up and he's gained four pounds since we've been home," she answered proudly.

Four weeks? I shook my head as anger fused through my body. My wife had damn near a year to tell me Verónica was pregnant and she hadn't said a mumbling word. My brother had to have known as well, and that was the hardest pill to swallow because he knew how much I had cried over my sons. He knew how hard it was for me to let my surviving son leave Colombia.

"Huh? Did you say something?" She didn't even look up. Her eyes were bonded with her baby.

"I questioned why your mother didn't tell me before now."

She looked at me, then quickly looked away, but not before I saw the distrust in her eyes. "Padre, we weren't sure how you'd react."

I jumped up off the sofa and started pacing the living room. "And you thought I'd react better learning this way?"

"Keep your voice down. I'm trying to get Li'l Moses to go back to sleep so we can finish our conversation," she warned.

I was walking a thin line. I wanted to forge a relationship with my daughter, but I was so angry I just wanted to punch something. "So, if all of this hadn't happened, I probably would've never known about your child, right? Is that what you are telling me?" I could not believe what was happening. Just thinking my family would go to such lengths to keep a secret hurt me to my heart, but I couldn't throw stones. Her mother and I had done the exact same thing so I couldn't really be mad.

I pushed my anger aside. "Never mind, don't answer that."

# CHAPTER SEVEN

## CARLOS MENDOZA

The front door was swung open, then I heard a deep voice, but the speaker's face was hidden from me.

"Honey, I'm home," the voice called out.

I was anxious to meet the man my daughter married. I heard a loud crash upstairs and the pounding of feet coming down the stairs.

"Verónica, is everything okay?" I came out of the living room and walked right into Moses.

His briefcase was on the counter and he was going through the mail. At first I thought he was following me, but I ruled out that thought because he was too comfortable. He was going through the mail like he had a vested interest. Then I remembered what Verónica had called the baby.

Moses looked up from the mail, surprise written all over his face. "Carlos, I . . . Shit."

My mind refused to connect the dots, even though the pieces were right in front of my face. "What . . . Why?" I was too stunned to get mad yet. I was still trying to get over the changes in my family that I didn't immediately understand what I was seeing.

Verónica rushed down the stairs so fast, I feared she would fall. "Padre, uh . . ." Verónica's eyes flashed from me to Moses as tears shined brightly in her eyes.

"Careful," I shouted. But that wasn't what I wanted to say. Looking back at Moses the pieces finally fit together. Moses and my daughter. I scowled at Moses. I was angry, but I was going to deal with that motherfucker later.

Moses stood next to my daughter, and even if I wanted to deny what was right in front of me, I couldn't. The question was how was it all going to play out.

"Who the fuck is this man and, more important, why does he have a key to your house?" With feigned ignorance, I measured my words carefully. I didn't want to intimidate Moses into exposing our previous conversation.

"Keep your voice down," Verónica admonished. Raw emotions flashed across Verónica's face, and I could tell she was upset but determined to defend her position. "Padre, wow, this is such bad timing. Can we all please go into the living room?"

"Fine." I immediately regretted consulting with Moses, and I wanted to punch him in the face for keeping the truth from me. He had every opportunity to tell me that he was involved with my daughter the moment he realized who I was.

Moses shifted from foot to foot as if he was uncertain as to whether or not he was going to follow us into the living room, but he came anyway and sat next to Verónica.

"Padre, I told you I was married. This is Moses . . . my husband."

"Are you kidding me?" I shouted. Outraged, I leaped up off the sofa. Visions of them having sex made my blood boil. *How the fuck could Moses not tell me that? Why him? This motherfucker has some explaining to do.*

"No, I'm her husband," Moses confirmed.

They grabbed hands and I had to physically force myself to unclench my fists. I didn't know what upset me the most, the fact that she was married with a child or that she married a black man. And, more important, this *particular* black man. There were so many thoughts running through my head, I couldn't speak for a moment.

Verónica said, "Padre, I know you're upset. I wanted to explain why we kept it a secret but Moses got home before I—"

"Mr. Mendoza, despite the circumstances, it's good to finally meet you."

Surprised, my head swung up. I felt like I was in a very bad television show and I was expected to perform brain surgery. After some prompting from Verónica, Moses stood up and held out his hand but I didn't want to take it.

I was unable to move. Even though I preferred to keep my business relationship with Moses a secret, I wasn't sure I could stomach having him as a son-in-law. Verónica had to know my views on mixed relations and I felt like Moses was being deceitful so I didn't trust him. My source of pain was that he looked me in the eye and didn't say shit about even knowing my daughter, let alone being married to her.

"Padre, say something please." Tears streamed from her eyes.

I didn't mean to hurt her but I was hurting too. "How long have you two been married?" The words were forced between lips that didn't want to open, but I was curious.

"We got married shortly after the baby was born and Victória got shot," Moses stated with a hint of attitude in his voice.

I raised a brow. "Oh, really?"

"It wasn't like that, Padre. I used to work for Moses and we fell in love."

Was this supposed to make me feel better? I didn't even know she had a job outside of the home. I stood up to leave because I needed to be alone to think. "It's late, we should talk about this at another time. Would you show me where I will be staying?" I walked over and grabbed my suitcase, anxious to be by myself. I saw Verónica move out of the corner of my eye, but Moses stopped her from showing me the way to the guestroom.

"Does this change what we discussed?" Moses asked when we were out of Verónica's earshot.

"Honestly, I don't know. You've certainly given me something to think about."

Our eyes locked, but neither of us said anything else.

# CHAPTER EIGHT

## VERÓNICA RAMSEY

"Honey, the baby is crying." Moses, my husband, nudged me in the back and rolled over.

I was beyond tired and a tad bit irritated with him because he didn't get up himself and give me a break. "Aw, come on. Can't you get him? I just got in bed."

"Verónica, you know I have to go to work in the morning."

I threw back the covers and searched in the dark for my slippers as LM's wails got louder. I felt insulted. I knew he had to work, but staying home taking care of a newborn was work too, and Moses was going to have to recognize it. "Taking care of our child is also a job, and it doesn't end at five o'clock." I stuffed my feet in my slippers. "I'm coming, boo," I mumbled, fighting through the tears that threatened to fall from my eyes. I didn't want resentment to build inside of me, so I knew I would have to tell Moses how I felt.

To be honest, I was surprised by the way Moses was acting, since he was so supportive in the beginning. I didn't know if it was the postpartum depression or the loss of my brother and first husband that was making me feel this way. I felt like Moses was taking me for granted.

"Mommy's coming, sweetie." I peeked in the nursery to assure myself LM was crying from hunger. His little arms and legs were flailing around as his whimpers became roars.

I wanted to keep the baby in our bedroom with us until he got a little older, but Moses felt it would lead to LM sleeping in our bed instead of his own. I totally disagreed with Moses, but not enough to pick a fight about it. If there was one thing that I'd learned from my previous marriage, it was to choose my battles.

I retrieved a bottle from the refrigerator and placed it in the microwave for twenty seconds to knock the chill off. Part of me was glad LM was making so much noise because that meant Moses wouldn't be able to get a lick of sleep until I returned with the bottle.

"Verónica, are you getting a bottle?" Moses called down the stairs.

I wanted to say something really stupid to him but I held my lips together, choking back the sarcasm. Instead, I ignored him and his stupid-ass question.


I put LM back in his crib and headed back to our room. I was still a little heated about being the one who had to get up all the time to tend to the baby, but I wasn't as angry as I'd been half an hour earlier. How could I be mad when I saw the way my son's eyes danced when he saw me? Like most men, he was only focused on one thing— my boobs. He fought me tooth and nail when I stopped giving him the boob and traded it for a bottle. I couldn't take the constant tugging on my nipple so I opted to pump my breast instead. "He got it honest." I chuckled, but my good mood soured almost immediately.

Mike, my first husband and LM's real dad, was killed a few days before he was born. My Uncle Monte ordered Mike's murder when he found out that I was pregnant. If Monte had his way, LM and I would be dead. A cold chill traveled down my back. I hurried up and got into the bed. Part of me wanted to snuggle against my husband, but the other part of me was still upset with him. Moses patted me on the leg as I burrowed into the sheet.

"Everything all right?"

He was snoring seconds after he asked without waiting for a response.

I moved away from his touch, but I doubted if he even noticed. I allowed my thoughts to wonder if things would have been different if Mike were alive. I loved him but I wasn't in love with him. I wanted more fire and passion, and it was probably my desire for more that got him killed. I started crying, something I found myself doing at least five times a day, and I was unable to stop. Perhaps I would have felt differently if I had had a chance to mourn Mike's death before I married Moses, but it was too late to change any of that now. I knew I was suffering from postpartum depression but who had time for that with all the other things going on?

I felt like the only person in my life who hadn't lied to me was my son. As I drifted off to sleep a tiny voice resonated in my mind. "Trust no one," the voice said. It wasn't the voice that sent off warning bells in my head, it was the words themselves that caused a galactic blast to flow through my veins. The voice was androgynous, neither male nor female, but it still sounded vaguely familiar. I struggled to keep my eyes open so I could ponder on the identity of the voice, but I fought a losing battle. I was just too tired to think anymore.

# CHAPTER NINE

## VERÓNICA RAMSEY

I secured LM in the middle of my bed and tickled him. "Hey, sweetie, things are going to be okay. Momma is just going through a rough time."

He smiled at me. The only thing that I didn't regret over the last six weeks was the birth of my son. He was the love of my life, and I vowed to do everything in my power to protect him—unlike how my parents had protected us. Even after everything went down, I wanted to believe that they loved us in their own way. But it wasn't enough.

LM was changing before my eyes. Initially, he looked like my first husband, Mike, but over the last month he started to look more like me. And, surprisingly enough, he was starting to look like my current husband, Moses. I pulled my baby closer to me. I didn't have much left in the world I'd die for. However, I was getting pretty tired of Moses' lackadaisical attitude toward us. He went through what I could only describe as phases: one minute he loved us and the next he acted as if he hated us.

I was bothered by the fact that my husband showed little to no interest in my son and seemed to be obsessed with finding the money and bonds Tilo had stolen from my family. I couldn't care less about the money, but Moses was determined to find Tilo and expose her. He was convinced that she was still alive, but I wasn't so sure because God doesn't like ugly and what she did to my family was straight-up ugly. Plus, investigators said that based on the amount of blood found in her car it meant she was more than likely dead. I thought she got what was coming to her, but I couldn't convince Moses of this. It just wasn't that important to me, and it was causing a rift in our relationship. If he showed one-tenth of the energy he spent on finding Tilo on us, I was certain we would have a great marriage. Getting him to shift his focus was the hard part.

"Are you awake?" My father came into my bedroom and I cringed.

My father knew nothing of boundaries. My bedroom door was closed so he should have knocked before he entered. I could have been doing anything before he barged in.

"I'm awake, but the next time you see my door closed, please knock. I may have been getting undressed."

His skin turned crimson red. I wasn't trying to embarrass him, but I was no longer a child living in his home. The situation was reversed, and he had to learn to respect it.

"I'm sorry. I have much to learn." Padre hung his head.

I felt ashamed for lashing out at him when it was really Moses whom I was mad at. I could only imagine how different our country was from his. "I wasn't trying to hurt your feelings, Padre, but if I didn't correct you, you might walk in on something you don't want to see."

He gave me a blank look like he had no clue what I could be referring to.

"Padre, I'm married now."

He turned red but I knew he finally understood.

"I may have ridden the short bus, but there is nothing wrong with what's up here." He pointed to the top of his head.

I almost choked. Did my father just make a joke? My father kept a straight face; it only made me want to laugh even more. I held it as long as I could until we burst out laughing.

He said, "It's good you laugh. It's not good to have so much tension in your life."

No truer words were ever spoken. Things were so hectic at the house. I was dealing with a new husband and a father who had been absent most of my adult life. I'd spent several months with an evil imposter who claimed to be my father and I almost died as a result. Now, my real father was back in the picture, and I was having a difficult time learning to trust again. "Come on in, Padre." I patted the bed to let him know it was okay to join me. We didn't have any other seating in the master bedroom. The furnishings in Moses' house were sparse, and I hadn't had the time or the energy to change this house to a home.

"How's my grandbaby?"

"This little fella makes sure I'm up every two hours."

"Do you want me to take him so you can get some rest?"

I could tell by the moisture gathering in his eyes that he really wanted to tend to his grandson, but he still had some explaining to do about the past before I could let him hold the future. "No, that's okay. With my luck, by the time I fall asleep you would be bringing him back with his greedy ass. I'm good. I'm about to get up anyway. I want to go to the hospital to visit Victória."

"I spoke to the doctors today and she is doing good. They called to say she is finally awake."

I jumped up, practically flipping LM off the bed in the process. "Are you serious? That's great news. Why didn't you tell me sooner?" My voice rose, and I was mad at my father all over again.

He stood up off the bed. "That is what I came up here to tell you."

I immediately felt stupid for jumping to conclusions. "I'm sorry, Padre, for barking at you. I've been so worried about Victória, I was beginning to believe she would never wake up." I had thought this many times, but this was the first time I'd said it out loud. I turned LM on his stomach so I could get dressed. I wanted to get to the hospital as soon as possible.

"Padre, can you give me a moment so I can get dressed?"

"Of course." He backed out of the room and closed the door.

I threw back the covers and slipped my gown over my head. I wanted to shower but I also needed to get to the hospital. I picked up the phone to call Ramón and stopped cold. I still couldn't believe he was gone.

I walked over to the closet to try to find something to wear, but nothing in the closet would fit my petite frame. I'd lost all my pregnancy weight but because I hadn't really been out of the house since coming home from the hospital, I hadn't gotten around to unpacking my regular clothes.

"Shit." I put my nightgown back on and went to the top of the steps and called to my father.

"Yes?" He stood at the bottom of the steps. He looked so uncomfortable, I felt sorry for him.

"I need to run to the basement to see if I can find something to wear. Could you come upstairs and watch the baby? He can't fall off the bed, but I don't want to take any chances."

He quickly climbed the stairs with a big grin on his face. I patted his shoulder as we passed on the stairs.

LM was not on the bed when I returned to my room with several pairs of jeans and tops to match. My father was also missing and I began to panic. My heart started beating real fast; I found myself gasping for breath. I'd asked him to watch over the baby. I didn't give him permission to move him. I threw the jeans on my bed and stormed off down the hall to the room that he was occupying. I stopped short at his door when I saw him cradling my son and whispering into his tiny ear. My heart swelled; I could not stop the tears from flowing down my face. I hadn't given my father any credit. I'd forgotten that he used to hold me in the same manner. I silently turned and went to my room to get dressed.

I needed to get to my sister and let her know I was alive and that our father had finally come home. I wasn't sure how I was going to break the news about Ramón. I would just have to cross that bridge when I got to it.

# CHAPTER TEN

## TILO ADAMS

"Do you like it?" The hairdresser swiveled my chair around.

I stared at my reflection in the mirror. My new hair came down well past my shoulders, and it was very full at the top. It actually looked good. I hardly recognized myself. "Excellent! You did a great job." I got out of the chair and moved in closer to the mirror.

She handed me a small mirror so I could exam my entire head. I wanted to make sure no tracks were showing. I wasn't about to walk around looking like a damn fool. "Shit, my own mother wouldn't recognize me."

If she thought it was something strange to say, she didn't say it. I had to be careful unless I wanted to pick up another body at the hairdresser's.

"That's what a weave does, creates a new persona and allows some people to be who they weren't at birth."

"Whoa, that's how you feel about it?" I was surprised that she would be so blunt with her description. But when I thought about it, she was absolutely correct. Weaves did allow people to be what they weren't. If you were bald, it allowed you to have hair. If your shit was thick and coarse, you could buy some slick and silky curls.

She said, "I'm glad you like it."

The weave was tight, and I was glad I'd taken the time to get it done. "Keep the change." I handed her $200. I was feeling extra good and sexy. I even felt like putting on makeup, something I hadn't done in years. I would indulge in that on the way to the airport in the morning.

# CHAPTER ELEVEN

## MOSES RAMSEY

"Moses, please don't get upset with me, sweetie. All I'm saying is that for all of our sakes, you need to give it up. You're never going to find Tilo."

"Verónica, I don't want to talk about it. Besides, I need to get to the office." Truth be told it wasn't so much a need to get to the office, it was a need to get away from her whining. She had been playing the same tune for eight weeks and I was sick of hearing it. I pulled on my pants and buttoned up my shirt. My tolerance for nagging was low and lack of sleep was starting to take its toll on me, so I knew I had to get out of the house before something happened that I couldn't take back.

"Are you going to let it go?" she said, continuing to push the envelope.

I almost lost it. "Yes," I agreed between clinched teeth.

When we were seeing each other, I never noticed how much of a pain in the ass she could be. But I was sure getting a good dose of it now. She was clocking my every move.

"Good, because I wouldn't want anything else to happen. Too many people already got hurt. I'm sick of all the drama. I just want our lives to go back to normal."

I stopped and looked around the kitchen. Did she honestly believe that what we had going on could actually be conceived of as normal? Everything about our lives, marriage, and love, was based on a lie. It was moments just like this that I questioned whether I'd ever loved Verónica.

"Moses?" She had this strange look on her face.

"Huh?" I'd zoned out and hadn't been paying attention.

"I asked what time you'd be home?"

"I don't know, babe, I'll call you." I knew that I was being unreasonable by getting an attitude with her, but I could not help myself. She could be so annoying sometimes, especially when she got something in her craw.

"Don't be mad, Moses. I'm just thinking about you."

"I'm not mad, sweetie. It's all good. I'll see you this evening." I bent down and kissed her on the head. I poured a glass of orange juice, which would serve as my breakfast. I told Verónica what she wanted to hear, but I had no intentions of giving up. She wasn't the only one telling me to let it go. The Feds all but confirmed Tilo's death from the blood in her car, but what they didn't know was that she was planning on stealing all the money and disappearing. I was caught between a rock and a hard place because the only way I could persuade the Feds to use their resources to find her black ass would be to admit I was in on the shit. That wasn't going to happen. I grabbed my briefcase and went through the garage to get to my car in the driveway. I was very distracted as I drove to work. Hell, I almost hit two cars in the process.

"If you don't focus, you dumb fuck, you're going to wrap this car around a pole," I said aloud. Finding Tilo wasn't going to do any good if I killed myself in the process. I pulled over to the side of the road to get myself together. In a way Verónica was right. This Tilo shit was driving me crazy. I imagined seeing her everywhere I went. I was so obsessed, it had me running up on strangers and making a fool out of myself. I wanted to give it up, but I could not get past the bitch tricking me. I didn't take that shit lightly.

When I pulled back into the morning traffic, I concentrated on the road and arrived at work with no other mishaps. I caught the elevator to the third floor and pulled out my keys to open the door. My thoughts were still flipping here and there so I didn't notice Verónica's father until I bumped into him.

"Excuse me, I wasn't paying attention."

"That's quite all right, son. I should have stepped aside when I saw you weren't paying attention to where you were going."

I looked up when he called me son. I was still trying to wrap my arms around having a father-in-law.

"Come on in." I was suspicious of the visit. I opened the door, turned on the lights, and adjusted the air conditioning. He took a seat in one of the chairs facing my desk.

"Can I get you some coffee or something else to drink, Mr. Mendoza?"

"Son, we don't have to be so formal."

"I'm curious about what brings you to my office instead of speaking with me at home."

"Because I want to know what type of progress you've made in finding Tilo. I want that bitch to pay for killing Ramón." He was quiet for a moment, then whispered, "Victória opened her eyes yesterday."

I was surprised. She had been in a coma so long I had begun to lose hope of ever questioning her. "Really? I didn't know. I'm surprised my wife didn't tell me."

"She just found out a little while ago and was so busy rushing out of the house with the baby and all, she probably just forgot to call you."

While it was a plausible excuse, I couldn't ignore the tiny tug in my gut that told me it could be more. "I'm sure." I nodded even though I didn't feel like it was true. I was ready for Carlos to leave so I could think about my next move. I was going to have to figure out a way to keep my investigation secret until I knew more about their family dynamics. For all I knew, Carlos may have a hidden agenda the same way his brother had. I was not about to be tricked again. "Have you been over to see Victória yet?"

"No, Verónica said I should wait until she had the opportunity to tell her about what happened."

"Don't you think you should be the one who explains your actions?"

He looked at me oddly. "That's very insightful of you. No wonder my daughter chose you."

I was stunned. He actually sounded like he was proud to have me in the family. I sat back in my chair, speechless. Based on the conversations I'd had with Verónica, I never thought he would truly accept me.

"I'm just saying, those two have been through a lot in a relatively short amount of time. It's understandable they will have trust issues. Trust me when I say I know that firsthand."

"I wish I could do it all over again only differently. I have to make it up to them."

"Mr. Mendoza, with all due respect, some things can't be undone. It is what it is. We're just going to have to move on and make the best of it."

He stood up. "You're a very wise man. Now find that bitch. I don't have to tell you that time is of the essence." He turned to leave.

"We should continue to keep this between us for the time being. I have to live with your daughter, and she doesn't want any part of this investigation."

"Fine, just find her."

If he only knew how badly I wanted to find her. It had been going on two months now since she'd disappeared and it was driving me nuts. To me it was personal. It really wasn't all about the money. The bitch played me for a punk-ass bitch, and I was having a difficult time swallowing it. I didn't care if it took me as long as it took to find Bin Laden, I was going to find her.

The phone rang.

"Private Investigator Moses Ramsey," I announced as I picked up the phone. My afternoon was turning out to be a busy one. I was flipping through my mail when I heard the voice that haunted me in my dreams.

"Moses, darling."

I dropped the mail. "Tilo." It wasn't a question, more like a confirmation that she was alive, and I knew she would taunt me. Now I was just waiting for it to begin.

"Do you miss me?" She was laughing, which only made my blood boil even more.

"What do you want, bitch?" I hissed. I logged on to my computer to trace the number she was calling from. However, she may have the ability to block it, but I wasn't ready to give up my chase.

"I understand some of your hostility, but it's not good to hold on to hatred for such a long period of time. Don't you agree?"

I was so mad, I couldn't even punch in the right numbers on my keyboard to activate the trace.

"Moses, are you there?"

"I'm here. I still want to know what you want."

"I thought you were a smart man, Moses. Surely you aren't trying to trace my call. You didn't underestimate me and think I would call you from my own phone, did you?"

I wanted that bitch so badly I could taste it.

"Humph, for what? You won." I punched the numbers again, trying not to pound so loudly on the keys.

"You may be a smart man, Moses, but you're a horrible liar. This is a throwaway phone; you'll never be able to trace it back to me."

She was right. With the disposable phone I could not trace it back to her, but I could trace the general area where the phone call was coming from.

"Oh shit," I muttered as the phone slipped from my ear. My dick got hard when I saw that the bitch was still in Georgia.

"I'm not going to lie, I would have liked to get to know you better, but you dipped your dick in another woman first. So don't even think about coming for me, or I'll tell her you tried to kill her." The line went dead. She had some nerve talking about where I had dipped my dick when she was pussy-bumping my wife's sister. However, the threat was not lost on me. I had to eliminate Tilo, period. It wasn't a matter of catching her and turning her over to the authorities, I had to kill the bitch.

# CHAPTER TWELVE

## VICTÓRIA MENDOZA

It began with a loud noise, more of a nuisance than anything. But this changed as the sound grew intense. It was so loud it hurt my eardrums and shook me from my deep sleep.

"Make it stop," I moaned, but my spoken plea didn't sound anything like it did inside my head. My lips felt like mush; I had no control over how they formed my words. I twisted my head to the right and felt a blinding pain that infused my brain with tiny stars. My body tensed from what seemed to be a massive revolt inside my body; every muscle woke up, engaged in some sort of motion.

I could feel my arms flailing, my legs jerking, my torso convulsing, and there was nothing I could do to stop them. I only wanted to go back to sleep, but each agonizing movement sent currents of pain to my brain. The noise in my head escalated. If I could've moved my arms with any controlled movement, I would have gripped my head to keep it still. Turning it to the right only brought more pain, but I couldn't keep my head still either.

*Stop.* I heard the word in my mind, despite the clutter in my head, but I wasn't sure if the word came out of my mouth.

*Where am I?* I tried to open my eyes but it felt like my lids were taped down. The more I struggled to open my eyes, the louder the noise in my head became. *God, I give up. If you stop this pounding in my head, I'll stop fighting.* I waited for the pain to stop, but I could only assume God was otherwise busy or couldn't understand me. My body continued to shake and shimmy on what I assumed was a bed. My arm exploded in pain when something hit it. My arm apparently connected with a solid object and pain shot up my limb. Whatever I hit was major because the pain in my arm was different from the pain in other parts of my body. It radiated up my left arm and centered in my chest.

"We're losing her," someone shouted.

*Who the hell was that and who are they losing?* The pain in my head subsided somewhat, but my chest was showing out.

"Code blue. Code blue," another voice shouted.

These motherfuckers were getting on my nerves. I felt additional pressure on my chest, and I wanted to tell them to leave me alone. I couldn't breathe. Someone was pressing down on my chest and my nose was covered. I struggled to open my eyes but they remained glued shut.

Someone shouted, "Clear."

*Clear what? I wish these stupid asses would speak English.* Couldn't they see I was in need of some assistance? My body lifted up off the bed and fell back with a thump. *What the fuck is going on?* Before I could get an answer, my body lifted again and crashed back onto the bed. My entire head was hurting now, not just the right side. I was convinced someone was trying to kill me. But just as suddenly as everything started to lose clarity, everything came in focus. The pain slipped away and my body relaxed.

"I got a pulse." A nurse bent over me and shined a light in my eyes.

"Welcome back," another spoke.

I looked around the room as best I could without moving my head. I was afraid to because I didn't want to trigger the pain I was certain was connected to my head.

"You gave us quite a scare," the first nurse spoke.

I tried to speak but my lips wouldn't cooperate. Frustrated, I started to cry. I didn't understand what had happened to me but it must have been bad—very bad.

"Don't try to speak. Give the medicine a chance to work. You're okay now."

Was this supposed to make me feel better? If it was, it wasn't working. I wanted to know where I was and, more significant, how I had gotten there. I let my eyes roam the hospital room, searching for a familiar face, but I didn't recognize anyone in the room. I lifted my hand and grabbed the nurse's hand before she could leave me. I searched her face, seeking information.

She reached for a cup with ice chips and coated my lips. "You're at Grady Memorial Hospital. You've been here for almost two months and up until yesterday you've been in a coma. You started convulsing yesterday, and we've had to use the crash cart on you three times."

"I almost died?" My words seemed muffled, but she obviously understood.

"Yes, but this is the first time that you've opened your eyes since you've been here; so, hopefully, the worst is over with." She smiled.

"Head hurts." My throat was parched and it hurt to talk.

She brought a straw to my lips. "Just take a sip or two. We don't want to shock your system. I'm going to call your doctor. Try to get some rest."

Panic overwhelmed me. I didn't want to be left alone. What if I crashed again? "I'm scared." I felt tears roll out of my eyes and puddle in my ears.

"I know, sweetie. I won't be gone long. I'm just going to go up the hall and call your doctor. Your family has been notified. I'll be back before you know it." She patted my hand and she was gone.

I couldn't have held her there if I tried. I closed my eyes and turned my head to the right. My eyes shot open as my brain was infused with pain again. I shifted my body to the left, which also woke up some nerve endings, but I didn't want to make the mistake of turning back to the right. Once I got comfortable, I silently prayed God would wake me up again.

# CHAPTER THIRTEEN

## MOSES RAMSEY

I spoke into the phone. "Dad, I need to speak with you. Is Mom around?" I paced my office nervously. I needed to get something off my chest, and my father was the only person I knew who I could trust with this information.

"She's in the kitchen."

"Good, what I have to say is for your ears only. Later you can decide whether to share it with Mom. Could you take me off speaker phone so she doesn't come into the room?"

"Moses, I don't keep secrets from your mother. Secrets are little lies that can ruin a relationship."

"I know, Dad, but can you just indulge me for a moment? I need to speak to you man to man."

"Sure, son, but I must say you have me concerned."

I waited while he took me off speaker and left whatever room he was in.

"Okay, son, go ahead. Your mother can't hear anything we say."

I released a sigh of relief. I didn't want to have to explain this shit to my mother and my dad. My mother would make a big deal about it.

"Dad, I fucked up and I could use some advice."

"Fucked up how? And you know I don't like that foul language."

"Sorry, Dad, but there is no other way to say it. I fell in love with a woman who was already married, and she worked for me."

"Son, didn't I tell you never to shit where you work?"

I could tell he was disappointed with me because he almost never cursed. It didn't take many words from my father to make me feel like a child all over again. "Yeah, you told me . . . but in the heat of the moment, I wasn't thinking straight. She was so beautiful I couldn't help myself. If it makes you feel better, she actually came on to me. I didn't have the willpower to turn her down."

"Better? How is that supposed to make me feel better? I thought I taught you better than to let your dick do the thinking for you."

I knew I would have to eat a slice of humble pie, but I wasn't prepared to eat the whole damn thing. If he was going to lecture me the whole time, then I'd just wasted my time. I didn't call him for a lecture, I needed advice on how I was going to deal with a wife, and a baby who most certainly wasn't mine.

"Dad, I know I messed up. I didn't call you to confirm it for me. I need your help, so can you please hold your opinions to yourself until I tell you the rest of the story?"

"I'm sorry. You know I only want the best for you. Your mother and I are worried about you being in Atlanta by yourself."

"I got that, Dad. After this is over I may even move back home, but I've got to get through this."

"Damn, sounds serious."

"It is. The woman I am involved with is Latino." I wanted to let this information settle in before I continued. My parents were very proud of their heritage and did not condone interracial relationships.

"Shit," my dad said. His outburst caused my heart to leap.

I didn't mean to ever hurt my parents, and judging by the way he was cussing, I could tell he was hurting. "Dad, I'm sorry. I didn't choose to love her, it just happened."

"Son, your mother is going to have a duck-plucking fit."

"I know. That's why I haven't told her. There's more."

"Oh, shit."

"She got pregnant. At the time I believed the child was mine. Remember when I called and told Mom I was having a baby?"

"Yeah, your mother and I argued about that for two days! I told her she was only hearing things she wanted to hear. Because of you, I couldn't get any for over a week."

"I wasn't lying. Her name is Verónica, she said I was the father. Dad, she changed my life, and I wanted to be that child's father. I was trying to persuade her to leave her husband and marry me."

"Oh, Jesus." He blew out a deep breath. I could tell he was smoking, which was something my mother forbade him to do.

"She said she loved me, Dad, and I loved her. To me it was simple, but she said it was more complicated."

"Okay, I got all that, what happened?"

"Dad, I have to tell this my way. I need for you to understand that I wanted to be there for my child just like you were there for me. But she was committed to someone else and it was driving me nuts."

"Father God! Don't tell me you did something stupid and had him killed."

"No, I said I was in love, not psychotic."

"Thank God."

"I'm sorry, Dad. I haven't done things the way you wanted me to but at least now you know I'm not gay."

"Under normal circumstances I would've been happy to hear that, but this mess you're involved in—"

"Have you ever had a woman in your face who did it for you on every level every day? I couldn't help myself when she came on to me. Shit, what was I supposed to do?"

He said, "Things have changed since I was a young man. When I met your mother, she wouldn't let me get with her until I married her. I realize things have changed, but why a Latino woman? Why not a black queen?"

"Dad, you know as well as I do that you can't control who you love. It was just something about her; it wasn't meant as a slight to black women."

"Okay, I can respect that. So what's the problem? Her husband found out and he wants to kill your dumb ass?"

I didn't appreciate the way he was making light of the situation. I needed him to care about it as much as I did. "It's a long story, but her husband was murdered."

"Whoa, you said you didn't kill him. Should I be worried?"

He didn't know the half of it.

"It was pretty intense at the time. I will go into it in more detail the next time I see you, but I have to get the rest of the story out before Mom comes looking for you."

"You got that right. I'd better put out this cigar."

"Verónica told me the whole time she was carrying the baby it was mine. I believed her, Dad."

"Wait, hold the fuck up. You said she was married, son, so how the hell could this child be yours?"

My dad was hopping mad—I heard it in his voice.

"Dad, I know you're upset but hear me out, please. She said she wasn't having sex with her husband and that he was incapable of having children."

"Son, that's the oldest line in the book. I can't believe you fell for it."

"I did, hook, line, and sinker, and to make matters worse, I married her."

I heard his phone hit the floor. "Holy Mother of God," he shouted.

I could hear the pain in his voice. I was his only child, and I hated being a disappointment to him.

"She lied to me, Dad. The baby is white. I feel like such a fool for believing her."

"Whether the baby is white or purple, if you love this woman it shouldn't make a difference."

"But what about the lies she told me?"

"Your whole relationship was built on a lie. So now the only question that really remains is, what you are going to do about it? Her husband is gone. Are you ready to abandon her?"

My father had a good point. While I was still hurt that the baby wasn't mine, a part of me still loved Verónica .

"I guess I'm going to make a go of this marriage."

"Good, and you're going to have to make an effort not to hold the sins of the mother against your child."

"I'm going to work on it; I really love her. Thanks for hearing me out, Dad."

"So are you trying to tell me we are grandparents?" my mother asked.

"Mom, how long have you been on the phone?" My stomach sunk. If she didn't hear the whole conversation, I was going to have to start all over again. Once was enough. If she did hear the conversation, I knew she was going to want to see the baby and see him quickly.

"I picked up as soon as your father left the room. He's no good at keeping secrets from me and he knows it."

My dad laughed. When I realized that she wasn't mad, I started laughing as well.

Mom said, "So when can I see my grandchild?"

# CHAPTER FOURTEEN

## VERÓNICA RAMSEY

Moses came into the kitchen and tossed his key on the counter. "Hey, sweetheart, did you have a good day?"

I stopped stirring the tuna salad I was making and looked around to see who Moses was talking to. I assumed he was on the phone because he hadn't called me sweetheart in over months. My first thought was, *who is this man and what have you done with my husband?* "Uh . . . actually I did. The baby slept good today, hopefully, he'll sleep through the night. How was your day?"

Moses gave me a happy-meal smile and it made me nervous. "It was very enlightening."

I didn't know what he meant by that, and I was afraid to ask. For some reason he was in a rare mood and I didn't want to ruin it. He leaned over and gave me a gentle kiss on the lips. An electric shock passed between us, which made us both jump.

"Ouch, hot stuff coming through." I pressed a finger to my top lip.

He kissed me again and this time I felt no pain, only passion. "Sorry I shocked you. Was that better?"

"Mmm, I'll say it was." I closed my eyes and savored the moment.

We didn't share moments like this often. His kiss was tender. I could actually feel the love it represented.

As he moved away, I felt the air conditioner cool my now warm face. I opened my eyes but he hadn't moved. He was still smiling at me, and it was kind of creepy because I didn't recognize him. He reminded me of the man I fell in love with.

I said, "Moses, what's going on? I'm not complaining, but you have me confused. When you left this morning you barely looked at me, and tonight I get not one kiss but three."

"Can't a man kiss his wife?" His smile lingered on his face but I was still uneasy.

"I wasn't complaining. I just wanted to know what happened so I could make it happen more often." I laughed it off, but I'd never been so serious in my life. I was sick of all the fussing and arguing we'd been doing. It wasn't good for me and it damn sure wasn't good for the baby.

"Where's your father?"

I froze. Something was definitely wrong. "Who are you and what have you done with my husband?" I grabbed a knife from the countertop. I'd been through that subterfuge bullshit before, and I was not about to go through it again.

"Sweetheart, put down the knife. Everything is okay. I just came to some conclusions today and they have changed my outlook on this." He reached for the knife and I allowed him to take it from my hand, but I still wasn't sure things were on the up and up.

I frowned. "What kind of conclusions?"

"Don't you worry your pretty little head. Just know that things are going to be different around here— starting tonight."

He unknotted his tie and left the room. I sunk down on the closest chair. Despite Moses' assurances, I did not feel relieved. I felt like I did when my uncle entered our house and pretended to be my father. I was certain the man who entered my house today was my husband, but that was as far as I was willing to go with that. I heard the shower running and I looked at the clock. It was already five and I wasn't done preparing dinner.

"Where did my day go?" I jumped up, dismissing my insecurities about Moses, and put some effort into finishing dinner. As I opened the refrigerator I heard LM whimpering through the child monitoring system we'd installed throughout the house.

I grabbed a bottle of breast milk from the refrigerator. From under the sink, I got a small pan to heat his bottle. To his credit, Moses had purchased a top-of-the-line bottle warmer. As far as I was concerned, though, it took more time than it was worth trying to figure out how to use the damn thing. Some things didn't need modernization. I placed the bottle in a little water and turned on the burner of the stove.

LM's whimpers were gathering intensity, so I turned up the heat and was careful to shake it every few seconds so it wouldn't have any hot pockets. The water had just started to simmer as LM began to cry in earnest.

"Hey, big guy. What's all the noise for?"

I heard Moses talking to his son. LM immediately quieted. I froze—total state of shock. Moses had never once gone to check on the baby when he was crying.

"What the hell is going on here?" I mumbled to myself as I edged closer to the monitor.

"Let's go see what's taking your momma so long with your milk."

I broke out of my trance, but I still felt like I was walking through a cloud as I walked around the kitchen in circles. Moses met me halfway and took the bottle from me. He gave me a sexy smile, which almost made my knees buckle, and he winked at me. He turned around and went back upstairs. I watched them until they disappeared at the top of the steps. Something very strange was happening in my own house and I didn't know what it was. I'd prayed that Moses would take an interest in my child, but I never thought God would've moved so quickly.

When Moses returned to the kitchen, he had changed into some jeans and a T-shirt that showed off his muscles. My heart swelled with love but I was still confused.

"Where's the baby?"

"After I burped him, he went right to sleep. I changed his diaper, so he should be good for another few hours." He took the paper off the kitchen table and winked at me again.

I gave him an uncertain nod as he walked into the family room.

"Where did you say your father was?" Moses asked again.

"Ah, he said he had some errands to run. He's been gone all day."

"Come here for a minute."

Nervously, I walked into the room expecting the worst. He was lying on the sofa. The paper was on the coffee table. Untouched.

"Come sit your sweet pussy on my face," he commanded.

"What did you say?"

He laughed. "You heard me." His baritone voice sent a ripple down my back straight to my pussy.

"What about my father?"

"Then I guess you'd better hurry up."

It drove me crazy when he spoke sexy to me. I still had on my panties, but Moses took care of that. He roughly pulled them to the side and put his face between my thighs. I exhaled. He pushed his tongue into my pussy. I was thirsty for his love. I wanted to come deep in his mouth.

"Ah . . . that shit feels good." I ground my pussy against his face without a care in the world. He fondled my breasts. He stuck his finger in my pussy as he gently sucked on my clit. I was close to a climax and we'd just started.

"That's it, baby, that's my spot."

He didn't respond because his mouth was full, but he heard me because he increased the pressure on my clit. His arms were wrapped tightly around my thighs, holding me in place. But he really didn't have to hold me, I wasn't going anywhere.

I said desperately, "Fuck me, baby." I had a lot of regrets in my life, but loving Moses wasn't one of them. This man took me to heights that I didn't even know existed.

He pushed me away long enough to breathe, my juices dripping off his face. "You like that?" he asked as he drove his face back into my pussy.

How did he expect me to answer when he was pleasing me like this? "Ah," I moaned with pleasure. If he was trying to drive me fucking crazy, it was working. All my insecurities were forgotten. "I'm cumming!" I squirted in his mouth.

My entire body shook with an intensity I'd forgotten existed. He pulled my body down and rammed his dick into my pussy. My walls wrapped around his dick like a warm blanket. He was such an energetic lover. I grunted when I felt his dick hit my wall.

"Oh my God," I moaned. "Oh, Lord," I shouted.

"Damn, baby, this shit is good. I've been dreaming about your pussy all day long." He rammed his dick inside me again. His brow was creased and his lips were pulled back. His eyes were wide open like windows to his soul.

"Don't stop." Technically, we should've waited. I had a difficult delivery and the doctor advised us to wait on sex for two more weeks, but I couldn't tell this man no. He just turned me on.

"Back that shit up for me then." He was asking me to back my ass up so he would fuck me doggie style and he only had to say it once.

"I got you, give it to me." I bent over and looked at him over my shoulder.

That was all he needed to hear. He pushed his dick so far up in my shit, I had no choice but to come on it. His weight fell on me as he came; it was cool, I needed the rest.

"Damn," he said.

"You got that right. That was awesome." He went to sleep; and for a minute, so did I.

However, LM made sure we didn't sleep long.

# CHAPTER FIFTEEN

## TILO ADAMS

I stared at my reflection in the mirror. "I should have never left that house without killing Moses. What the fuck was I thinking?" I brought my hand down hard on the countertop. When he came for me, and I had no doubt that he would, it would be my own fault. I felt like kicking my own ass. I shouldn't have taunted him, but every time I closed my eyes I saw his face. I didn't want to spend the rest of my life running from that motherfucker. He should've been plant food by now. If he didn't give up the chase, I was going to make it happen.

If he had shown half the balls I'd given him credit for when we were plotting to steal the money, I might've brought him along with me. "Naw, bitch, who you fooling? You never learned to share as a child, and you're too damn old to learn how to do it now. He can kiss my black ass. That's what he can do for me." It didn't bother me at all that I was having a conversation with myself. *That's because you killed everyone else in your life who mattered to you.*

I looked around for the voice inside my head. It started yapping the moment I used my gun for greed instead of serving and protecting. Some might call it a conscience, but to me it was just another fucking pain in the ass that I cared not to deal with. "Shut the fuck up," I shouted.

I took one last look around my apartment then I placed my final items in my suitcase. With my new look, I was finally comfortable enough to chance leaving the country. I was blond now. The dreads I'd spent so much time grooming were a thing of the past. I had a new identity and with it a new life. I looked like Bianca. I regretted my decision not to leave town immediately after the murders. My logic, at the time, was to take my time deciding where I wanted to live so I wouldn't risk additional exposure by hopping from place to place. Historically, most criminals were caught after or during their travels. They were most exposed because they could not control things and the people around them. I didn't want to make the same mistake. I wanted to find a locale where I could grow old, fat, and happy.

In order to do this, I had to find out if anyone other than Moses was searching for me. The last thing I needed was to show up at the airport and get arrested. Hence, my call to Moses. He didn't appear surprised to hear from me, so I concluded he hadn't given up and would be a major thorn in my side until I found a way to eradicate him. I already knew money wasn't the answer, or, at this point, an option. I was gonna have to either kill the motherfucker or make him wish I had. Didn't much matter to me whichever way it went down.

As I gazed into the mirror I didn't recognize myself. It wasn't just the hair, it was in my eyes. They were blank and no longer filled with light. Tears flowed out of my eyes, and I was certain that life as I knew it was over. I'd killed two innocent people and stolen their inheritance. I bought myself a front-seat ticket on a one-way, custom-painted rollercoaster ride straight to hell.

# CHAPTER SIXTEEN

## VERÓNICA RAMSEY

"I'm not going to be able to take you to the hospital until my Moses gets home from work. I don't want to keep taking the baby to the hospital and exposing him to all those germs." I had just put LM back to bed. If I didn't need to go to the hospital, I would've gotten into the bed myself.

"Why can't we get a babysitter?"

I looked at my father like he had lost his damn mind. What did he mean, we? I wasn't sure about letting him go to the hospital. Victória had only been awake a few days and I didn't want to upset her. He was reading the paper but put it down as he watched me.

"Babysitter? That's not about to happen. Moses and I haven't even broached the subject of babysitters yet. I'm terrified about leaving my baby with strangers. You never know what they could be doing while you aren't there to protect them."

"When will he be back? I really want to see Victória."

For some reason his statement angered me. I felt like he was getting comfortable with a very uncomfortable situation. Most days I could catch myself before I went off on him, but those days were getting harder and harder. I swung back and forth between loving and hating him. If he was so eager to see us, why did it take the death of our mother to bring him home? I spoke before I could get a hold of my thoughts. "What's the rush now? You missed most of our lives. You missed all of Ramón's." I shocked both of us with the brutal truth. I promised myself I would keep my negative feelings to myself but all the anger I felt rolled out of my mouth unchecked. Before I knew what was happening, I had assumed the ghetto chick, neck-rolling posture of someone about to kick ass in the streets. He didn't know nothing about that shit and something deep inside of me wanted to be the one to show him.

"He will be home when he finishes taking care of his business because, unlike you, he provides for his family. He doesn't just send money. He's here for his son." I didn't have to finish the rest of my statement because he knew what I was going to say. I slumped down on a chair, ashamed of myself. It had to be hormonal because I would never intentionally be mean.

He said, "Your words hurt, but nothing you can say can hurt me more than my own inaction. I know I have my shortcomings, but there are a lot of things you don't understand. I've always provided for this family."

I shook my head because he still didn't get it. Being a father wasn't about the money. We needed him but that time had come and gone. I wasn't feeling well and I was taking it out on my father. "Padre, I'm sorry. I wasn't trying to start an argument with you. A lot of things have gone on over the past few months and my body is playing tricks with me. I want to make sure Victória is okay, and then we can deal with all this other stuff later." I felt defeated.

"Verónica, I spoke to Moses the other day and he made a very valid point. He said I should be the one to explain myself to both you and Victória. He, uh—"

"When did you get to speak with Moses? He didn't say anything about it to me."

Padre turned red and looked very uncomfortable, but I was not about to let him off the hook.

"Well, I, uh, I . . . uh—"

"What are you not telling me?" I was imagining all kinds of things, so I needed him to tell me what really went down so I could stop coming to my own conclusions. Moses was different yesterday, and I needed to know if my father had something to do with it.

"It's nothing really. I didn't realize your husband didn't mention it to you." He walked into the kitchen and I followed him.

I was really getting mad. The way he said it, his tone implied there was something wrong with my marriage.

"It must have slipped Moses' mind. He normally tells me everything."

My father stared at me like he didn't believe a damn thing I said. Of course it could have been my hormones making me act all crazy and shit.

"Have you said anything to Victória about me?"

I paused, distracted. I wanted to know why Moses didn't tell me about speaking to my father. I also wanted to know what else he was hiding from me.

He said, "Verónica."

My father brought me back to the present. I'd forgotten what we were speaking about.

"Huh?"

"Have you told Victória anything about me?"

"I haven't told her that you are here. She's still getting herself together, so I don't want to bombard her with too much information at one time." I started to get nervous. Truth was that I hadn't told Victória anything, not even about our brother Ramón. I was waiting for her to ask me what happened.

"She hasn't asked any questions?"

I fidgeted. "Well . . . she's curious about what happened to her."

"She doesn't remember anything?" He pulled a glass from the cabinet and poured some water in it.

"Uh, she believes you have something to do with her being in the hospital."

A vein in his neck stuck out; he stopped moving, glass halfway to his mouth.

"Me? Are you serious? And you're okay with allowing her to believe this when you know I had nothing to do with it?" He was ass-kicking mad. He slammed his glass down on the counter and started pacing back and forth.

"Padre, I don't know what I'm doing right now. She looks so frail, I don't know how much she can take. Hell, what do you think we should do?"

He didn't hesitate. "I think we should tell her right now! There's been too much deception as it is, and I'm ending this shit today. No more deception." He looked as if he wanted to strike me.

"I'm not the one who started this shit." I followed him into the living room.

He put me on the defensive as he stood over me. Who the hell did he think he was? *He can't come in my house and tell me what the fuck to do. That shit is over and done with.*

"It doesn't matter who started it, Verónica. It has to end. I can't have Victória thinking I harmed her or her brother." His voice was more subdued and authentic.

"She doesn't know about Ramón, either." Since I was being honest, I confessed to the rest of it too.

"That's it! I'm going to the hospital now." He rushed toward the door.

"Padre, wait, at least let me go with you. She doesn't know you."

He looked like he was about to refuse but he lowered his hand.

"Fine, hurry up. This shit has gone on long enough." Tears rolled down his cheeks as I reached for the phone to call Moses.

I had mixed emotions about his tears. While I understood he wasn't responsible for the actions of his brother, he created the circumstances that allowed the situation to happen. And I was not about to let him go to the hospital and possibly destroy all the progress my sister had made toward recovery. That was not about to happen if I had anything to do with it.

Padre stumbled, falling back onto the couch, clutching his heart. His face turned blue; he looked like a Smurf. I immediately regretted lashing out at him.

"Padre!" I screamed, running toward him. "What's the matter? Are you okay?" I knelt in front of him, uncertain of what I needed to do. The last thing I needed was another parent dying right before my eyes.

"I need to see Victória," he said, gasping for breath. Padre changed right before my eyes, suddenly looking old and sickly.

*He's faking. There's nothing wrong with him,* I thought.

"Padre, are you ill?" Even though I didn't believe his little act, my heart started beating a little faster. What if he wasn't faking? I didn't think I could stand to lose both my parents, even though he'd been absent most of my life.

"I need my pills. They are in the side pocket of my suitcase," he moaned and rolled over on his side. His tongue hung from the side of his mouth. He appeared to struggle for air.

Faking or not, I rushed to his room and grabbed his suitcase and brought it back to the living room. I beat myself up for being so mean and hateful. As much as I wanted to hate him, I still loved him. My hands shook as I dug into his case. I kept looking over at him to see how he was doing. "Should I call for an ambulance?" I was getting nervous.

He shook his head and I continued to search.

"Do you have them?" he asked as my fingers closed around a small prescription bottle.

"Yes, here they are. How many do you need?" The directions were on the front of the bottle but the words would not come into focus.

"One."

The fucking bottle wouldn't open. It had one of those child-safety caps on it, which were designed in my opinion to piss folks the fuck off. A few seconds later I opened the bottle and shook out a single tablet into his hand. He held it, his eyes beseeching me for assistance. I raised his arm, guiding his hand to his mouth. He placed the pill under his tongue. He leaned back against the couch and closed his eyes. I was scared.

"Are you okay?" My face was inches away from his nose.

He didn't answer, just nodded his head. I sat down next to him and watched him like a hawk. His color slowly started to return. I wondered what was wrong with him that he could have an attack so quickly and recover seemingly in minutes. However, those minutes seemed like hours. Slowly, he opened his eyes. His breathing had slowed down as well.

"That was a big one," Padre replied as he struggled to sit up straight.

"How long has this been going on?"

He eyes didn't meet mine.

He said, "About five years, but there's nothing to worry about. It's all under control."

He didn't appear to be in control to me. What if I wasn't there and he couldn't reach his pills? What would have happened then? Would he have died?

"How come—" I didn't have to finish my statement. My parents were the masters of deception.

"It's not so bad . . . as long as . . . I keep my medicine close . . . no stress."

He was in the wrong house for that shit. Part of me wanted him to go to a hotel, but the daughter in me wanted to keep him close so I could look out after him.

He looked at me, sadness filled his eyes. "So much wasted time." A tear slid out of his right eye.

I reached up and wiped it away. It was a tender moment, filled with forgiveness and remorse. We both turned when we heard a key in the door.

# CHAPTER SEVENTEEN

## TILO ADAMS

I jumped up out of the bed, drenched in sweat. I was convinced someone was in the room. I grabbed my gun from underneath my pillow, ready to shoot whoever had managed to get into my hotel room.

"Who's there?" I whispered, afraid of the answer. My heart slammed against my chest, its vibration pounding in my head. My arms shook as I tried to hold my gun steady. I slid my legs over the side of the bed and crouched into position. If someone was going to attack me, I preferred them to do it while I was standing.

My eyes struggled to see in the dark, but the sweat in my eyes made it difficult to see clearly. I pivoted around in a circle but nothing jumped out at me. This was the third time tonight I'd awoken from the same dream.

"It was the dream again, you idiot." I slowly lowered my arm and exhaled. Even if I was dreaming, it was very vivid. I would be lying if I said it didn't have me all shook up.

I went into the bathroom and ran some water in the sink. Part of me wanted to jump into the shower to wash off some of the sweat. The other part of me just wanted to get back in the bed and pretend it never happened. Again.

I allowed the water to get hot and grabbed a wash-cloth from the stack on the counter and rubbed it over my face. I refused to look into the mirror because I didn't want to see what my face looked like. There was nothing cute about being scared half to death.

The dreams were getting on my fucking nerves. They started the day I shot my former lover, Victória. Her eyes plagued me, and she reached out to me in my dreams. Each time I walked toward her she always disappeared before I could reach her. I turned off the light and made my way back to the bed. The sheets on the side of the bed I'd been sleeping on were soaking wet. It looked as if I'd peed on myself. If I had, it wouldn't have been the first time. I turned down the sheets on the other side of the king-sized bed and climbed in. I pulled the covers up under my chin and tried to pretend the dreams never happened.

"Shit," I said aloud to the empty room. I hadn't slept for more than four hours in over two months. I checked under my pillow to make sure I'd put my gun back within easy reach. I sighed when I felt the cold, hard steel against my fingertips. My dream was always the same. It started out so beautifully and ended so terribly wrong. I wanted to forget the details of my nightmare, but my thoughts had a mind of their own and took me right back to where I'd left off. I was scared to close my eyes, fearing the images would flash once again through my mind. The shit was getting old. I knew I would feel some remorse for my actions, but I had no idea it was going to be like this.

"This is some bullshit!" I exclaimed. I was exhausted and had not anticipated all the guilt I'd feel while I was planning the caper. Obviously, I didn't know myself as well as I thought I did. When all else was said and done, I found out I too had a heart, and I broke it the day I pulled the trigger.

"You pussy," I said, beating my pillows to get comfortable. I was mad at myself for being so weak. This wasn't my first kill, so I couldn't understand why I couldn't shake it and it be done. Having sex with Victória may have contributed to my discomfort, but enough was enough.

However, I could not get her face out of my mind. It was in her eyes. I didn't think she believed I would pull the trigger. Truth be told, I didn't believe it either. I thought I was going to punk out at the last minute but I didn't. I shot her in cold blood like I had her brother. In my dream, her eyes blazed with love and forgiveness. They begged me to save her, but I didn't.

She would never understand. Her brother had to die because he knew everything. He worked for Moses, and he knew the operations of the family business. He also harbored hatred in his heart, and it wouldn't take much for him to transfer that energy to me. He was a liability I couldn't afford to have hanging around. I shot Victória because I knew that she'd hunt for me for the rest of my life for killing her brother.

I allowed Verónica to live for two reasons: one, I didn't want her son to grow up without his mother; and two, I wanted to piss Moses off. He was already mad that the child she bore belonged to another man. He would be equally pissed when he realized he was actually married to her. "I wish I could've seen Moses' face when he realized his wife wasn't dead." I laughed out loud.

Laughter always came before the tears.

# CHAPTER EIGHTEEN

## CARLOS MENDOZA

I jumped up off the sofa a tad bit too fast. My head was a little woozy, but I refused to succumb to the dizziness. I stumbled a little bit but, otherwise, I remained on my feet. "Can we go now?" I was nervous to see my daughter and to clear my name.

"Padre, don't you think you should rest some more?"

"I'm fine, let's go." I shot Verónica a warning look. I didn't need her telling Moses about my little episode. Even though I made a deal with him to find Tilo, he still hadn't earned my trust. I was going to be watching him as much as, if not more than, he was watching me.

Moses walked through the front door. "What's going on?" Moses put down his briefcase and gave Verónica a kiss on the cheek.

I shot Verónica another warning look, but she either completely missed my warning or I sucked at it and she ignored it.

"Padre isn't feeling well. He wants to go to the hospital, but I think he should lie down and take a nap," Verónica insisted as she slung her purse over her shoulder.

"I said I'm fine. Can we go now?" I didn't want to get into a fight with Moses, but I would if I had to. I was going to the hospital either with Verónica or without her.

Moses said, "How long has my little man been asleep?"

If Moses felt the tension in the air, he obviously chose to ignore it.

"About an hour. We shouldn't be gone long. I'm taking my car just in case Padre wants to stay a little longer."

Perfect. I would have suggested the same thing because I didn't want to have the discussion about my health with her right now.

I was tense as we approached my youngest daughter's hospital room. Never in a million years would I have believed that our lives would come down to this.

"Brace yourself, she's frail," Verónica said before she pushed open the door to room 521.

I paused for a few seconds while trying to gain the courage to enter her room. I knew Verónica tried to prepare me, but nothing could prepare me for the sight of my little girl lying in a hospital bed. Nothing. Everything else in the room disappeared as I looked at her. "Sweet Jesus." I rushed forward and touched Victória's arm.

Verónica came up on the other side of me and placed her hand on my shoulder. I made no attempt to stop the tears that washed my face. I felt like God was punishing me for every mistake I'd ever made, and He was doing it all at once. I closed my eyes for a brief moment and when I opened them, Victória was staring back at me.

"You're awake," I said as relief flooded through my body, but I was also scared.

Victória didn't know me and distrust showed in her eyes. She didn't have old memories to fall back on. She was so young when they moved, four, maybe five, and I wasn't around much. To her I was just a voice on the phone. She had no real memories of me. I wanted—no, scratch that—I needed to hear her voice.

Victória gave me but a moment's glance. This hurt my feelings but I tried not to let it show on my face. I gained solace when she didn't flinch from my touch. My children had reason to hate me. I needed for them to give me another chance to make things right. Her eyes connected longer with Verónica's than they did with mine. She never spoke; I was worried that she wouldn't speak. Her eyes went back to Verónica. I felt like I shouldn't even have been in the room. Her look said she didn't want to see me.

Verónica said, "Hey, sweetie, how are you feeling today?"

Victória looked at me again. She didn't seem to care one way or another about me.

"Ramón? Where is he?" Her voice was hoarse and we could barely hear her.

Verónica shook her head and sat down on the bed with Victória. I didn't know what to do. I wasn't sure if I should move closer to the bed or leave the room. Victória didn't help me because she never acknowledged me. I tried not to take it personally.

I said, "There's something that I—no, we—need to tell you, and it's not going to be easy."

Victória looked at me again. Her eyes became hard like two small pebbles. Verónica caught the exchange and helped me out.

"I know you don't remember him and I'm sure this is going to come as a surprise, but this is our real father."

If Victória was shocked by this bit of information, she didn't let it show. She continued to stare at Verónica like she was the only person in the room.

I said, "Hi, I . . . uh—"

Victória help up a hand in front of my face. "Where's Ramón?" she asked again.

"I think you should call the nurse and let them know that she woke up." My heart started beating faster.

"Good idea." Verónica jumped off the bed and practically ran out of the room.

"Sweetheart, I'm so happy to see that you are doing better."

She continued to stare at me as she tried to pull away from my touch. I refused to let go. I knew this was going to be my only chance to win her over. If I didn't do it now, I might never get another opportunity.

"Where's my brother?" She stretched her words, showing anger with each syllable. Her lips were clenched as she looked straight ahead, refusing to meet my eyes.

"Victória, I don't think you should be getting upset."

She pushed my hand off her arm with an energy and strength I didn't know she possessed. I didn't know what to do. As much as I wanted to hug and hold her, I was sure it wouldn't be a good idea. I frantically looked around, wishing Verónica would come back.

"Don't you dare tell me what I should and shouldn't do. Who the fuck are you?" she screamed at the top of her lungs.

Tears were flowing freely from both of our faces. I never meant to inflict such pain on my children. What bothered me more than anything was the fact that I'd probably never get them to understand what motivated their mother and me to make the decisions we did. "Victória," I said a little more sternly.

She turned to me with a look that could only be described as hatred. "Where's my fucking brother, and who the fuck said you could come in my room?"

I couldn't take it anymore. I started backing out. The nurse burst in and immediately took control. She told me to step out into the hallway while she examined Victória. I was grateful for a reason to escape. I was shaken to the core and felt so helpless to do anything.

"Are you okay?" Verónica asked as she placed a hand on my shoulder.

I needed her touch. More than anything, I needed a hug. "Oh God, I'm so sorry." I wasn't talking to anyone in particular, but I had to say it just in case. I knew seeing her would be difficult, but never in a million years could I have imagined how bad it was going to be.

"Do you want to sit down?"

"Stop fussing over me. I'm fine." I immediately regretted taking my frustration out on Verónica. Obviously hurt, she withdrew her hand.

"Sweetheart, no, I'm sorry. That didn't sound quite the way I intended it to. I just meant that I don't want you making a big deal about what you saw earlier. I'm fine . . . really I am; it doesn't happen often. I am stressed and that doesn't help the situation. You have to understand that—"

"You can go in now. I've given her a shot so she can rest. Please don't stay long," the nurse instructed as she exited the room.

I understood the warning in her voice. Verónica went in first and I reluctantly followed. I knew it wasn't going to be easy coming back into their lives, but damn, I never expected this.

# CHAPTER NINETEEN

## MOSES RAMSEY

The baby and I were sitting in the living room when Verónica came home from the hospital. I could tell she'd been crying so I assumed it had something to do with her sister. I had not gotten the chance to go to the hospital to visit Victória yet. It was something I needed to do, but I wanted my visit to be kept a secret.

"Hey." She put her purse down on the sofa and stared at the television.

I was surprised she didn't make a beeline for the baby, but I didn't think she even realized that I was holding him. "Where's your father?"

"Said he wanted to be by himself." Verónica wasn't being very talkative, which was highly unusual for her.

"How'd it go?"

"Bad."

I waited for her to elaborate, but she just stared at the television like she was watching *The Real Housewives of Atlanta*. I might have thought so, too, if it weren't football. Verónica hated football.

"Is your sister okay?"

She tore her eyes from the television and stared at me like I'd said the dumbest shit on the planet. "Would you be okay if you found out that everything your parents had ever told you in life was a fucking lie?"

"Is that a rhetorical question?" I could have confessed to my own deception while the door was wide open, but I punked out.

"Seriously, they lied about everything."

What was I to say? I was just as guilty. "Stay here, we need to talk." I went upstairs and put M down for what I hoped to be the night. It felt good taking care of him, watching our first game together, and being responsible. I hoped that what I was about to tell Verónica wouldn't change our future together. I poured both of us a double shot of rum on the rocks before I returned to the living room. Verónica was still staring at the TV as if she really understood what she was watching.

I turned it off. "Here, you're going to need this."

"Oh, shit. If this is more true confessions, I've had enough today."

"I understand. But there is something I need to get off my chest, and it's best you hear it now rather than later."

"Is it going to be bad?" Tears started leaking from her eyes.

I didn't want to hurt her, but I was ready to start the healing process. "Your meeting me wasn't by chance."

"Excuse me?" She put her drink down on the table without touching a drop.

I drained my glass and reached for hers. If she wasn't going to drink it, there was no sense in letting aged rum go to waste. "Now don't go getting all upset and shit, it's not as bad as it sounds. Your Uncle Monte, posing as your father, hired me to follow your mother. He believed she was having an affair but I never confirmed it. The only reason I am telling you this now is because I'm tired of keeping it inside. I want us to build a solid foundation together, and it can't be done if it starts out on a broken slab."

She sat back, despondent. I could tell she was a little leery. She looked like she was about to bolt from the room at any moment.

"One day I followed you."

She gasped and started to get up, but I stopped her.

"Honey, wait. Before you start jumping to conclusions and shit, let me finish."

She sat back down with her arms folded across her chest.

"You were looking for a job and I created one just for you." I hung my head. This conversation was going to go one way or the other. She was either going to be flattered that I put so much energy into meeting her, or she was going to flip the fuck out about the invasion of her privacy. I braced myself for her reaction.

She started watching the television again. Only problem, though, was it wasn't on. Damn, I didn't anticipate silence. Silence was a motherfucker because folks started confessing to shit they didn't even do just to fill the void. I was not about to get tricked into that shit so I waited her out.

"Can you fix me another drink?" she said and nibbled her bottom lip.

Perfect. She must have read my mind. I went to the bar and grabbed the entire bottle, hoping we didn't need it. After Verónica drank what I would have easily called a triple, she was ready to start talking.

"So, was my mother cheating?" She filled her glass again.

I was relieved she wasn't focused on my deception. I wiped my sweaty brow and tried to keep the smile of satisfaction off my face. "Not that I could tell. Whenever she left the house, she was with Ramón."

Verónica nodded her head but she wasn't finished. "What else?"

"Huh?" If she was requesting something specific, she was going to have to spell it out for me because I was not about to start confessing all willy-nilly.

She poured another drink, and I began to worry things wouldn't turn out as planned. Even though this marriage started with deep deception, I really did want my marriage to work. I only had to remind myself of how I felt the day I found out she was having a baby, and I knew that I wanted what my mother and father had, and I believed I could get it with Verónica. I reached out to put my arm around her shoulders, but she pulled away.

"Were you a part of the scam my uncle pulled on my family?"

I was outraged. *I did some fucked up shit . . . but that other shit with your uncle, I didn't even see it coming.* "Hell no! I didn't know the man like that. He fooled all of us."

"How am I supposed to believe you?" She was on a slow boil—the alcohol contributed to the heat.

"Seriously? Are you fucking serious? Honestly, you should be flattered I went the extra mile just to meet you."

"Flattered? Are you high?" Her voice reached a high-pitched squeal, which grated on my nerves.

"Honey, calm down. You will wake the baby."

She jerked away from me again.

"Don't you see I couldn't say anything to you because I couldn't explain why I was watching your house? So I kept watching the house—and you—while collecting a check from the person I thought was Carlos Mendoza for absolutely nothing. One day I decided I had enough of the charade. Instead of watching out for Mrs. Mendoza, I followed you to the unemployment office."

She still didn't say anything, so my stupid ass kept on talking. "I went back to my office feeling excited. I was about to take matters into my own hands. I sat down at my desk and composed an ad to appear in the paper for an office assistant. See, I had no idea what your skill level was and, to be honest, I didn't give a damn. It took a month before you finally took the bait and came in for an interview." I sat back, confidently smug about the way I explained my actions.

"Is any of that supposed to make me feel better? I feel violated."

"Honey, don't . . . I'll admit it was a fucked-up situation. But when I saw you, I was already in. There was no way I could change it, and I didn't want to lose the opportunity to get to know you. I'm a private investigator. It's what I do, but I never expected to fall in love with you. That was never part of my plan." I reached for her again, but she still moved away from me.

She poured herself another drink, and I was still working on mine.

"Are you finished with true confessions?" She was mean-spirited and sarcastic, but I could understand it.

I ignored her apparent attitude. I'd probably feel the same way if the shoe were on the other foot. "I turned down so many applicants waiting for you to come through the door. I didn't even care if you knew how to turn a computer on, let alone use it." I started laughing but she didn't join in. "I wanted to get to know you. My heart practically skipped a beat when you walked into the office. Remember, I didn't have a receptionist, so you walked up to my door and knocked. This was the closest I'd been to you, and you were even more beautiful up close than you were from a distance.

"My dick was hard as a rock, just smelling your perfume. You broke my heart when you told me you were married. It felt like you'd thrown a bucket of ice-cold water on me. I felt so dumb. I'd spent so much time watching the family, it never even dawned on me to follow you home. I just assumed you were single."

"So why did you give me the job?"

"I convinced myself that you were off-limits. As far as I was concerned, you had AIDS and therefore were untouchable."

Verónica shot me a dirty look, shaking her head, but she didn't look as mad as she originally had. "You should have told me the truth."

"You're right and I have to admit it was hard. When you told me you were married, I almost told you the job was filled but I was caught. If I said no, you could have sued the shit out of me for marital discrimination or something stupid like that." I was lying through my teeth, and I was mad at myself for not being more thorough in my investigation. I began to second-guess myself as to what else I'd missed.

"So, no regrets?" She was clearly drunk, swaying to music that didn't exist.

"Uh . . . of course not." In reality I was full of regrets, but I was stuck like chuck. I was going to have to spend at least eight hours a day with a woman who I was deeply attracted to. My gut told me that this was going to be very hard to deal with. Despite my fears I was still excited about getting to know this exotic creature who stood before me. Perhaps if I listened more to my gut instinct instead of my dick, things wouldn't have turned out as badly as they had.

"Hey, I wasn't going to sleep with you. That's not why I hired you. I just wanted to be around you. I promise."

"But you fucked me anyway."

"That was your idea, remember? You came on to me." Damn, I didn't mean to say that out loud. It didn't quite sound the way that it happened.

"Ouch, I thought we came on to each other."

I'd hurt her feelings. Shit, I didn't want to waste time talking. With the baby and her father, Verónica and I had so little time alone. I was missing my wife. "Damn, baby, I didn't mean it like that. All I'm trying to tell you is that I fell in love with you the moment I saw you. I had to have you, and I'm so happy to have you as my wife."

She looked as if she didn't believe me, but one kiss ended any further discussion.

# CHAPTER TWENTY

## CARLOS MENDOZA

"Verónica, how well do you know this man you are married to?" I wanted to confess to my involvement with him. There had been so many lies and so much deceit flowing through our family, I just wanted to pump the brakes. If only for a little while.

"Padre, Moses has been wonderful to me and Ramón. He's my best friend and he loves me and the baby."

Her face was animated, and I could see the love in her eyes. Her mother used to look at me like that before our sons were killed. I felt a pang of regret for all that could have been but could be no more.

I found her eyes with mine. "I hear what you are saying, but how much do you know about him? Have you met his family?"

"Well . . . no, I haven't met them yet. We've only been married for a few months and it was a spur-of-the-moment wedding. Besides, his parents live out of state. I'm sure once Moses calls them and lets them know that we exist, either they will come see us or we will go visit them."

"He hasn't even told them?"

"To be honest, I don't know. We've never discussed it."

I didn't like the sound of it. Regardless of the timing of the marriage, if Moses had legitimately good intentions toward my daughter and her child, he would've contacted his family by now. I could understand that it might have been difficult for him to accept a child who wasn't his, but from my understanding, he knew this before he married my daughter.

"He should have told them by now." I was heated and ready to confront him myself.

"No, Padre, there really hasn't been any time. With what is going on with Victória, telling anyone really had slipped my mind."

I wasn't sure I believed her. We were sitting in the living room after Moses came into the house and went directly to his office. "I'm not trying to bring trouble into your home, but I would be lying if I said this doesn't concern me." I could see the worry lines on her face and could tell I had planted little seeds of doubt in her mind. That was good —it was what I intended to do. As far as I was concerned, he should have told the world he was married to my child and the fact that he didn't even tell his family worried me.

Regardless of how good things appeared on the surface, I didn't trust Moses. I felt like he was in this deeper than he let on. I was determined to find out what his involvement was. I wanted to confront him but I also knew that he wouldn't tell me the truth. The fact that he wasn't the first person to call me when all of this was going down told me he couldn't be trusted.

I was no longer living with my daughter but I visited every day. I had moved back into our old house. I could not believe that my brother had the nerve to put it up for sale, but I managed to stop the proceedings. I was waiting for Victória to get well enough so I could show them what was hidden inside.

# CHAPTER TWENTY-ONE

## VICTÓRIA MENDOZA

Verónica walked into my hospital room with a bundle of flowers.

"What the fuck is going on, Verónica? I feel like I've been on some other planet and the whole world has marched forward without me."

"I know, sweetie. Things have been so crazy. Once you're better, I will explain everything that I know."

"No, I'm not waiting 'til then. I need to know now." It wasn't often that I pressed my older sister to do something she didn't want to do, but I was tired of being in the dark. I felt like I had been asleep for a decade instead of the last two months.

"Sweetie, calm down. This can't be good for your condition."

"My condition? What the hell is my condition? Why am I in this hospital in the first place?"

"Tilo shot you." Verónica looked like she wanted to swallow her tongue.

"Huh? Why?" I couldn't breathe. I felt like someone was choking me. I knew something was wrong but I had no idea it was this bad.

"How much do you remember?" She set the flowers on my bedside table.

"Huh?" I couldn't concentrate on what Verónica was saying to me. She must have been mistaken. There was no way Tilo could have tried to kill me. Why? She loved me. I started crying; there had to be some mistake. Nothing was making sense.

"Victória, should I get the nurse? Are you in pain?"

Yes, I was in pain but not from my injuries. My heart was the source of my pain, but I couldn't speak about it now. I needed time to wrap my arms around what Verónica had just said. "I'm fine but my head hurts." I didn't want to talk anymore. I turned over on my side. My head wound wasn't as sensitive, so I was able to lie on my side.

"Okay, boo, I'm going to let you get some sleep. The doctors said you can go home tomorrow."

Home, what did I have to go home to? Everything I cared about was gone, except for Ramón.

"Ramón, where is he?" I sat up again as I was starting putting two and two together. I remembered Ramón being in the house with me.

Verónica pulled me into her arms and rubbed my hair away from my face. "He's gone, honey. Tilo shot him too, but he didn't make it. They said he died instantly, so he didn't suffer."

I pushed away from my sister. This was too much to take. Ramón wouldn't have even known who Tilo was if I hadn't introduced them. "Oh God, no!" I screamed, but in my heart I knew it to be true. It had to be because it hurt too badly for it not to be. I felt like someone had placed a humongous stone on top of my chest and it was pressing down on me. Verónica held me so tightly I felt faint.

"It's okay, it's okay," Verónica chanted.

She lied. How was anything ever going to be okay? Ramón hadn't even had a chance to live his life and he was dead because of me. I wanted to be alone. I needed to be alone. "Leave." My voice was muffled against Verónica's shirt.

"What did you say?"

"Leave. Please." I pushed away from my sister. I understood her desire to comfort me, but I couldn't handle it right now. I needed to be by myself.

"I don't think I should—"

"Go, dammit!" I tried it the nice way but it didn't work. If yelling at her was the only way that I could get her the fuck out of my room, so be it. "Go now, please," I whispered.

She jumped up from my bed and walked reluctantly toward the door. She was visibly upset by my outburst, but at the moment, I couldn't care less for her feelings. I had to get a handle on my own feelings before I did something I would probably regret.

"I'll be back in the morning to pick up you. If you need anything before then, call me," she said as she quietly closed the door behind her.

I summoned the nurse.

"Yes, may I help you?" the nurse said through an intercom system.

"My head is hurting. Can you give me something for the pain so I can sleep?"

"Sure, let me check your chart and someone will be there shortly."

My head was hurting, but not enough to require drugs. I wanted them to escape reality. I didn't want to think about what my sister told me. It was hard enough thinking about Tilo trying to kill me, but she took things to another level when she killed my brother.

"That bitch had better run 'cause when I find her, her ass is mine!" I meant that shit. I was going to find that lying bitch and when I did it was not going to be pretty.

# CHAPTER TWENTY-TWO

## VERÓNICA RAMSEY

I cried all the way home from the hospital. I felt like I'd failed my younger sister and brother. Even though I had nothing to do with the madness that caused Ramón's demise and her attempted murder, I still felt responsible because I was the eldest. I pulled into my driveway with a heavy heart. I didn't want to go in the house. Behind those doors I had to be Supermom. I had to have everything under control. And today I just didn't damn feel like it. I sat out in the car until it grew too warm inside for me to stay any longer. I walked toward the door with leaden footsteps because I didn't know if I could carry out my charade today.

"How is she?" Padre asked as he handed me my sleeping son.

I wanted to chastise him because I knew that he probably held LM the entire time I'd been gone. I understood his protective nature, but he made it difficult for me when I was home alone and trying to do other things.

"Have you been holding him the entire time?" I tried to keep the censure from my voice, but I was sure he could detect my irritation.

"No, I just fed him and he fell asleep."

My father was a liar and the truth was not in him, but I didn't want to fight. I wanted to lie down and sleep myself. I carried LM to his crib and fell across the bed, hoping for at least an hour or two of uninterrupted sleep. LM was finally sleeping through the night, but this latest round with Victória was weighing heavily on my mind. I never had a close girlfriend. Victória was the only friend I ever had. That was another reason why it was so difficult for me to see her in the hospital. It was nothing short of a miracle that she was going to be released tomorrow. Physically she was okay, but I wasn't sure how she was doing mentally. I was waiting for her to show some sign of emotion, but every time she got to that point, she sent me away.

Padre came to the doorway and knocked softly. "Unless you need me to stick around, I'm going to head on home."

"Sit with me for a moment please."

He looked a little unsure but he came into the room and sat down on my bed.

"I told Victória about Ramón."

He lowered his head. We had many conversations about when we'd tell her.

"I wanted to be there when you did. Is she okay?"

"She's as okay as she can be under the circumstances. I wanted to wait until you were around, but the timing was right. She wanted to know what happened to her, so I told her."

"Do you think she remembers anything?"

"She might. It's so hard trying to read her mind. She keeps so many of her emotions inside. It's hard to tell."

"Your mother was just like that."

"She was? She didn't seem to have a problem expressing her emotions to me." I laughed as I rubbed my butt. I had my share of whippings, so if she held something back, I'd hate to see it.

"Trust me, she held a lot back. I see your mother in both of you."

"Oh, yeah? What do you see in me?" I was enjoying this conversation. This was the first time that I'd sat down with him and didn't feel like pointing fingers at him.

"You got her diplomatic side. She was about harmony and balance."

We sat in silence for a few seconds as I absorbed his words.

"I knew she needed help, but I was too selfish to come."

I looked up, surprised by the way the conversation changed. "Padre, I was with her most of my life, she never said she was unhappy."

"Don't you see, that's how she was. I knew her well enough to know what she wasn't saying."

"Moses said Monte hired him because he thought Madre was having an affair."

Padre quickly inhaled but he blew the air out just as rapidly. "To be honest, in all the years we were together, I never entertained that thought."

"Did you care?"

He didn't answer. For a moment I thought he was going to ignore the question.

"Our relationship was complicated. Your mother didn't love me. She respected me, but she didn't love me. There is a big difference."

"Why did y'all stay together so long?"

"We didn't know any better. It wasn't like that for us coming up with the choices you have here in America. Our marriage was arranged . . . and for me, I never thought about doing anything else than what I was told to do."

Wow, I wasn't expecting this type of honesty from him. I expected him to paint this rosy picture, especially since my mother wasn't there to dispute anything he said.

"Regrets?"

He didn't hesitate to answer this one. "Plenty. My biggest regret is that I didn't come home sooner. I could've, there was nothing holding me in Colombia. My parents were gone. But I think I was afraid, too much time had passed."

"Did Uncle Monte have a family?" I was curious about the man who lived in our house but rarely showed any kindness toward me.

"His wife died before they had children, so no. I was his only family."

"Wow, maybe he was jealous of you. You had five children. You had sons."

He shook his head in the affirmative. "We'll never know."

He was right, we wouldn't.

"In case you're wondering, Moses said he never found any evidence of an affair." I saw him smile before I drifted off to sleep.

# CHAPTER TWENTY-THREE

## VICTÓRIA MENDOZA

I was facing the door when it opened. I was relieved he got there in time. "Thanks for coming on such short notice." I attempted to sit up straight as I raised my bed.

"Not a problem. I've been meaning to come, but I wanted to make sure you were up for visitors." Moses stood at the foot of my bed.

"Where's Verónica?"

"She's home with the baby. She said she was coming to get you tomorrow around twelve."

"Good." I nodded my head. I wasn't sure how to start my conversation with my sister's husband. He was a virtual stranger to me. The only things I knew about him were the things my sister told me. My brother Ramón worked for Moses for a while and idolized him, and this meant a lot to me.

"How much do you remember?" Moses made it easy on me by cutting directly to the chase.

"Pretty much everything, I think. I needed to speak with you to help me fill in the gaps." I was partially truthful. I did have a few holes in my memory, but more than anything I wanted to know if he knew Tilo and I were lovers. If he didn't know, it was a secret I was prepared to take to my grave.

He took a seat in the only chair in the room and pulled it up close to my bed. He really was a handsome man. He reminded me of LL Cool J, only younger.

I said, "How is it that you came to know Tilo? I remember her saying something about you being her boss."

"It's kind of a long story. The short version is she was looking for you. Apparently you hadn't shown up for work for several days and would not answer your phone. I was dropping off Ramón and she followed me. I busted her following me and she starting filling me in on what she thought was going on in the house."

"Is that all?"

"She thought all of you were in danger. Ramón confirmed it, so I got involved."

He still wasn't answering my question.

"So you hired her? I still don't understand how all that came about."

"Like I said, it's complicated, but our relationship was strictly professional."

He knew, I could tell by the way he answered the question. Now I needed to find out if he had shared that information with my sister. I took a moment to think about how to phrase my next question.

"I think you should know that your father has asked me to find Tilo; however, your sister is totally against it, and I would appreciate it if you wouldn't mention it to her. She would like to let sleeping dogs lie."

"And?" I was nervous but I tried not to let it show.

"I'm gonna find the bitch."

"Perfect. I want in for personal reasons."

"I was hoping you would say that. So far I haven't been able to find out anything about her. Her FBI records are sealed. They believe she's dead and refuse to allow me access to her files. They wouldn't even tell me what she was working on."

"I still can't believe she was an FBI agent. If she was working on a case, it was obviously dealing with my family. My guess is that she wanted the bonds that Ramón got from Madre's safe-deposit box."

"That's a safe assumption, but I don't think that was the reason. Call it intuition or call it superstition, but I think it goes deeper than the bonds. If you want my opinion, the bonds were an added bonus. I think she was looking for something else," he said.

"This shit is crazy. Tilo never appeared to be that type of person. Shit, she was scared of her own shadow." My heart felt like it was breaking into little pieces. Tilo was the only person I'd allowed into my personal space, into my heart, and she deceived me. Suddenly, I didn't want to talk anymore. I didn't want to know any more details of what had happened to me. "Moses, I think I need to take a nap. I'm not feeling so well. Can we talk later?" I still had questions, but I wasn't ready to deal with the answers.

"Sure. I'll see you later at the house when Verónica brings you home."

"No offense, I don't want to come to your house. I'm not going to feel comfortable, and I honestly ain't ready to play aunty."

"I can understand that. Sometimes LM makes so much noise, I want to leave too, but I love my little man so I'm staying. Where do you want to go?"

"My apartment, if it's still available."

"What are you going to tell Verónica? You know her feelings will be hurt if you don't come home with her."

I allowed my head to sink down to my chest as I thought of a solution. "I'll make her understand. Trust me."

"Okay. Call me when you're ready to work." He handed me his card, which I stuck in my drawer.

"Moses, this one is personal. Can we keep things between us?"

"I'm good with that, but I've already told you your dad wants in. Are you good with that?"

"Honestly, I don't know. I have to wait and see. For now don't tell him I'm on board. There are a few things that I don't want to explain to him, or even my sister, for that matter."

"Gotcha. I think I can handle that."

# CHAPTER TWENTY-FOUR

## CARLOS MENDOZA

Moving into my old house was easy. The new owners wanted it renovated before they rented it out, but I was trying to convince them it was easier to sell it back to me, because if they didn't, I'd have the property held up in court for the next few years with a protest. They weren't happy, but neither was I. My brother practically gave the house away, and it cost me an additional $20,000 to buy it back.

I explained to them that Monte had no legal authority to sell my house, so I returned their money and a little extra to make them go away. They weren't happy because they wanted rental property close to downtown, but they were going to have to find another house. It was a lot of money, but there was more than enough money hidden inside the house to make up for it.

Over the years, not only was I sending the bearer bonds, I also sent cash the likes of which had not turned up yet. Alelina told me she was hiding it in the house, and I was going to find it. No one knew of this stash so I was fairly confident it was still there. I intended to use a good portion of the money to find Tilo. She killed my son and harmed my daughter. I was looking forward to teaching her a lesson for fucking with my family.

I looked around the house. I didn't feel any connection with it because none of our old furnishings were

left in the house. The walls were painted white and bar-
ren. The rugs that used to cover the hardwood floors
had been removed. Everything that made it a home
was gone.

Since I was alone, I didn't bother to hide my tears. I
stepped into the kitchen. All of our old appliances had
been replaced with the latest technology. This only
added to the unfamiliarity of the house. I had asked my
wife several times, in fact, to update the house using
some of the money I'd sent her, but she never did it.
She claimed the old stuff worked just fine for her. She
was a frugal woman by nature; it was one of the things
I loved about her. For a moment I was overwhelmed
with sadness for a love that started out so right but
turned out so wrong.

My footsteps echoed across the hardwood floors as
I walked from the kitchen back to the living room. It
wasn't a bad house. It was old but it was built during
an era when builders actually cared about what they
were building. This wasn't some subdivision shit that
they threw up in a matter of days. This house had style.
I hadn't realized it until I saw it empty. In fact, if things
worked out with my family, maybe I would stay in Atlanta and make this house into a home.

As I walked around I was reminded that it was in this
room that my son was taken from me. I walked around
the room to see if I could detect where he had actually
fallen. Just thinking about Ramón lying in a pool of his
own blood was enough to make my legs grow weak. I
knew my youngest son resented me, and I would have
done anything to have been able to go back through
time and undo the hurt and pain that I'd caused him.
Even though I hurt my other children as well, with
them, I still had time to try to mend the damage I'd
caused.

I left the living room and went to the bedroom I once shared with my wife. The time passed so quickly, it was hard to believe I hadn't been there in over ten years. I paused for a second at the door to get my emotions in check. I wasn't big on displaying my feelings, but since I was alone, I allowed myself to go with the emotions I felt. As I pushed open the door I pretended things were as they should have been and waited for my wife to greet me. But of course they weren't— and never would be again. The thought tugged at my heart and I lost my composure completely.

I sank to my knees as my sobs overwhelmed me. The force of my tears was so hard I rolled onto my side and brought my knees to my chest and rocked from side to side. A lot of plans for our future were made in this room. This was the only place in the house where I freely spoke to my wife and she talked back to me. This was the only room in which we shed façades. We were forced to wear and rejoice in a love we weren't allowed to share.

I continued to rock back and forth until the sobs became muted whimpers. It was a good cry, long overdue. I continued to cry, but my tears weren't just for the death of my wife and son. It was the end of my vision and my dreams. Things would never be the same and there was nothing I could do about it. It was a bitter pill for me to swallow since I always prided myself on being in control. But someone I didn't even know had taken that power from me and I wanted it back.

I indulged myself for more than an hour. It was an hour that I didn't have to spare, but I didn't have much choice—my grief knew no bounds. As I wiped away the last tear I struggled to my feet. I wasn't as young as I used to be, and getting my legs up under me was harder than I thought it would be. If my brother were still alive, I would have shot him myself because I ultimately felt it was because of him that my life was ruined. I closed the door behind me when I left, and vowed to never go in that room again.

I turned on the light to the stairs leading down to the basement. The bulb that normally lit the top of the stairs had obviously blown out, but there was enough light coming from the window at the bottom of the steps for me to see my way. I carefully walked down the stairs. The last thing I needed to do was to fall and break a hip or something.

Like the rest of the house it was empty of furnishings with the exception of a washer and a dryer. I guessed the new owners decided to keep them, even though they were old as hell. For the first time since I entered the house, I smiled.

# CHAPTER TWENTY-FIVE

## VICTÓRIA MENDOZA

Verónica was picking me up today so I had to get my mind right. Part of me was excited, but the other part of me was worried about where I was going to stay. I didn't know what awaited me back at my old apartment, and I definitely didn't want to stay with Verónica and Moses.

I was sitting on the side of the bed when Verónica pushed open the door. The nurse had already removed my IV and had given me my discharge papers.

"Hey, you, you ready to go?" she said with a gorgeous smile on her face.

"I'll say. I didn't sleep at all last night. It was like they were trying to give me every test under the sun before I left. I'm so needled out it ain't even funny!"

"I hear ya. I was only in the hospital for about ten days but they gave a new meaning to *running a few tests.*"

"I guess I shouldn't complain because they obviously did something right, and at least I get the chance to leave."

"You ain't even lied. There were times that I didn't think you were going to make it," Verónica said.

She had a point. The nurses all told me how lucky I was to be alive. I thanked God every day for sparing me. I got up off the bed and started gathering the last of my belongings. I didn't have much, but all that I had I was taking with me. Hell, they were charging me for it so I might as well have taken it. I even took the notepad and pen with the hospital's name on it. I was sure that when I drilled down into the detail of my bill, somewhere on it would be a charge for it.

"Let me get that for you," Verónica said.

I stepped back, surprised. I wasn't used to having her waiting on me, it was usually the other way around. Especially when she was pregnant with LM. She had me doing everything, and I do mean *everything*. This was like poetic justice.

"It's not heavy, I can carry it," I protested mildly for appearances.

"Girl, it ain't often that I get to wait on you so you'd better enjoy it while it lasts. Trust and believe as soon as we get to the house, you're on your own."

I cringed when she mentioned going to her house. Not only did I not want to go there because of Moses, I also didn't want to be up half the night because of a crying child, nephew or not. "Where's Moses?" I asked as we walked through the door.

"At work, honey, where else?"

I could not help but to laugh at the way she turned up her lips when she said it. "Why you say it like that? You knew that man worked a lot. Shit, you used to work with him so you know firsthand how he rolled."

"I know you're right, but once I went home, I never knew how much longer he stayed in the office. I could only assume. It's been a damn culture shock now that I'm at home waiting for him. After sitting at home with the baby all day, I need adult interaction. That's why I'm glad that you are coming home with me."

I missed a step and stumbled when she said that. I didn't want to burst her bubble or anything, but I wasn't feeling that at all. "Uh, Verónica . . . I'm not so sure that going home with you is a good idea. I mean, you and Moses are still honeymooners. I don't want to be like a third wheel. Plus, we've got a good relationship; I'm not trying to ruin shit by moving in with you." I hoped my explanation and misgivings were enough to make her change her mind.

"Girl, Little Moses is a third wheel. You would be more like an intervention. We've lived together most of our lives. It won't be anything different, so stop tripping."

Damn, she was making me feel like shit. We'd just passed the nurse's station when the head nurse looked up and saw me.

The nurse said, "Hey, wait, you can't just walk out of here. Let me get someone to assist you."

"Nurse Walker, that won't be necessary. My sister will help me if I need it."

"It's hospital policy." She put down her pen and called someone over her radio to assist.

"For crying out loud. Can't I walk out with my dignity?" I whined. I was beginning to develop a headache. Everyone had plans for me except me, and it was getting on my nerves. I patted my foot in agitation.

"Calm down, sis. It will only take a minute and we will be on our way."

She was so giddy, I wanted to slap the fuck out of her. I leaned up against the station and tried to hide my irritation with the whole nine yards.

It took another ten minutes before we were finally able to leave the hospital, by this time I was fit to be tied. I just wanted to go someplace and be by myself. I still wasn't up to full strength so I was so agitated. I really needed to be alone before I said something that I would later regret.

"You comfortable? We should be at the house in no time," Verónica said as she pulled out of the hospital parking lot.

"What about Padre? Where is he these days?" I said, taking in the scenery.

"He's at the house, watching LM. He's moved back into our old house, so unless he's watching the baby, I hardly see him."

Being in the hospital I'd completely missed winter but it didn't bother me one bit. I hated the cold.

"Hey, when you feel up to it, you might even consider moving in with him."

"Pump your brakes, sis. You may be feeling all lovey-dovey and shit, but I don't know that man, so you can nix that shit."

"He's not that bad, Victória. He's actually a sweet man." She was all smiles and shit, but I wasn't feeling it.

"He may be, but I'm going to wait until I get to see that for myself. It's only a matter of time before we see if it's all an act or not. And you really are going to have to think of another name for your child. You can't keep calling him LM. I can understand how it would be confusing calling him Moses and you sure can't call him little. The little girls will have my poor nephew traumatized by second grade."

We both laughed.

She said, "I see it's going to take more than one to the head to change that wacked sense of humor you have."

"I'm just saying, *Li'l?* Even after he explains why y'all call him that, kids are still going to be curious. You going to have folks following him to the urinal to find out what's really going on. God forbid his dick . . ." I held up my pointer finger and thumb, squinting as I looked between my parted fingers. "Lawd, you should start working on this right away before the name sticks. I'm not calling him that. I just won't be party to that nonsense, and you can best believe I'm going to tell him just as soon as he's old enough to understand."

We couldn't stop laughing.

Verónica said, "His middle name is Ramón."

The car became so quiet I could hear the crickets chirping outside the window. "Damn, I ain't ready to call him that either." I looked out the window, trying to think of how to get back to the happy wave we were just riding.

"It's all good. We'll think of something. I don't want my baby traumatized."

"Can we stop by my old apartment before we go to your house? I want to see what Tilo did with my things."

"Victória, you've been in the hospital for close to two months. Chances are the landlord has already evicted your things, and they are probably sitting up in some junkyard somewhere or in one of your neighbor's houses."

"Can you just humor me?" I said quietly, but my mind was made up. If I hadn't been evicted, I was moving home. "Wait, where is my car?"

"Moses drove it over to our house. But I'm not about to let you drive. You just got out of the hospital. You should be thinking about getting in bed, not riding all around town and shit."

"Verónica, we can do this the easy way or the hard way." I was done discussing it. I just needed my keys so I could be on my way. "So what's it like having Padre around?" I was trying to change the subject to avoid an argument.

"He is not the same man I remember. He's more . . . mellow and relaxed," Verónica answered.

"Are you sure that it's him?" I asked. We had been duped once and I for one wasn't ready to be duped again.

"I'm pretty sure. He's very remorseful for staying away so long, and that's more than I can say for his brother who pretended to be him."

"Shit, that wouldn't be hard to do . . . The fucker didn't show one ounce of compassion toward Madre."

We sat in a comfortable silence for a few minutes as Verónica drove. I was still going through it and trying to come to grips with the fact that my brother Ramón was dead and was never coming back. We both started speaking at the same time.

"I was thinking about Ramón," Verónica said.

"I know. I was thinking about him too, and our mother." I felt the tears I'd been holding back drench my cheeks.

Verónica said, "Cut that out. If you keep crying, I'm going to crash into a tree or something. Why don't we think about something else?"

She was right. We had had enough pain over the last few months. It was time to heal. "You're right. I'm sorry. So, how are things going with you and Moses?"

Verónica wiggled in her seat. I was trying to read her body language to see what that meant, but I was clueless. I wasn't sure if she was wiggling because she was uncomfortable speaking about him or because she had a hot, freaky flashback and had to fan the cootie.

"It's going good, I guess. When I first came home from the hospital, he was very standoffish, but he's warming back up to me now. I think we are going to make it."

"You were worried?" I was surprised. I knew Verónica loved Moses. She risked her first marriage on him, and he appeared to love her as well. But who was I to judge? I thought Tilo loved me.

"I hate to say it, but yeah, it was rough at first. If I didn't know better, I might even go so far as to say Tilo started it. Her name came up a lot, and I finally had to check him about it. I don't even want her name mentioned in my house."

My hands started sweating. Tilo wasn't my favorite person these days either, but it would really fuck me up if I found out that she was screwing Moses too. I tried to play off my concerns. "Are you serious? How? She didn't even know either of you until all this shit went down, right?" A forgotten memory bounced around in my head. Tilo did know of Verónica. I told her about the affair, her marriage, everything. Damn.

"She may not have known me personally, but I think it's mighty strange she was the one who found me and took me to the hospital after I got away from Monte's madness."

*Motherfucker, this shit keeps getting deeper and deeper.* I was so confused, I didn't know who to trust.

"What could she have possibly said? I mean, think about it. I could tell the moment I saw Moses that he was in love with you."

Ramón said the same thing to me when he saw the way Tilo looked at me. I was learning a valuable lesson: looks could be deceiving.

"Things are better now. We've gotten past the bad stuff," Verónica said.

"So how did he react to the baby? I can't wait to see him."

"Girl, at first he wouldn't go near him. If LM was crying, Moses would walk right on by him like he didn't even hear him. I swear I cried myself to sleep every night for a solid month."

"Aw, sweetie, I'm so sorry you had to go through all of that."

"It's better now. He's come around."

"So, what prompted the change?"

"To be honest, I don't know. But I am glad it happened because I don't think I would have been able to continue down the same road we were going."

"Well, for your sake, I'm glad."

We arrived at Verónica's house. I was eager to get going, so I immediately gathered my things.

"Wait, give me a minute to check on Padre and the baby, and I'll ride over there with you."

"No, I need to do this by myself. There is a chance she's gotten rid of everything but I have to see it for myself. If that's the case, I'll be back. Either way, I have my phone and will call you to let you know what's going on." I didn't want to argue with her about it, but I would if I had to.

"Victória, I don't have a good feeling about this. I bet if I look through your discharge papers it probably says you shouldn't drive."

"Whatever. I'm going. I'll call you after I see what I see." I left her sitting in the car.

# CHAPTER TWENTY-SIX

## TILO ADAMS

I leaped up from the bed in a cold sweat, shaking from head to toe. My eyes swung around my hotel room, frantically looking to see who or what had scared me so badly. I was trembling. I held my hands in front of my face, and they looked like they didn't even belong to me. I didn't want to admit it, but I was losing touch with reality. My life had become a series of bad dreams and sullen memories. More than anything, I wished I could have a do-over. If God granted me one, I was certain I would do things differently.

"This shit has got to stop," I said out loud. Every time I closed my eyes it was the same damn thing and the shit was old, but I didn't know how to make it stop. The sleep that I managed to get was sporadic at best. It took me hours to fall asleep, but when I did I was tormented with dreams, visions, and other unspeakable horrors.

I never imagined life as a criminal would be so hard. Now I understood what it meant to be on the lam and it was not a pleasant feeling. My cell phone sat on the vanity but it was just a paperweight because there wasn't a single person listed who I could call just to get me through times like these. My mom thought I was dead. With the exception of Moses, everyone else did too.

"I need to get away." It was time to make a move. I had been saying this every morning for the last two months, but I had yet to act on it. I was still holed up at the Omni Hotel in Atlanta. Fear kept me there. I was afraid to trust the fake ID and passport that I obtained, even though I'd gotten it from a reliable source. "Bitch, stop talking about going away and do something about it." Talking to myself had become second nature. It didn't bother me that I was having a full-blown conversation with myself. With the nightmares I was having, it was a miracle I wasn't walking down the street babbling like an idiot.

I walked into the bathroom to pee. I was so exhausted. I flopped down on the toilet seat and rested my forearms on my thighs. I peed like I hadn't used the toilet in a month. I was so tired, I didn't have the strength to stand up. As I rested my head on my knees, I drifted off to sleep. My nap, however, was cut short by another scary image of Victória's face after I had shot her brother.

"Shit." I wiped my cootie and pulled up my underwear. I went over to the sink to wash my hands. As the water got hot, I grabbed a washcloth from behind the door. The water felt good on my face and soothing to my eyes. For a moment I considered using it as a compress and crawling back to bed, but I was sick of the nightmares, and I was truly ready for a change in scenery. It was time that I did something about it. It didn't make sense to have all this money and be afraid to leave the hotel. I tried to leave the bathroom without looking at my face, but my eyes had a mind of their own. The vision before me repulsed me. My eyes were bloodshot as if I'd been crying, and the dark circles underneath my eyes looked like I'd been in a fight and lost.

"Damn, girl, you've got to pull your shit together." I threw the washcloth in the basin and left the room. It was time I did something about my situation. Before I had a meltdown, I had a plan and I was about to execute it. To make money, you had to have money, and I was about to make mine work for me.


I had always wanted to go on a cruise. Now that I had money, I was going to treat myself to one. I booted up my laptop and did a Google search for "cruises." The list was seemingly endless, and I was about to give up my search. I didn't want just any old cruise. I needed to get away and anonymity was key. I refined my search to "celebrity cruises" because I knew they weren't traveling on the average cruise ship. Bingo!

"'Aw, sookie sookie now.'" I clapped my hands with enthusiasm. Suddenly things were looking brighter. I looked at the different videos and decided I was going to take a world cruise. Mapping out the different cities I wanted to visit, Cunard Cruise vacations, based out of England, seemed like a great choice. I saved the trip to my Yahoo! Trip Planner and looked at the logistics of getting there.

"This bitch is going to set me back about thirty stacks, but it will be worth it. At least I won't have to worry about running into anybody I know. Hell, I might even see Oprah on the ship." I was giddy with the possibilities, but I was also grateful for the break from my reality. Planning the cruise allowed me time to plan for a future and to forget the past. I double-clicked on the *Queen Mary 2* and pulled up the 2011 itinerary.

"Oh shit, they have a cruise leaving on April thirteenth from New York." I pulled out my BlackBerry and checked the date. Being locked up in this hotel room, I'd lost all concept of time.

It was March twenty-fifth so it only gave me a few weeks to get to New York and purchase some clothes for my upcoming trip. I spun around in my chair and started to check out flights to New York. If I could get out of Atlanta today, I was going for it. I'd been pushing my luck by staying in the city anyway. It was time for this eagle to spread her wings and fly.

# CHAPTER TWENTY-SEVEN

## VERÓNICA RAMSEY

I didn't want to admit it, but I was slightly relieved that Victória didn't want to stay with me. I loved my sister and I was glad she was home, but I was still learning how to be a mother and balance my life. It also didn't help that Moses and I were still getting to know each other. In fact, I was learning something new about him every day, and if I was truly honest, not all of them were good.

I felt a little guilty for not sharing all the dynamics of my relationship with Victória, but she had enough on her plate without carrying around my bullshit, too. Things between Moses and me had gotten better, but we were not the same two people who fell in love.

"Hello?" I could hear the television in the living room, but I needed to get a grip on my emotions before I went to check on the rest of my family.

"Yeah."

I was a little put off at Moses' greeting. He used to say "hey, beautiful" when I walked into the room, but I guessed now that he had me he felt he didn't have to do and say all the things that made me fall in love with him in the first place. If Victória had been with me, I would have felt compelled to explain our evolution.

"Is everything okay?" I tried to keep the pain that I felt in my heart out of my voice.

"Yeah, why wouldn't it be?"

Part of me wanted to pick up this ball and run with it, explaining to him all the things that could have gone down while I was away, but I didn't want to spend the rest of the night arguing with him. Luckily, my father moved into Madre's house so we didn't have that added pressure to deal with, either.

"I didn't mean it that way. I turned my phone off when I was in the hospital, so I wanted to make sure you weren't trying to reach me."

"If I needed you, I would have left you a voice mail."

I ignored what I felt to be sarcasm in his voice. I let out a heavy sigh before I continued. "Where is the baby?"

"Walking down 285," Moses responded.

Despite my resolve not to let his lack of enthusiasm bother me, I started to get mad. "Dammit, Moses. Would it hurt you to take your eyes off the television and pay me some attention?"

"What is wrong with you? Are you on your period?"

I wanted to hit him. Why do men think the only reason we argue with them is because we're on our periods? Was it too much to ask that he at least acknowledge my presence with a kiss or something? Hell, he could have told me to kiss his ass and take the trash out on the way to doing it. Something. Shit.

"Never mind." I started to walk away but he grabbed my hand.

"No, seriously, what's up?"

I had his full attention now, but I didn't know what to do with it. He'd made me mad and I wasn't ready to get over it. I yanked my hand away. "Nothing. I'm going to take a walk on 285."

"Aw, man, it was a joke. Don't tell me you are going to take me seriously and shit. What happened to the woman who used to laugh at my jokes?"

"I don't hear anything funny." I folded my arms across my chest. I was still a tiny bit annoyed, but starting to come around.

. "Where's your sister?"

"She might not be staying here after all. She went by her apartment to see if her stuff was still there. If it is, she said she's going to stay there."

"What? She didn't want to come play house with us?"

I laughed for the first time because of something Victória had said about the baby crying all night. "I guess not. How long has the baby been asleep?"

"That boy must have known you left the house because he cried almost the entire time you were gone."

This was not what I wanted to hear, and I immediately started to panic. "Is he okay? Do you think he has a fever? Should I call a doctor?" I was throwing questions over my shoulder as I climbed the stairs.

"Honey, stop. He's fine. I was just fucking with you."

"Moses, that's not something to joke about. Do you even know how hard it is for me to leave my baby? Don't play around like that."

"Honey, chill. I'm sorry."

Even though I accepted his apology, I still went to check on LM. When I was satisfied that he was okay, I went back to the living room where Moses was watching the news. "How was your day?" I was trying to get things back on an even keel, and hopefully Moses and I would spend the rest of the night like the young lovers we really were instead of the boring parents we'd become.

"Huh?" Moses' eyes were glued to the television, and he really wasn't paying attention to me again.

Once again my feelings were hurt. I tried not to take it personally but twice in less than thirty minutes was a little too much for me to take in my moody condition.

"Forget it." I started to go into the kitchen to figure out what to fix for dinner. This was another thing I was rapidly getting tired of doing. I felt more like a fucking maid, but this maid wasn't getting paid.

"Wait." Moses pulled me down in his lap. "I just want to hear the rest of this story."

I turned toward the television. A commercial was playing so I didn't know what had captured his attention.

He started kissing a trail of kisses from my cheek to collarbone. "Mmm, you smell so good." His lips acted like fire to brush, lighting a passionate flame that burned throughout my body.

"Ah," I murmured, but Moses pumped the brakes when Barbara Walters came back on for her special report. *Thirty Days and Thirty Nights* was the name of the special. It wasn't so special to me. I wanted to get back to the kissing, but Moses appeared to have lost interest.

He said, "Have you been following these stories?"

I wanted to tell him what I really felt but I bit my tongue. "No." I was pouting and didn't give a fuck what was on television.

"I have. The violence in Mexico is out of control. Ever since the raid on the Cali Cartel happened here, the drug violence over there has gone through the roof. They are cutting off people's heads and leaving them in the streets with notes on them and shit. It's crazy."

He piqued my interest. Moses eased me off his lap while we both watched the set.

"How long has it been on? Did you record it on the DVR?"

"Sorry, babe, I didn't even think about it."

I got the remote off the table and started recording the show. I was sure Victória would want to see it when she was ready to catch up on the news.

The TV anchorwoman said, "The bodies of eighteen men were found in a mass grave in South Acapulco. Authorities suspect the bodies to be those of the missing members of a group of men who vanished while vacationing on September thirtieth—" The TV screen went to an emergency test broadcast.

"Nah, are they serious? I wanted more information."

"Yo, this is crazy. What the fuck were eighteen men doing together on vacation? That's what I want to know."

"Eww, Moses, that's just nasty."

"I'm just saying. I don't know ten motherfuckers willing to go on vacation together, let alone eighteen."

The show came back on. "Gunman kills fifteen men at a carwash. Thirteen of the men worked at the carwash but they also were clients of a drug rehab center. Mexican authorities have apprehended a single gunman responsible for this latest massacre."

"Damn, sounds like a pissed-off woman to me."

Moses didn't say anything, his eyes glued to the television.

The anchorwoman continued. "The case of the eighteen dead men doesn't add up. Authorities say relatives of the men insist they were ordinary guys with no affiliation to the bloody drug wars plaguing Mexican cities. Police are skeptical about what the travelers were up to."

Moses said, "But it's more than that, boo. Mexico is showing its ass. Let me show you a chart I'm working on." Moses moved, but I didn't pay attention because I was so surprised by what I'd been watching on television.

As a nation we did not act like the people I saw looting and protesting in the streets. I could not imagine what could have happened to push them to the streets.

Moses grabbed my hand and pulled me away from the set.

"Enlighten me because I don't understand." I was hurting inside for the state of the world. Tears rolled down my cheeks as I tried to forget the terror on the faces of the Mexican people.

"Honey, don't cry. I probably shouldn't have even let you see that with all that we've been through. Things are definitely getting out of hand over there."

As we sat down at the kitchen table, I could hear LM beginning to stir around through our monitor.

"I'll get him," Moses offered.

I was glad because I really didn't feel like dealing with him at the moment. I looked through the papers that Moses had given me. The pages extrapolated five years of violence and what appeared to be six months and counting of retaliation. The citizens of Mexico were fighting back, which made sense since Padre said the leaders of the cartel were leaving Mexico in droves.

"Do you see a trend to the violence?" Moses asked when he came back with LM.

"I see that the citizens are angry about the violence and they are fighting back. What do you see?" I already knew I had missed something fundamental, and I needed Moses to help me focus.

"So much of the violence is centered around the police. Yeah, there are some random shootings, but most of it is stemming from the people being tired of a corrupted government."

Moses was so animated it was contagious, but I didn't see where he was going with it. Why was it so important to him and he never lived there? I was watching Moses intently when a thought hit me so powerfully I felt like I'd been slapped. I didn't even want to say out loud what

I was thinking because I didn't want it out in the universe, but I didn't have a choice.

"This is about Tilo, isn't it?" I wanted him to tell me that I was wrong. I was praying that he would say I was tripping, but his brilliant smile confirmed what I feared the most. My heart felt like it was skipping a beat.

"Yeah, I think so," he whispered.

# CHAPTER TWENTY-EIGHT

## MOSES RAMSEY

Verónica wasn't exactly thrilled to hear Tilo's name mentioned in our house. She forbade me to mention her, but I led her to cross the line with my painstakingly staged evidentiary trail. I really had no conclusive evidence that Tilo was involved in the upheaval in Mexico, but I played my long shot so I could work the case without ending up in divorce court.

I felt bad about deceiving Verónica; however, I could not think of any other way. Now that Victória was home from the hospital, Verónica was going to rely more and more on me to care for our son, so I had to make a way to bring my work home without any unnecessary cloak-and-dagger bullshit. I wanted to believe that Verónica would respect the privacy of my office when I was not there. But since she used to work for me, she might not believe in the same sanctity.

I pulled my phone from my hip as I went back downstairs. I quickly dialed the last number on my phone. Putting the phone up to my ear, I waited for it to be answered.

"Did you do it?" a man said.

"Yes, it's done." I peered upstairs to make sure that I was still alone.

"Good. Any problems?"

"No. Everything went fine." I kept a close lookout for Verónica. I couldn't let her sneak up on me.

"Okay. Now just try to relax and wait," the man said.

My palms and armpits started to sweat. "That's so much easier to say than do."

"Well, you're going to have to do the best that you can. You've waited this long, a few more weeks won't hurt you."

"I hear ya. Look, I've gotta go. Verónica's father is pulling up in the driveway." I closed my phone and went into the kitchen and pulled out a bottle of Absolut and two glasses from the cabinet. I carried the glasses into the living room and waited for Mr. Mendoza.


Verónica came into the living room looking sexy as ever.

"Are you feeling better?" I was a little tipsy and feeling pretty good.

She said, "My headache is gone. What are you doing other than having a few libations?"

"Your father and I were getting acquainted."

Verónica looked around with a surprised expression on her face. "Padre? Where is he?"

"He left." I drained my glass and was thinking about pouring another even though the ice had melted.

Verónica went into the kitchen and grabbed her own glass and joined me. "You know we don't have long before little man gets up, right? Even though he's not actually sucking my tit, my boobs start to get tight and feel real heavy right before it's time to feed him. I guess they know it's time to get the pump."

"You want me to rub them for you?" I was only playing, but if she wanted to put her titty in my hand, I damn sure was gonna handle it. When she didn't take me up on my offer, I went in the kitchen to get a bottle ready for the baby.

"Hey, what are you going to do with that?" She had a sexy smile on her face. For a minute it was almost the way it was in the beginning when we had fun and played with each other.

"I was hungry," I jokingly replied. I missed those days of fun and flirtation before we became man and wife and I desperately wanted them back.

"Oh, really? Well, that bottle is reserved for the baby, but if you play your cards right, mister, I'll let you taste the milk from the sprout! Fresh, not that bottled shit."

"Oh, I love it when you cuss. You're so sexy with it." All of a sudden I was in a playful mood, and I wanted to recapture the passion that used to flow between us.

"Oh, daddy, I like when you talk to me like that, but it's going to have to wait 'cause LM's alarm is about to go off any minute." She walked up close to me and gave me a deep, soul-searching kiss. I wrapped my arms around her and tried to hold on to the feeling. This was my biggest problem these days—holding on to the love that drew me to Verónica in the first place. It wasn't another woman who drove a wedge between us, it was the fatherhood of our son. I couldn't help but to feel cheated, even though I knew she was married when we first started dating.

I stepped away as soon as I heard LM wailing in the speaker. I tried not to look at it as a mood killer, but my dick wasn't listening. I pushed away from the counter as Verónica took the bottle and went upstairs. While I waited for her to return, I went through the mail stacked on the kitchen table. The stack, mainly bills, had been sitting on the table all day, but this was the first time that I'd bothered to look through them. One postcard-sized letter stood out. It was a blank card with no discernable postmark, which was odd. I looked closer at the card. Written on the card were the words:

Wish you were here—not! LOL.

I didn't need a psychic to know who the card was from. The bitch was taunting me and it was pissing me the fuck off. It was bad enough she lied and got away with the money. Now she wanted to play games.

"Why is this bitch still fucking with me?" I slammed my fist into my hand. Every time I got to the point where I thought about letting it go and getting on with my life, she did something to stir the shit up again. There had to be a reason she was still fucking with me. She couldn't be that stupid, so I had no choice but to find out why she couldn't let it go, but neither could I.

# CHAPTER TWENTY-NINE

## VICTÓRIA MENDOZA

It felt good being alone but it was also a little scary. I never had my own room until I moved into my apartment, but I shared the place with Tilo. Initially, we were roommates, but we soon became more than that. Much more. And it was hard for me to turn this part off. It tormented me in my sleep and caused me to doubt everything in my life.

I parked in front of our building with the engine idling. Part of me felt sure Tilo would be inside with an explanation on her lips. If it was true, I honestly didn't know what I would do.

Our subdivision was quiet, but this afternoon it was almost too quiet. It seemed like the entire building was in mourning with me. Even though my brother had been dead since January, to me it was still fresh and a constant battle not to cry. It was warm in the car so I rolled down the window, but it was still too quiet and the silence was killing me. I turned on the radio but the music sounded foreign. I was trying to get up the nerve to go inside but my feet would not cooperate.

I studied the foot traffic in the surrounding buildings, but our building was strangely void on human activity. Rather than going into our apartment, I decided to visit the rental office to make sure my things weren't put on the street. When we first got the apartment, management made us pay a deposit equal to a year in advance. At the time we were pissed off. I was grateful now because, even though I'd missed a few months paying the current rent, it should still have been okay. And if it wasn't, I still had my sister to fall back on.

Lucky for me, the rental office wasn't crowded like it normally was when I went inside. I assumed that was because most people were at work. "I'd like to speak to the manager please," I said to an attractive reception-ist.

"Are you looking for an apartment?" She handed me a brochure with the different floor plans that they had.

"No, but I still would like to speak with the manager."

"He's on the phone right now. If you would like to have a seat, I will let him know that he has a visitor."

"Will he be long?"

"Uh, I'm not sure."

"Thanks." It was a dumb question and I realized it as soon as I had said it. I sat down on the sofa feeling nervous, but I wasn't sure why. Luckily, I didn't have to wait long. The manager came out of the office. I could tell by the look on his face he was surprised to see me.

"Ms. Mendoza, wow! It's Ms. Mendoza." He looked to the receptionist and bobbed his head, clearly excited.

I was thankful I didn't have to go through a big spiel explaining who I was. We stood there staring at each other for a few uncomfortable seconds.

"Can I speak with you in your office?" I felt like a lab rat under observation. So naturally I wanted to get out of there as soon as I could.

"Absolutely. I am so glad to see you," he said as we walked to his office. We weren't close friends, so I didn't know why he was feeling all giddy and shit.

He closed the door behind us and took a seat at his desk.

"Uh . . ." I searched his desk for a nameplate but there wasn't one. "Sorry, I've forgotten your name." The sad part about it was that his face didn't even look remotely familiar, but it could have had something to do with my partial loss of memory.

"Not to worry. My name is Richard Peyton."

"Thanks. Richard, I'm not sure if you remember me but I lived in—"

"Of course I remember you. I'm so sorry about your family." He paused. "I follow the news."

"Wow, really? I wasn't aware that it was on television." I was going to have to speak to Verónica so she could fill me in on exactly how much of our business was public knowledge.

"Yeah, it was the number one story for days. The most excitement we've seen around here in years, no disrespect."

I didn't even know what to say. He was talking about my life like it was some soap opera on television.

"I'm glad you survived. The news didn't say a lot about how you were doing, so I'm glad to see you."

*If you were so concerned, you fucker, why didn't you bring your ass down to the hospital and ask?* It was a mean thought but I meant it. "It's my apartment that I want to speak to you about. It's a two bedroom and I won't be needing the second room. Can I switch to a one bedroom, and what would that entail?"

Richard didn't appear to be surprised by my request.

"That's not a problem. We've been holding your things in storage waiting for someone to come and claim them."

I was confused. Why would my things be in storage? "Storage? Someone moved my things?" I felt violated. I couldn't believe that someone had actually touched my stuff. It was a weird feeling. It was bad enough that it felt like someone was stomping around in my head. I was relying on being able to go home and trying to piece together the puzzle my life had become. I never contemplated anyone moving those pieces around. It was a bit disheartening, to say the least.

"Um, yeah. Uh, someone vandalized your apartment and the entire building had to be cleared. Whoever did it poured gasoline throughout the apartment. There was a phone tip before any permanent damage was done. Since we didn't know how you were doing, I had your things put in storage."

I was speechless, but there was no doubt in my mind of who attempted to torch the apartment. Richard confirmed my suspicions that Tilo was not dead.

". . . police but they never came."

My mind was spinning and I wasn't really paying Richard any attention until I heard him say "police."

"What? Excuse me?"

He looked flustered and uncomfortable but I didn't care about that.

"I said I was surprised the police weren't interested in searching your apartment with all the other stuff that was going on."

I wanted to slap the fat, pompous fuck right in the face but he wasn't worth the time or the trouble. He was a mini-drama queen, and I didn't have time for that shit.

"Okay, whatever." I wasn't about to go into my personal business with him. I rolled my eyes, letting him know exactly how I felt about the situation. "So what now? I really want to get settled."

He logged on to the computer and found me another apartment, then handed me the keys. "I will have your things moved within the hour. You will need to switch the utilities over to your name. I believe we were able to save everything except the beds and the sofa. You might also want to get your clothes cleaned just in case they still smell from the gas."

"Thanks for your help." I wanted to tell him to kiss my ass so badly, but I held my tongue until I got outside. Even though I was mad about the violation and destruction of my property, I took it as proof that Tilo was still alive. I didn't know how I was going to do it, but I was going to find that bitch and make her pay! I was sure of that much.

# CHAPTER THIRTY

## MOSES RAMSEY

I left for the office early today. Last night's tempera-
tures had dropped down to the thirties, so I wanted to
get an early start before all the idiots and fools hit the
streets. The weather was absolutely crazy these days.
One minute it was seventy degrees and the very next
day ice was on the roads. Due to the recent rains, the
streets were still wet so I wanted to get off the road
before the rest of Atlanta started moving and killed
someone.

I sat down at my desk and pulled a cigar from the
humidor. I rarely smoked in my office, but today I was
going to make an exception. I snipped the tip off the
cigar and lit it up quickly before I changed my mind.
With any luck, the remnants of the smoke would be
gone before my staff arrived.

The cigar relaxed me somewhat, but I was still feeling suspicious. I felt like I was missing something that
was staring me right in the face. I turned on my computer and started scanning the headlines as I pulled
deeply on my cigar.

"Ah." I exhaled. I missed smoking my cigars. Ever
since the baby, I hadn't been able to smoke in the
house. I didn't want to smoke in my truck either because there would be times that they would be in the
vehicle with me, and I didn't want the baby to smell the

fumes. I wasn't worried about Verónica so much; she claimed to enjoy the smell. So rather than feel guilty about lighting up at work, I cherished the stolen moment.

I studied my cigar as I blew smoke rings at the ceiling. Tilo enjoyed a good cigar as well. I had already contacted the local cigar shops and left pictures of her and asked them to contact me if she came to their stores. It was a wild shot, but I was trying to think of every angle to get some type of lead on her whereabouts. My gut told me she hadn't gone far. With each passing day, however, the chance of losing her forever was becoming more of a probability than a possibility.

Every time that I thought about that bitch beating me at my own game, I wanted to hurt someone. I wasn't used to losing. It was a bitter pill for me to swallow.

"Verónica must think I am a total failure," I mumbled to myself. I swung around in my chair and focused my attention on the scenery outside my window. I needed to relax and get my mind off the case.

The case was only one of the reasons that I came into the office early. I was supposed to hear from the doctor today about the DNA test that I'd had performed on LM. My mother insisted I test the baby after I sent her a photo. She claimed that I used to look exactly like LM when I was his age. I didn't pay much attention to what she said. Frankly, I thought it was wishful thinking on her part, but I indulged her nevertheless. I wasn't holding my breath, but I was spending more time with LM and I was enjoying it. I'd already forgiven Verónica for letting me believe she wasn't sleeping with her husband. I even accepted her baby as my own, but in the back of my mind, he would always be her child. I had been fooled once before and I had no intention of getting fooled again. I blew another plume of smoke into the air as I reached for my coffee.

"Yuck." I spat the coffee on my desk. I expected the coffee to be warm, but it was downright frigid and it left a nasty taste in my mouth. I slammed the cup on the desk, causing the coffee to slosh over the side of the cup.

"Shit." As I scrambled to grab a napkin out of the center drawer of my desk to wipe up the mess, the phone rang. "Not now dammit," I yelled at the phone as if it would hear me and stop ringing.

"Hello," I barked into the receiver.

"Uh . . . may I speak with Moses Ramsey please."

"This is he." I didn't recognize the voice, and this only added to my irritation.

"Oh, okay. Is this a bad time?"

"No, of course not. Who is this?"

"Uh, I'm sorry, this is Dr. Richmond's office. I have some test results for you, and I was trying to schedule a time for you to come into the office to discuss them."

"Is that really necessary? I mean can't you tell me over the phone?"

"No, sir. Dr. Richmond will not allow us to read the results over the phone. You understand confidentiality and all. . . ." Her voice trailed off, leaving me to fill in my own blanks.

"Fine, what time do you want me to be there?" I was beyond pissed at this point. Part of me understood the need to deliver the news in person, but the other part of me was irritated and eager to hear the results.

She said, "We have a ten o'clock and a two o'clock available today."

I glanced at the clock. It was nine and their office was only twenty minutes away. "I'll see you at ten." I hung up the phone without waiting for her to confirm. When I got to the office, I would apologize to her for my rudeness. I took my cup over to the little wet bar and rinsed it out. I didn't want to admit it but suddenly I was nervous.

"Nigga, don't let this get you all twisted in the head." Even though I knew that LM wasn't mine, my heart wanted to believe there was a chance. I tried not to get emotionally attached, but I couldn't help myself. I turned off my computer and grabbed my suit jacket from behind the door. I also grabbed my overcoat and slung it over my arm. I was feeling a little warm. I knew it had everything to do with the news I was about to receive and nothing about the weather.

# CHAPTER THIRTY-ONE

## CARLOS MENDOZA

As I suspected, the basement was also emptied of furniture, and I wondered what happened to our furniture. I wouldn't mind getting it back because, even though it wasn't worth anything, there was sentimental value to it for me. The only piece of furniture in the whole house worth its weight in gold was my wife's old desk. I would have paid handsomely to have retained that piece. I made a mental note to ask my daughters if they knew anything about it. Not only was the wood handcrafted, the desk had many secret compartments that Alelina used to hide important documents in.

The washer and dryer that I had purchased from a secondhand store when we first moved to Georgia was still there. I breathed a sigh of relief. If someone had disposed of them as well, I don't know what I would have done.

I probably would have dug up my brother, the son of a bitch, and shot him again. I laughed but I was dead serious. I pushed a button, hidden from view, which lifted the appliances off the floor and slid them away from the wall. I entered the combination that would unlock the door to the secret room hidden beneath the appliances. I held my breath as I walked down the stairs. I hadn't been in the room in years, so I wasn't sure what to expect. I was fairly certain it hadn't been detected but I was still nervous.

Secrets of our past and the hopes of our future were in this room. The books lining the walls would be a gift to my daughters. In them were firsthand accounts of what we were forced to do to ensure their safety. Perhaps if they read the journals, they would find it in their hearts to forgive us for the deep deception we perpetrated.

I turned away from the books. I didn't come for them. I came to make sure the money we hoarded was still safe. This money was going to be the means of our escape from the grips of the Cali Cartel, but unfortunately we waited too long. Another tear slid down my cheek. I thought I'd left all my tears upstairs in the bedroom but I was wrong.

Greed kept us in the game, and I knew that I would pay for that sin for the rest of my life. My brother Monte sucked me into his world and used the threat of my family's safety to keep me in it.

I pushed back the wall of books and stared at the stacks of money. I had no idea how much was there, but I was sure it was more than we could spend in a lifetime. The realization should have comforted me but it only made me cry harder.

"Why didn't we get out sooner?" Weeping again, I fell to my knees.

"I'm so sorry, Alelina . . . so sorry. I really did love you . . . I thought I knew what I was doing." The walls of our makeshift safe seemed to shake as my wails shook the rafters of the seven-by-eight-foot room that I was in. I stayed on the floor until I was ready to lift my head without sorrow.


"Verónica, did your sister come home yet?" I said into the phone.

"Uh . . . yeah. I got her."

I could tell that she was still uncomfortable speaking with me. "Is she okay?"

"Yeah, she's fine."

She wasn't offering any additional information, which really bothered me. Something was wrong, but it was obvious she wasn't going to tell me about it.

"Great. Listen, I really need to show both of you something. Can you come over to our old house?"

She hesitated before she responded. She let out a loud sigh. "Padre, I'm not sure I—"

"Will you come over?" I tried not to sound overly eager. They had been through so much, and I didn't know how much more they could take.

"Now?"

I could feel her irritation even through the phone line. They had every right to resent me. I couldn't blame either of them if they decided to completely cut me out of their lives. "I'd really appreciate it. But if you think Victória is not up to it, we can do it later." I tried to prepare myself for the rejection I was sure was coming.

"I'll have to ask her, hold on."

I held my breath as she muted the phone. "God, please." I prayed like I had never prayed before. It felt like an eternity before she came back on the line, even though it was only a few seconds.

"We're on our way."

I let out a huge sigh of relief. "Okay, I will see you when you get here. Thanks."

# CHAPTER THIRTY-TWO

## VICTÓRIA MENDOZA

"What is this about?" I had so many other things that I could have been doing, so I didn't feel like participating in this little outing with my dad.

Verónica said, "Your guess is good as mine. He didn't offer any explanation when he asked us to come." She held my adorable nephew in a baby carrier.

We were standing outside of our old home, but I didn't feel anything. I'd already said my good-byes, so I wasn't feeling this reunion at all.

I turned up my nose. "This is some bullshit. You may have accepted him into your life, but I don't give a rat's ass about him."

"It's not about accepting him into my life. He's still our father; you can't change that. You haven't spent any time with him. He's really not that bad." She pushed a pacifier in LM's mouth.

My sister was always the gullible one, but this time I thought she went too far. We went through hell, and I wasn't the forgive-and-forget type of person. Since I didn't really know who the fuck my parents were, I didn't know who I got that shit from. So if she was willing to forgive our father for the sins he committed against us, fuck them both. "Whatever." I wasn't up to debating with her at the moment. I wanted to get back to my apartment to see if I could learn something that would help me to find that lying-ass Tilo. If someone wronged me, I was all about payback being a motherfucker. As far as I was concerned, Tilo won round one, but I intended to take home the prize and hang that bitch out to dry.

"Do you want to leave?" Verónica asked as I paced back and forth in the driveway.

Part of me wanted to leave, but the other part wanted to know why he wanted us to come. If he was going to provide any answers, I was willing to stay. "Naw, we're here now. Let's see what that motherfucker wants."

"Victória, he's still our padre," Verónica said with a hitch in her voice as she smiled at LM.

"Well, the jury is still out on that as far as I'm concerned. Being a father is more than donating sperm, and that's all he ever did for me." I opened the door and led the way into the house. If I was going to do this, I wanted to get it over with so I could get back to my business back at the house. "Hello?" I yelled. I refused to call this man Padre until he showed me he was worthy of the title. I tapped my foot as I impatiently waited for his response.

"Padre, it's Verónica and Victória," my sister yelled.

We walked into the empty living room. This was the first time that I'd been in the house since the night I was shot and Ramón was killed. A flashback of the night he died almost brought me to my knees. "Victória, are you all right?" Verónica gripped my arm, but it felt like she was a million miles away.

"Yeah." I snatched my arm away from Verónica. "He needs to hurry the fuck up. I can't be in this house too long. Too many memories." I had no idea I would feel this way. I wanted to get out of there so I could grieve again in private. I looked toward the stairs expecting our mother to come down them, but that wasn't going to happen. "Where the fuck is he? Call him, I don't have all day," I barked at my sister like she was to blame for my feelings. She wasn't in the house the night of Ramon's murder, so she couldn't possibly be feeling the same emotions I was feeling.

Verónica whipped out her phone. "Padre, where are you? We are here." She nodded her head and closed her phone. "He's coming."

I heard footsteps but they didn't appear to be coming down the stairs. I looked around in confusion. "Where the fuck was he?"

"Victória, your mouth is filthy," Padre announced as he slowly came into view.

I wanted to tell him to kiss my entire ass but I held the words inside.

"We're here, now tell us why," Verónica said.

I would have phrased it differently, but he got the message. I wanted to know what was so important that he brought me back to the scene of so much heartache without regard to our feelings.

"Victória, I know this is hard for you, and I sincerely apologize, but I need you to see this."

My father sounded humble. A part of me hoped that I could feel love for him again.

"What is it? I need to get back home to rest." I was lying my ass off; I just wanted to get out of there.

"Of course, I understand and I thank you both for coming. Will you follow me?" He was being so formal, I was scared to follow as he turned and walked out the same doorway that he had come from.

I looked at Verónica and she looked as scared as I felt. I thought my nephew even picked up on it.

Verónica said, "Give him a chance, Victória. He's trying."

I wanted to smack her up against her foolish head. I didn't want to blame her for all the bullshit that had taken place, but she was knee-deep in the shit and I resented her for it. If she hadn't gotten involved with Moses, our lives might have turned out much differently. I knew I was being irrational but I could not help myself.

"Please," Verónica begged.

I could not ignore the begging in my sister's voice. I would indulge her; but if I smelled bullshit, I was out—even if it meant turning my back on the only family I had left. "I just want you to know, I ain't feeling this."

LM started to get fidgety.

"I know. But please indulge him."

We followed my father through the kitchen and into the basement. I kept my eyes averted from the living room. I didn't want to be where my brother had died. The urge to run out of the house crying was overwhelming.

"Where are we going?" I demanded as I stopped midway down the stairs. If this was some dog-and-pony shit, I'd have rather he tell us about it before I walked down the stairs. For all I knew, it could be another trap we were walking into blindly.

Verónica said, "Victória, please, this won't take long." She tried to calm LM.

*How the hell does she know how long this shit is going to take?* I let loose a loud sigh as I counted backward. Verónica grabbed my hand and practically dragged me down the rest of the stairs. She was working her way up the list of people that I wanted to tell to kiss my ass. As far as I was concerned, he had years to make this shit right and he chose to do nothing. He allowed his brother to walk into our lives and destroy them. I wasn't about to forgive him for it anytime soon. "Why do we have to do this? We've been in the basement before. He's not showing us anything that we haven't seen before," I mumbled.

"Chill, Victória," Verónica hissed.

I stopped short. I didn't like the way that she was siding with him instead of me. Did I miss something? Last I checked he was the one who had abandoned us. Padre stopped at the bottom of the steps, causing us to bump into him. This just irritated me even more.

"Dumb fucker," I mumbled as Verónica jabbed me in my stomach.

She was lucky I wasn't feeling all that strong or we would have been fighting all over the basement.

"Ouch, bitch," I said, ready to let her have it, wishing she weren't holding my nephew.

"Victória . . . enough."

My father didn't have to raise his voice to let me know he was serious. It was a tone I wasn't familiar with but it brought tears to my eyes. I felt like I'd been transported in time and I was a little girl again. I was going to play his little game—one last time—and I was done. Padre led us to where the washer and dryer normally sat but they were pushed off to the side.

"What's going on here?" I asked as I peeked down twelve steps to what appeared to be a subbasement. I turned to my sister. "Did you know this room was here?"

"No, I didn't. Padre, what is this?" Verónica asked. Her voice was gentler and less accusatory than mine. She was working hard to keep the peace.

"I can show you better than I can tell you," my father replied.

# CHAPTER THIRTY-THREE

## VERÓNICA RAMSEY

My cell phone scared the shit out of me when it rang. I whipped it out of my holder and placed it up to my ear. "Hello?"

"Hey, baby, where are you?" Moses asked.

"I'm over at my old house. My father wanted us to meet him here. He wanted to show us something."

"Oh really, what?"

"Don't know yet. What's up?" I could feel all eyes on me as I tried to get off the phone with my husband.

"I was just checking to see what time you would be home. I've got some running around to do." Moses was getting bored.

"Padre says it won't take long, so I'll be there as soon as we're done."

"Oh, one more thing, my mother and father are coming to visit."

My heart skipped a beat but I tried to sound calm. "Oh, really? What's the occasion?"

He said, "It's no occasion. It's just time they met their daughter-in-law."

He had a point, it was time, but I could not help but to wonder why now? We'd been married for months and I hadn't heard boo from them.

"Wow, when are they getting here?" I was in panic mode. There were so many things I wanted to do before I met my in-laws. I needed to get my hair and nails done; the house could have used a thorough cleaning.

"They will be here at four."

If he said anything else after that, I didn't hear it because my mind was working overtime.

"Let me get off the phone, I have a lot to do. I'll see you at the house." I closed the phone. "Victória, we have to get going, I have to get home."

"What's wrong?" She looked alarmed.

"I need to get home. My in-laws are coming and I've got to prepare."

"Wow, did you know they were coming?"

"No, Moses just sprung it on me."

Victória cringed. "Ouch. I've never met in-laws before, but I think I would prefer advance notice."

"Tell me about it. Padre, what's this shit about!" With one phone call I'd forgotten about being the peacemaker. My ass needed to get home with a quickness.

# CHAPTER THIRTY-FOUR

## TILO ADAMS

I woke up in a cold sweat once again. I pushed back the heavy covers—damp with my sweat—and rushed to the bathroom. My stomach was so queasy, I felt like I was about to throw up, but nothing would come out. I felt hungry all the time but every time I tried to eat, I threw up.

"This shit is getting old," I mumbled to my reflection. I looked like hell but I felt even worse, if that was possible. The nightmares were driving me fucking crazy. I couldn't sleep because I felt like someone was chasing me all the time. I thought my conscience died with my former lover, but I was obviously wrong. I was disgusted with the weakness I was showing. I had dark circles under my eyes and my whole face appeared sunken in.

I pushed away from the mirror. I refused to spend another second looking at my tired reflection. I couldn't wait for my cruise to start. I needed the fresh start so I could get my head on straight and get back to the business of making money. I was scheduled to leave in a few days for New York, and I hadn't done a lick of shopping.

Truth be told, I was afraid to leave my hotel room. Even though I knew it wasn't true, I felt like everyone knew who I was and was waiting for me to step out of the room to apprehend me. This kind of pressure was not good for anyone, but I was sure most of my issues were related to guilt. The people I killed before were unknowns. They weren't a part of my everyday life. Therefore, it didn't bother me. Someone should have schooled me on that so I could have hired someone else for the hit. I got dressed so I could do some shopping. I didn't need much, but I needed something to go with my new look. I planned on doing my major shopping on the cruise. I grabbed my key card and purse and headed out the door. When I got to New York, I intended to hit shopper's row and buy some banging outfits.

I was good until I reached the lobby. I broke out in a sweat when I saw all the people rushing around. I thought they all were looking for me and my heart started beating real fast. I could feel my blood rushing from my head. I was feeling faint.

"Are you all right, miss?"

I leaned against the wall. I was trying to balance my weight without appearing drunk. This was totally unexpected. The feeling unnerved me so much, I couldn't answer right away. I stumbled over to one of the sofas in the lobby and lowered my head between my legs. I tried to control my breathing and my nerves. Slowly my heart rate became normal. I lifted my head and realized that no one except for the bellhop was paying me any attention.

"Can you get me a cab please?" I said.

"Sure, it would be my pleasure."

I watched him go out the door to hail a cab. I should have followed him but my legs were shaking. I waited until he started waving at me before I got up and tried to make my way to the door. I was halfway to the door before my legs gave out on me and I crumpled to the floor. It wasn't a blackout. I was totally aware of what was going on around me, but I didn't have the strength to do anything about it. However, by the time the ambulance arrived, I had gotten a second wind.

A female paramedic said, "We just want to examine you, miss."

"I'm fine. I told the bellhop not to dial Nine-one-one but he insistent upon doing so." My eyes locked with the bellhop's. If eyes could communicate, mine were begging him to corroborate my story if he wanted a good tip.

The bellhop said, "She did tell me not to call, but the hotel requires we do it for insurance purposes and for the safety of our guests."

Thankfully, he got the message. I winked at him. He was going to get a big, fat tip.

"I understand, but since we're here, why not let us take your blood pressure?" she said, preparing to examine me.

I wanted to choke the fuck out of this preppy bitch who just wouldn't go away. I hated to get ugly, but I was about to show my ass for real. "If my blood pressure goes up, it will because you won't leave me the hell alone. Now go somewhere and save someone who really needs your help."

I wanted to end my sentence by calling her a bitch, but I held it back. However, if she came at me again with the cuff, it was on. I definitely didn't want them to take my pressure because I hadn't been taking my medicine. I left my medicine at the apartment, and since I was presumed dead, I couldn't get a refill.

"Fine, we can't force you to accept treatment, but we can advise you that refusing our assistant may have dire consequences, which we will not be held responsible for."

I felt bad about being such a bitch, but I had no other choice.

"Rome, don't tell me to calm down. Those idiots you are dealing with have just cost me a million dollars," I yelled into the phone. I knew my pressure was through the roof, but I couldn't pull back. I couldn't stand incompetence. Since I couldn't be seen, I was forced to allow others to handle my business for me—for a small fee of course.

"I'm just saying, we have no way of knowing how the Mexican officials learned of the new shipment. It could have been a fluke," Rome said, sounding irritated.

"Fluke, my ass. Perhaps you don't understand how this shit works. If I lose money, you don't get paid."

"Tilo—"

"Don't call me that again—ever. The person you are referring to is dead, got it?"

"Yeah, I got it, but what do I call you?"

I thought about it for a few seconds, but since my head was hurting so badly, it was difficult to think. "Call me . . . Boss. Yeah, that's it: call me Ms. Boss. I kinda like that shit 'cause if the boss ain't happy, nobody is happy. You feel me?"

He probably wished he could kick my ass, but he didn't have a choice but to follow my instructions. I owned Rome. He had a gambling problem, which kept him out of the FBI. It wasn't big enough to keep him out of civil service. At least, it wasn't at the time he applied for a job with the Atlanta Police Department. And if I found out that he was the reason why my guns had been hood-jacked, I was going to kill his ass personally.

"Ms. Boss," Rome stuttered, not wanting to say the words. "It's not my fault. Everything on our end was on point. Shit got fucked up over the border somewhere," Rome whined.

"I don't give a flying fuck where it happened. It happened! And as a result, I don't fucking get paid," I shouted into the phone. If I could've done everything myself, I would have. But I needed to rely on Rome to do at least 95 percent of the things I asked him to do right. If his percentage dropped, so did he.

Rome was lucky I was talking to him over the phone instead of face to face, which I would have preferred because I would have shot him right between his motherfucking eyes.

"Well, I'm just saying, get my fucking guns back or be prepared for the consequences. And you might start thinking about ways to take out that mayor. He's messing with my money and I don't appreciate that shit."

"But this is the second mayor we've handled since the election."

"And your point would be?" I wasn't trying to hear that shit. I was done talking to Rome. I didn't care how he made it happen, I just wanted it to happen. I had one more call to make before I left the country.

I hung up on him and dialed another number. "Yeah, it's me. I just got off the phone with Rome. The motherfucker is scared. I need for you to sell that stupid ass the same shit you took from him but double the price."

"He can't afford it."

"You idiot, tell me something I don't know. I need that nigga dirty."

"Okay, all right then."

"Wait a week and leak another story saying the guns were jacked. This gets Obama and his administration off my ass and you move up again. You feel me? Obama's team will think they are doing a good job and move their nosey asses out of Mexico so we continue to get rich." I was feeling pretty good because everything seemed to be going as planned.

"What about the kidnappings?" my anonymous malefactor said.

"Damn, man, do I have to tell you everything? You've got to keep things poppin', keep the violence spread out. Don't do too much in any one area or we'll have more attention than a little bit. Get creative. Do something to surprise me for a change. Shit! If I have to tell you how to do everything, what do I need you for?" I slammed down the phone. "I ain't trying to change the name of the game, I'm just trying to be the winner." I rolled over for a few hours to get some much needed rest. When I woke up, I promised to try, once again, to eat something and hold it down.

# CHAPTER THIRTY-FIVE

## MOSES RAMSEY

My stomach was filled with butterflies. I'd never been so nervous in my entire life. I didn't know what scared me most: the fact that I'd actually fathered a child or Verónica's reaction when she found out I had a paternity test done without her knowledge.

Mom and Dad were excited about meeting their first grandchild and my wife. I was still trying to digest the fact that LM was actually my son. Part of me was beaming with pride, and the other half hated the way I treated him when he was born. I despised myself for allowing Tilo to fill my head with nonsense that almost made me kill his mother. This made finding Tilo a number one priority because I could not ever let it be known what I'd planned to do.

Verónica loved Olive Garden, so I went by to pick up something for dinner for all of us. I happily paid the bill and rushed home to make sure that everything was perfect. On a whim, I stopped by the liquor store and bought some wine and their best champagne. I was in the mood to celebrate. To my knowledge, Verónica still thought LM was Mike's baby, but my plan was to reveal it to her tonight. I hoped that by showing her my baby pictures she'd be convinced of his parentage.

For me, I had a newfound commitment to the love I had for Verónica. I wanted and needed for us to grow as a family. Tonight I was going to tell her that. The fact that my mother and father would be there to witness it was a bonus because at least they would be convinced I wasn't gay. Being a black man living in Atlanta wasn't easy. Every woman assumed I was gay. I was tired of defending my manhood. My wife would walk through the door any minute and validate me.

I quickly set up the table with candles and flowers after I called Verónica to make sure she was on the way. Mom and Dad were resting in the guest room and eager to meet their first and only grandchild. As I lit the last candle my mother came down the stairs.

"Sweetie, do you need any help?"

"Mom, I thought I told you to get some rest." I wasn't surprised she didn't pay me any attention. Hell, my dad had been complaining about her being hardheaded for years.

"Who can rest at a time like this? Do you know how long I've waited for this moment? Your father and I aren't getting any younger. Well, your father is getting older, I'm just getting better."

I couldn't hold back the laughter. My mother was a piece of work.

"Mom, you haven't changed one bit."

"Why should I mess with perfection?"

We laughed again.

"Is Dad still resting?" I was fussing with the table settings because I was nervous. I wanted my parents to love Verónica the way I did. I had a lot of making up to do with her, and I planned to start tonight. I never wanted her to know I'd planned on killing her and running off with Tilo. My hand tightened around the stem of the glass that I was holding. I still had a hard-on for that bitch and couldn't wait to get my hands on her skinny neck.

"He's snoring, so I guess you could say he's resting. I don't understand how he can sleep with all the racket he's making."

"You love it because you've been sleeping with the racket for over fifty years."

It was her turn to chuckle now. "Boy, get away from the table and sit down somewhere. I don't know why you didn't let me cook."

I pulled out a chair at the kitchen counter and sat down. "I couldn't ask you to fly here and then put you to work as soon as you got here."

"Shoot, I got to eat too."

She had a point but I wanted to do all of this myself. I wanted everything to be perfect when my wife came in. I even went out and upgraded her wedding ring. We fell into a comfortable silence for a few minutes.

Mom said, "So tell me about your wife, not that stuff you told your father. I want to know what made her special to you?"

"That's a long story, but the short version is that she used to work for me and we fell in love. She has a beautiful spirit, Mom. Please give her a chance," I pleaded.

"Son, she is the mother of my grandson. She already has cool points with me. Try to relax. Everything is going to be okay."

I wished that I could feel as confident as she did, but she didn't know all the details of my relationship with Verónica. I loved my mother, but I couldn't share my deep deception with her.

"What is it, son? You looked troubled." Worry lines were etched on my mother's forehead.

"It's nothing. I just wish they would get here." I looked at my watch. It had been forty-five minutes since I'd talked to Verónica and I was getting antsy.

"I think you need to have a glass of the wine you bought. While you're at it, pour me one too."

She was right; I was wound tighter than a drum. I went over and grabbed two glasses off the dining room table and poured some wine into both glasses. I handed one to my mother and we clicked together in a toast. "To the good life," I whispered.

# CHAPTER THIRTY-SIX

## CARLOS MENDOZA

I wanted my family back, and I was willing to do anything I had to do to make it happen. I held my breath. In my heart I knew this was my last chance to prove to them that their mother and I really did love them.

I never thought all our deepest deceptions would be revealed, but showing them our secrets was the only thing I could think about doing to restore their trust. I wished Alelina could've been with me, but there was nothing I could do about it. The only thing I could do was pray they would learn to love me after they knew the extent of our deception. I had to make them understand that we did what we thought we had to do in order to survive.

"Why are we here, Padre?" Verónica demanded again.

I was taken aback by her tone, and I almost snapped on her. However, I waited until they were fully in the basement before I turned on the auxiliary lighting. They say a picture is worth a thousand words. The walls of the subbasement were bloated with one hundred dollar bills. I watched their faces with great anticipation.

"Oh my God. Are you serious?" the girls cried in unison.

"Is this shit real?" Victória cried.

I knew this was going to be a big shock to them because it blew me away too and I knew about the room. I was surprised by the amount of money tucked in the walls, but it appeared my wife held on to every penny I sent her. "I told you we had money," I boasted. I didn't intend to shock them like I did, but I knew that if I didn't win over Victória soon, she would turn Verónica against me and I needed them in my life.

"Is this blood money?" Victória demanded.

"It's your money. It represents everything your mother and I worked for over the years. It's the least I can do to gain forgiveness." I looked at LM, who was all eyes.

"You can't put a price tag on love. We needed a father in our lives," Victória shouted. She was clearly agitated while Verónica walked around apparently in a daze.

"I can't change the past, as ugly as it is, but I would like to change the future." My heart was pounding as I waited for their reaction.

Verónica and Victória were grown. I missed the most precious years of their lives and no amount of money could change that. I got it, even if they didn't believe it. I only wanted a chance. Not to be their father, I missed that boat, but to be a friend and ultimately someone they looked up to. I wanted the opportunity to be the man I should have been, and I wanted to have an active role in my grandson's life.

I held out two large duffel bags so they could take some of the money with them. It would take many more trips to get it all. I didn't know what I would do if they turned their backs on me and walked out. The waiting was torturous. Verónica was the first one to take the bag from me. I held my breath while I waited to see if Victória would as well. After several more seconds, she accepted the bag and I relaxed somewhat.

I watched them fill up the bags. There was more than enough money there for all of us to live extravagantly for the rest of our natural lives. My plan was to use some of it to continue the search for the bitch who ended my son's life.

Victória stopped packing and startled me with a question. "Are you planning on leaving anytime soon?"

I didn't detect any of the animosity that I earlier felt. "No, Victória, I'm going to stay awhile. Maybe even make this my home. Plus, I want to spend some time with my grandson." I didn't mention my desire to find Tilo. I'd broach that subject when the time was right.

"Wow, should I be impressed or is this just lip service?" Victória asked.

If the news stunned Verónica, I couldn't tell. She was so busy stuffing money in the bag, I didn't even know if she was paying attention to our conversation or my grandson.

"I'm sincere. I messed up. I allowed things to keep me away from you both. It was never a case of my not loving either of you."

Victória said, "We read some of the letters you sent to Madre."

I was surprised by this information because with the nature of what we were doing for the cartel, I always told her to shred the letters after she read them. "Where did you find the letters?"

"I found them in Madre's desk after she died. We were trying to make sense out of what was happening."

I was not pleased with this turn of events, but it wasn't what I said in those letters, it was more of what I didn't say that mattered. The average person wouldn't have understood. Once again there was nothing that I could do to change it. I exhaled deeply. Mending our relationship was going to be a lot harder than I'd anticipated. Tension in the room was so strong, I felt like it was a tangible thing that I could reach out and touch.

Victória was getting agitated. I think LM was too. Before she could say anything, Verónica's phone rang. She turned her back to us to answer the call. She spoke a few words in a hushed voice and ended the call.

"When you're ready, everything you want to know is in these journals." I could tell they didn't even notice the journals lining the walls.

"Can we continue this later? I need to get home," Verónica said as she attempted to throw her weighted duffel bag over her shoulder. The bag weighed almost as much as she did.

Victória dropped her own bag and attempted to help her sister, but I gently pushed her aside so I could assist.

"I'll help you with your bag, Victória, when I return," I said over my shoulder, scooping up LM's carrier in my other hand.

"I'm going to stay for a while if that's okay with you," Victória said, surprising the hell out of me.

"I thought you were riding with Verónica?" I didn't have a problem with driving her home later. I was just curious.

"I have my own place."

I got the hint as I gave her the key to come and go as she pleased. I had very little secrets left, and I wanted to get to know my baby. "I'll give you a few hours and I'll be back." I wasn't sure how I felt about her staying by herself, but she was grown and I had to keep reminding myself of it. This was not the way I wanted this visit to end, but I was powerless to do anything about it. My daughters had gone on with their lives, and it was up to me to catch up. I helped Verónica to her car and waved sadly as she drove away.

# CHAPTER THIRTY-SEVEN

## VICTÓRIA MENDOZA

"So what's your take on this bullshit?" I phoned Verónica as soon as I heard Padre leave. I wanted him to think I was staying, but I was testing him to see if he trusted me alone in his house.

"I really don't know what to think. Shit, I thought Tilo took all the money there was."

I couldn't help but laugh, even though it wasn't funny. "Yeah, I bet she thought so too. What she got was chump change compared to what's in that room."

"I know, right."

Just thinking about Tilo's trifling ass pissed me off. I could not believe that she played me like she did.

"I doubt if you will ever find her," Verónica said.

"Oh, I'm gonna find the bitch, trust and believe that. And when I do, I'm gonna do to her what she tried to do to me! Rock-a-bye baby for real."

"Victória, you can't mean you would . . . shoot her?"

Was she serious? "You're kidding, right? I mean, the bitch shot me; she killed our brother! You damn skippy I'm gonna shoot the bitch." I was done with people trying to do me any way that they thought they could and thinking it would be okay. The incident with Tilo changed me. I was about to be the bad bitch and I had no regrets.

"Sis, you're scaring me. I'm about to turn this car around and come back so I can talk some sense in you."

"Pump your brakes, Verónica. This ain't got nothing to do with you. She didn't shoot your ass, so please save it. I will shoot the bitch even if it means that I'll spend the rest of my life behind bars. You don't understand, she played me big time. She became my friend for a specific reason, and then she tried to kill me. That's something I don't take too lightly."

"I hear ya, sis, but don't do anything foolish. I can't afford to lose my sister too."

"I've got to find the bitch first and when I do, it's on."

"Well, I gotta go. Wish me luck."

"Yeah, go handle your business. I'll give you a call tomorrow and maybe we can get together and read some of these journals. Are you going to tell Moses about the money?" The line was silent and for a minute I thought the call was dropped. "Verónica, you still there?"

"Yeah, I'm here. I was thinking. I will probably show him the money, but it won't be tonight."

"I feel ya, I feel ya. All right, I'll speak with you later." I grabbed a few of the books off the shelf and dragged my bag up the stairs. Padre was still an enigma to me. He appeared remorseful, but I felt like he was hiding something so I wasn't ready to let my guard down with him.

The whole experience with Monte and Tilo had changed me. I wasn't the same trusting person anymore and it scared me because I felt like Verónica would be a fool to show Moses all the money she had. I learned the hard way that money made some people do some crazy shit.

I had mixed emotions about going back into the apartment that I shared with Tilo, but it was necessary for closure. I had successfully moved into another building and retrieved most of my clothes. The furniture was soiled but our electronics survived. I needed to walk around the old apartment one last time so I could formally say good-bye to those demons that woke me up at night. Knowing your lover tried to kill you is a bitter pill to swallow, and I hoped by coming to the apartment I would find an adequate chaser. Part of me was surprised the key to the door still worked, but the other half of me wanted to burn the bitch down myself. I put my purse inside the front door and went down the hall to check the mailbox.

I wasn't surprised to find it jam-packed with bills and junk mail. Since no one was taking care of my affairs while I was in the hospital, my credit was going to take a serious hit, but I would deal with it later when things calmed down some.

"Hell, with all the money our father threw at us, who needs credit?" My voice echoed off the walls, sounding distorted and alien to me. The kitchen still had some of our personal items. Magnets were still attached to the refrigerator and our grocery list was still hanging from a hook on the wall. A brown, singed oven mitt and matching pot holder sat on the counter waiting for the next meals to be cooked, requiring their services. Other than the kitchen no room held memories for me. I looked under the cabinet and got a box of trash bags to put my mail in, and left the bag next to the door as well.

The light on the answering machine caught my attention as I was leaving the room. I was scared to listen to it so I unplugged it and stuffed it in the bag as well. I would listen to it later when I was more comfortable in my new apartment. This place, without Tilo, was giving me the creeps. I walked through the other rooms but didn't see anything that I wanted to take with me. I was officially done with this part of my life.

I was about to leave when my front door was kicked open and I was roughly pushed against the wall. My face smashed against the wall, and for the second time in my life, I had a gun pointed at me. I didn't know what to do as warm piss flowed down my leg. I stood in place—too scared to move—with my hands framing my face against the wall.

"What . . . what do you want?" I whispered. I assumed it was about the money, but I'd left it in the car. The keys were on the floor. They could have it if they would just let me live.

"Shut up."

I didn't have to be told twice. I wouldn't say another fucking thing if it would keep me from going through the same shit I just went through. I heard additional footsteps behind me. A second person entered my apartment, closing the door behind him.

"If you scream, I will shoot you. Do you understand?"

I couldn't answer him if I wanted to. I was trembling so badly my lips were shaking. I nodded my head in acknowledgment. My legs were shaking, but since they didn't shoot me right away, I was hopeful. I wasn't trying to piss them off so I waited to see what they wanted.

"That ain't her," the second man said.

I needed him to shut the fuck up because he obviously made the first guy mad, judging by the way he was pushing my ass into the wall.

"Where's Tilo?" the man holding me asked.

The only thing I could tell was that he was light skinned with a slim build. I could tell this because he had thrust his leg between mine as he did a slow grind on my ass. His movements could have been sexual if he weren't holding a fucking gun.

"The bitch shot me and left me for dead so I have no idea." I adopted a hard-core attitude, even though I was crying like a motherfucker. If these were friends of Tilo, they could kiss my ass too.

"Bitch fucked you too?" The guy holding me relaxed his grip somewhat.

The shorter guy said, "How do we know she's telling the truth?"

If I had a gun, I would have shot that motherfucker myself. I wanted to turn around so badly so I could see his face. I wanted to remember him.

"Look at her. She done pissed herself." He shoved me but I had no place to go.

"Sounds like Tilo hasn't changed. What did she clip you for?"

I started to relax a little bit. I wiped the tears and saliva off my face as I told them how she killed my brother. I also showed them what she did to me. "What did she do to you?" *Bitch, is you crazy? This ain't no social gathering and these motherfuckers ain't your friends. How you gonna start asking questions and shit?*

"Come on, man, let's go. It stinks in here." His heavy footfall signaled his retreat.

A tiny spark of hope started to flicker in my body. The guy holding me turned around to leave, but as much as I wanted them gone, I wanted some more information about the woman I used to love. "Please, what did she do? I need to find the bitch and make her pay." I wanted to turn around, but I was afraid if I looked at him he would have no choice but to shoot me.

His silence was tormenting me but he finally spoke. "It's best you don't know about this little bit. Stay out of this. We are going to find her."

This chilled me because I knew he was going to kill her. As much as I hated Tilo, I didn't want her dead unless I was the one to pull the trigger. "Real talk, I don't know if I can do that." I was being honest with him and myself. Tilo tried to kill me, and I wouldn't let it go as long as I had breath in my body.

"Stay out of our way or next time you won't be so lucky."

With that he was gone, and I didn't even know what he looked like. I waited with my hands up just in case they decided to come back. My legs were still shaking but my heart was slowly coming back to normal. I couldn't get the voices out of my head, and I knew I was going to have to share this information with someone soon to help me sort it out. I got my things and left.


I threw the mail on the kitchen table in my new apartment and carried my bags into my bedroom. I was tired and wanted nothing more than to climb into the bed and go to sleep, but I needed a shower. I took off my clothes and tossed them in the corner. I ran the shower and pulled a nightgown from my dresser. Although I normally didn't sleep with anything on, I didn't feel comfortable being naked in the new apartment alone. I paused in front of the mirror before I stepped in the shower. Despite the fact that I'd been in a coma for two months, my body still looked good. I was always slim, so I didn't have to worry about doing a bunch of physical therapy to get my muscles in shape. Exercise was a part of my normal routine so the momentary break didn't do too much damage. My hair had grown longer than I was used to having it, but overall I still looked good.

"So what are you going to do with yourself?" I asked my reflection in the mirror. I was hoping the mirror held an answer because I had no clue. I was even questioning my sexuality. Since the only people who knew about my sexuality were either missing or dead, I could honestly go either way. Tilo was my first and I responded willingly. I never gave myself a chance to know how I would have responded if I was approached by a man. Shaking those thoughts from my head, I stepped into the shower and allowed the hot water to wash away my stress and my pain. My body was healing, but I had no idea how to heal my heart.

# CHAPTER THIRTY-EIGHT

## MOSES RAMSEY

"She should be here by now." I was trying to keep the food warm without burning or overcooking it. I paced back and forth while anxiously watching the clock. I wanted things to be perfect. I'd even gone shopping and bought her a proper wedding ring. When we got married, it was rushed. I didn't have time for all the pomp and circumstance, but now I wanted to rectify it. My plan was to get down on one knee and propose to her in front of my parents and my child.

"My child," I whispered. I couldn't stop saying it, and each time I did I smiled.

Mom said, "Relax, son, all this pacing back and forth is making me nervous. Get out of the kitchen and go keep your father company. I got this." My mother was right.

I was acting like a teenager meeting my girl for the first time instead of a married man. "I don't know, Mom, but ever since I found out LM was my son, I feel different inside. Is that normal?" My heart was hurting because I was carrying around a lot of guilt. I actually wanted this marriage to work, and I was ready to put in work.

"Of course it's normal, son. But it usually happens before the baby comes." My mother started laughing, but I was too tense to join in. She knew some of the circumstances surrounding my sudden marriage, but she didn't know everything and I planned to keep it that way.

"You got jokes. Today is the most important day of my life and you want to be a comedian."

"I'm not making jokes. It's the truth, but you've never done things the way you were supposed to, even as a child. You probably got that from your father's side of the family, but you obviously did something right because otherwise Verónica wouldn't have agreed to marry you in the first place."

"I hope so, Mom. I really was an ass those first couple of months."

"It's never too late to show Verónica how you feel, but you have to mean it, son. You can't just go changing your mind." She gave me one of her momma looks that let me know she meant business. She grabbed my hand and pulled me over to the kitchen table.

"Sit," my mother instructed. She had her hand on her hip.

I could tell she was about to read me the riot act. My dad, who was about to enter the kitchen, turned around and walked back out. He must have known things had taken a serious turn and decided to run while he had the opportunity.

"Mom, I don't want to burn dinner." I started to get up, but she pushed me back and turned off the low flames.

She took a seat across from me and grabbed my hands, looking me straight in the face. "Son, I got that your marriage didn't start off in the conventional way, but isn't she the same woman you fell in love with?"

"Yeah, but—"

"But is for assholes and I didn't raise an asshole." Her analogy was so bizarre and out of the blue, I wanted to laugh. One look at the serious expression on her face stopped me. My father cleared his throat, and I could tell he was ear hustling and having a difficult time trying to remain serious as well. She shot him an evil look but he didn't see it; he was still hiding behind the newspaper.

"I understand, Mom . . . But, Mom, I've made some major mistakes in my marriage. Things you don't know about. Part of me wants to tell her, but I'm sure if I do she'll leave me in a New York minute." This was as close to asking for advice as I was going to get.

"Then don't tell her," my father broke his silence.

"Shut up, Ricardo. You ain't in this conversation."

"And you shouldn't be either. That boy know's what he's got to do, and if what he did was so damn serious and he wants to keep that woman happy, then he should shut the hell up and keep it moving." He got up from his seat in the living room and came into the kitchen.

"Ricardo, now is not the—"

"Hush, woman, this is between me and my son. Now you know I ain't much for getting into other folks' business—especially grown folks—but you 'bout to fuck up. Do not—let me repeat this—do not tell your wife something that you know is going to hurt her unless it's a matter of life or death. If you are truly sorry and it's never going to happen again, and—let me repeat this—and if it won't affect her health or welfare, keep your damn mouth shut."

"Ricardo, don't tell this boy to go into his marriage lying."

"First of all, he's not a boy, and second, he's already married. There is no logical reason to stir up some shit if you don't have to, that's all I'm saying."

Mom said, "If she loves you, all things are possible."

I understood where both of them were coming from. The guilt was killing me, though, and I had to tell somebody. "I tried to kill her." Tears flooded my eyes when I thought about how far I was willing to go for the almighty dollar.

"Son, like your father was saying, ain't no sense in stirring up some shit if you don't have to. All that matters now is whether or not you love her." She got up from the table and took over tending to the food.

I sat at the table stunned and confused. "I do." I wiped the tears from my eyes. I wanted to look at my mother but shame prevented me from doing so.

Dad said, "People make mistakes every day. If Jesus can forgive you, why can't you forgive yourself?"

"I'm trying, but every time I think about what could've happened, I feel like I should tell."

"And who would benefit from that?" My mother had such a smart-ass mouth.

I knew she was speaking the truth, but she didn't understand how heavy the guilt was. My dad said what he had to say and went back into the living room. I thought he was finished dishing out advice but he wasn't.

"Son, your mother is right. If you tell Verónica the truth, there is a good possibility she will walk out on your ass and we'll never get to see our grandson. And let me just say this, if that happens and I have to live with your evil-ass mother for the rest of my life because of it, I'm not going to be happy about that. You feel me?" He flipped the paper for emphasis.

"I beg your pardon, Ricardo. I'm not evil," my mother huffed.

"You are when you don't get your way. I can't blame you, I spoiled your ass so it's my fault. Besides, she needs someone else to love besides me." He was grinning from ear to ear when he said this, and I couldn't keep a smile off my face even though my heart was still heavy.

My mother shared a look with my dad. I could feel the love radiating from them. I wanted the same relationship with my wife.

"You're right, Mom. I'm going to take that secret to the grave."

"What secret?" Verónica asked as she stepped in the room, carrying my son.

# CHAPTER THIRTY-NINE

## VICTÓRIA MENDOZA

"I need some answers and I think you're the only one who is going to give it to me straight." I walked into Moses' office without stopping to knock.

He seemed surprised to see me. Before I could say anything else, he grabbed me by the arm and dragged me out into the outer office.

"Shush." He pointed to the walls and pointed to his ears.

"What the fuck?"

He put his fingers to his lips and shook his head angrily. I wanted to yank my arm from him but I decided to play nice. I didn't know Moses well, so he certainly didn't have permission to put his hands on me. Once we were in the hallway he spoke to me.

"I think my office is bugged. Until I find out who is listening, I don't want to talk in there."

I was skeptical. He came off like he'd just stepped out of the cuckoo house.

"I know what you're thinking. Better safe than sorry, though." He had a point.

If there was any validity to his concerns, I didn't want my business put out on Front Street. However, I needed to speak with him. He looked worried as he peered back at his closed office door. He drew some keys out of his pocket and locked the door.

"Come on." Moses turned and walked toward the elevator with me following close behind.

I was still trying to decide if I liked my sister's husband. He was fine and funny. Did I mention fine? But I wasn't sure I trusted him.

"Does this type of shit happen to you often?" I asked when we were in the elevator. No wonder my sister was fascinated with him. Life with him would certainly be interesting.

"Actually, this is a first time, but I'm pretty sure I know who planted the device."

We walked the rest of the way in silence to a small coffee house on Peachtree Street. He walked in front of me, and I got a chance to admire his broad shoulders and his tight ass. I could also see the imprint of his hamstrings as they pushed against the fabric of his pants. I had to admit, he was a well put together package. He held open the door of the coffee shop, and I chose a table near the window so I could look out to the street as we talked.

"Coffee?" he said.

"Please, cream and sugar."

He walked toward the counter and pulled out his wallet. I looked away as I felt a familiar twinge in my panties. The last thing I needed was to become attracted to my sister's husband. I was, however, excited to know I was capable of being turned on by a man. Maybe once this mess settled, I could speak to Moses about hooking me up with one of his friends.

He came back to the table and said, "I didn't know how sweet you liked it."

He drank his coffee black. I grabbed some cream and three sugars and fixed my cup. He sat back in his chair and watched me until I started to feel uncomfortable.

"What?" I asked defensively.

"I didn't say anything. I was waiting for you to tell me why you wanted to see me."

"Oh." I felt embarrassed, and I was sure it showed all over my face.

"You blush just like your sister," he said with a chuckle in his voice.

I took a sip of my coffee and burned my damn tongue. "Shit."

He burst out laughing and I laughed with him. I sat back in my chair and relaxed. He was not the enemy and, even though I didn't agree with the way that he came into my sister's life, he was here now and I had to deal with it.

"Sorry about not visiting you in the hospital. Time kind of got away from me."

"Damn, you should have lied and said you came. I wouldn't have known."

"True, but I don't believe in unnecessary lies."

"Hmm, interesting."

He raised an eyebrow. If he wanted to know what I meant, he didn't ask.

"So let's get back to the business at hand. What can I do for you?"

"I need some information about the night I was shot."

He frowned and suddenly looked uncomfortable. "Victória, I don't think I can tell you anything that your sister hasn't already told you."

"Verónica is spoon-feeding me information. She doesn't want to tell me anything until I've regained all of my strength."

He nodded his head as if he understood where I was coming from. "She told me. I don't necessarily agree with that, but I'm sure she has her reasons."

"I need to know what happened that night."

"I understand. Aside from arriving at the house with Tilo, I was downstairs so I don't know what transpired. The only person who can answer your questions is Tilo because she was the only one, other than you, who walked away. Do you remember anything?"

"Not really. I have little flashes when I sleep but when I wake up it's all gone."

"Did she tell you Tilo shot Ramón?"

I felt like someone had reached inside my chest and pulled out my heart. I clutched my chest in pain. No matter how many times I heard the same thing, it still felt the same. "She told me but it's so hard for me to believe. She just wasn't like that with me. I mean, how can you be so sure that Tilo did this to us?"

"I can't say with a hundred percent certainty, but my gut tells me she did it."

"What if some other members of the cartel stormed the house and shot us and took Tilo as a hostage?"

"That theory doesn't make sense because the cartel had issues with your family and not Tilo. If anything, they would have shot Tilo and taken you and your brother hostage."

I could see his logic. Getting my mind to accept it was a different animal. The part of me that still loved her wouldn't let me accept it. "Please don't treat me like a child. I get enough of that from Verónica," I snapped. I was taking my frustration out on him and I knew it.

"I'm sorry, that wasn't my intent, but you're grasping at straws. If a member of the cartel actually stormed the house, which I doubt, they would have not missed. I believe Tilo shot Ramón without blinking an eye, but when it came time to shoot you, it wasn't as easy and she didn't bother to check to see if she actually killed you. That's the only explanation that makes sense to me. My only question is why?"

"Yeah, you're right. I was just hoping that it wasn't true. I keep thinking she is going to put her key in the door and come back."

Moses passed the test. I remembered the envelopes of money that Ramón had given me before he was killed. If Moses mentioned the money, it would be a clear indication that he was involved in it as well.

"I don't believe that is going to happen. Everything Tilo did, with the exception of her botched job on you, was planned to perfection."

I frowned. "Why do you say that?"

"Well . . . I know she faked her death. I know she's somewhere alive and well, and I also believe she has the bearer bonds that Ramón told me about."

"I didn't know you knew about them."

"I wasn't positive it was the motive for the killing, but it makes sense. Everything she did makes sense until now. She really exposed herself when she left me a voice message. If I thought it would do any good, I'd take it to the FBI and try to convince them to reopen the case."

"What! She called? Why didn't you tell me that sooner? What did she say?" I jumped out of my chair and rushed toward Moses.

"Hey, hold up now." He was on his feet and trying to get me to sit back down before everybody in the coffee shop was all up in our business.

I stopped ranting when I realized how crazy I sounded. I backed up a few paces but I didn't sit back down. "I'm sorry. I'm good now." I took a few deep breaths to calm my nerves, but I was still wound tighter than a drum.

"I didn't tell you because I didn't want you to think I was a nut. First she sent me a postcard at the house, today she called and left the message." He took his seat, but I was ready to run to his office to listen to the tape.

"Why is she contacting you?" I snapped at him, feeling jealous.

"You are in a coma, remember?"

"I'm in a coma? What do you mean, I'm in a coma?" I laughed because I thought for sure he was joking; but from the look on his face, I could tell he wasn't.

"Your father and I thought it would be a good idea not to let anyone, with the exception of your family, know about you coming out of the coma. You're old news now so it doesn't matter."

"My father? What's he got to do with anything? He just got here and part of this is his fault." I was immediately turned off at the mention of my father.

"I know how you must feel, but he's as determined to find Tilo as I am. Verónica wants me to let it go but I can't."

"Moses, you couldn't possibly know how I feel. Hell, most days I don't know myself." I was conflicted. I wasn't sure how much he knew about my relationship with Tilo. "Can I listen to the message?"

Moses studied me for several minutes before he dialed his voice mail. He passed me the phone when he got to Tilo's message, and I confirmed that it was indeed Tilo's voice. My heart felt like it was about to bust out of my chest.

"Did you know Tilo tried to burn down our apartment?" This time Moses was the one jumping out of his chair.

"Shit, when?"

"I think I need something stronger than coffee. What about you?"

"Fine. Do you want to come by the house?"

"No, meet me at my place in an hour." I turned to leave.

"Where do you live?"

I smiled. If he didn't ask for directions then it meant he already knew and could be a suspect in the attempted torching of my apartment. I hated to be so suspicious of people, but until my full memory returned, I was being extra observant about the people around me.

# CHAPTER FORTY

## VICTÓRIA MENDOZA

I was feeling slightly better about my sister's choice in Moses after our meeting this morning. He kind of scared me when he dragged me out of his office, but I would keep my eye on him just in case. I was pretty much settled into my new apartment, but I still had piles of items that I hadn't put away.

The reason why I wanted Moses to come to my apartment was so that we could compare the voice on his answering machine to the taped greeting on my answering machine. If it was her voice, I would have no choice but to get with the program. Why else would she call Moses? As I waited, I decided to go through the stacks of mail from the mailbox.

I sorted the mail into two piles: hers and mine. Hers was mainly junk mail since all of the bills were in my name. At the time, Tilo told me her credit was jacked up so she asked me to put them in my name. In hindsight, she probably did this so no one would know where she lived. At the time, I didn't think about it because I thought of it as additional security. She couldn't get tired of me one day and kick my ass out without proper notice. My theory worked on one hand since she didn't kick me out, but she fucked me on a whole other level I didn't even think was possible.

I shook my head as I went through the mail. I was going to have to spend the better part of the day paying the overdue bills. Thank God I had a boatload of cash to do it with. I wondered if Verónica told Moses about the money, so I called her up.

"Hey, what's up?" I said.

"We're about to go shopping."

I could hear the happiness in my sister's voice.

"We?" Damn, she wasn't wasting any time spending her money.

"Yeah, didn't I tell you Moses' parents were coming to visit? His mother and I are going to hit the malls to get some things for LM."

"Oh yeah, I forgot." I was disappointed that she didn't invite me to come along.

"They got here yesterday. I was going to call you later to see if you and Padre wanted to come over to dinner. Are you feeling up to it?"

"Huh?" I was jealous because her life didn't miss a beat. Even though she lost her husband, she continued to march forward with a new band. I wanted to get on with my life but I had to find all the pieces to put my puzzle back together.

"Dinner? Where is your mind, child?" Verónica said.

"Sorry, I completely blanked out. Uh, I'll get back to you about dinner. Have fun on your shopping trip."

"Cool, thanks."

"Hey, did you, uh, tell Moses about the money?"

There was a long pause.

"No, I haven't had time. When I got home, girl, Moses had this romantic dinner and shit all laid out and everything. It was so nice. And, of course, his parents were here. They were fussing over the baby, so it really slipped my mind."

"Oh, okay. I was just checking."

"Why?" she said.

"I don't know, I just wanted to know."

"All right . . . I guess I'll talk to you later."

I said, "Yeah, I'll call you if I can make it over later."

"Fine. Get some rest. You don't sound all that hot to me."

As I hung up the phone, I never felt so lonely in my life. I never had a lot of friends, but I did have family. Right now, I didn't feel a part of Verónica's family. She had moved on with her life while I was still circling like a plane in a holding pattern.

"I need to put my hands on this bitch who ruined my life." I crushed a bill in my hand without even realizing it.

Someone knocked on the door. I tossed my Master-Card bill on the table and went to answer the door. It was Moses. "I just got off the phone with your wife."

Moses stopped like a deer caught in headlights.

"Relax, I didn't tell her you were coming over."

He came in and closed the door behind him. "Don't get me wrong, I'm not in the habit of hiding things from my wife, but she really doesn't want me involved in chasing Tilo. As far as she's concerned, Tilo is dead. Until I can prove otherwise, I'm not saying anything to her."

Prior to Tilo's deception, I might have busted Moses for lying to my sister, but I understood where he was coming from. My sister could be a royal pain in the ass. "What do you want to drink?"

"Actually, I stopped by the store before I came over here. Do you like Moscato?" He pulled the bottle out of a brown bag and set it on the table.

I went to get glasses and placed the answering machine in the center of the table.

He said, "What's this?"

I pressed play and Tilo's greeting filled my apartment. "You've reached 678-555-5555. We can't come to the phone so you know what that means—"

I pressed stop on the machine as the greeting finished.

Moses practically choked. "Damn, that's her. She sounds just like the voice on my answering machine. She didn't even attempt to disguise her voice. Were there any other messages?"

"No, I guess we weren't that popular. Where do you think she is?" I said.

"Seriously, I don't know and the postcard she sent didn't have a postmark on it."

"If she sent it through the mail, it would have to have a postmark on it. Do you have it? Can I see it?"

He pulled the postcard out of his briefcase, which I hadn't even noticed when he came in. "Is this her handwriting?"

I studied the short note as tiny hairs stood up on the back of my neck. I read her words. *Wish you were here. What the fuck does that mean?* I was angry. Tilo was flirting with him.

He said, "So is this her handwriting? If not, somebody is fucking with me."

I studied his face before I answered. I had so many questions but very few answers. "Yeah, it's her handwriting," I grudgingly admitted while the wheels turned in my head. "Moses, I'm still not clear as to how you even know Tilo."

He sat back in his chair and took a sip of wine. "I really don't *know* her know her if that's what you're thinking."

"Well, it did cross my mind." I put it out there for him to explain.

He sighed. "One night I was bringing your brother home. It was late and I didn't want him to catch the bus. When I dropped him off, a car followed me. I led the car down a one-way street and I cornered Tilo before she could get away."

"Why would she follow you? I don't understand."

"She said she was checking up on you. We went to get some coffee and she told me the whole story once she found out that Ramón worked for me."

"What do you mean the whole story?" I started sweating. Strange because it was cool in my apartment. I fidgeted and squirmed in my seat as I gulped my wine.

Moses continued to stare at me, which only heightened my feelings of discomfort. He said, "Uh . . . she told me you didn't come to work and she was concerned. And she told me about the letters your mom wrote."

"Damn, she told you all our business and she didn't even know you. That's strange, don't you think?" I was watching Moses like a hawk; he appeared as uncomfortable as I felt.

"In hindsight, yeah, it's strange. But there was a lot of things going on at the time, so I didn't pay attention. I was more concerned about Verónica and the baby." He had a point. Who had time to pay attention to details?

"Did Tilo tell you about us?" Since she had blabbed about everything else, it only stood to reason that she told him about me.

"She said you were lovers and that you lived together. If you're worried about me saying anything, don't. What you do behind closed doors is none of my business."

I didn't know what to think. If he meant to make me feel more at ease, he was wrong. He only made me more suspicious because this was the second secret

that I knew he was keeping from my sister. "Um, wow."
I sighed. I felt dirty and I wanted to take a bath.

"Victória, don't go there. She fooled all of us. I'm just
telling you this so you know it's just part of the game."

"She was my first." I don't know why I told him that.
It was none of his business. He didn't ask, but I needed
to tell someone. I was so confused about everything;
nothing was making sense to me. I started crying and
I couldn't stop. I felt so exposed, and I didn't like the
feeling one bit.

"Victória, one experience does not define who you
are. You're young and you have a whole lot of life to
live. You're going to make mistakes, but you have to
brush yourself off and keep it moving." He didn't reach
out to comfort me and I appreciated it. At that moment
I didn't think I could have stood to be touched. We sat
quietly for a few more moments.

"When I went by our other apartment," I said between sniffles, "some guys busted in the door asking
for Tilo. I didn't get to see their faces, but I'm positive
one of them was black. They must have been watching
the apartment, so we're not the only ones who know
she's still alive."

"What did they want?" Moses' voice rose with alarm.

"I don't know. They asked for Tilo. I told them I was
trying to find her myself, and they basically told me to
stay out of their way."

"Shit, who were they?" Moses started pacing.

"I have no idea. We never had people over; our life
was very private. My sister doesn't even know where I
live. Ramón knew but that's it as far as I know."

"It doesn't matter. I'm finding Tilo. Period."

"If you don't, I will."

\*\*\*

After Moses left, I went to several banks and got safe-deposit boxes in each one, which I stuffed with money. Since I couldn't account for where the money came from, I couldn't put it into my account. I was tired by the time I got back home, but I wanted to pay the bills that had accumulated while I was in the hospital. My Master-Card statement was the last one I opened. I was actually surprised to see the bill because, unlike my other cards, this one should have been current because I rarely used it. I kept this card for emergencies such as car repairs and to build my credit.

"Shit, this is a joint account." My hands started shaking as I opened the bill. I dialed Moses as I read the charges.

"Moses, oh my God, Tilo used my credit card. There's a charge on my card for AirTran Airways and I didn't make it. Can you call my father? I'm on my way to your office."

# CHAPTER FORTY-ONE

## CARLOS MENDOZA

I really didn't have time to stop by Moses' office. I went anyway, especially when he said Victória would be there. Victória and I still hadn't had an opportunity to sit down and talk, so I was hoping to knock out two birds with one stone. If I had to use Moses to get this accomplished, I didn't have a problem with it.

"Hello, Moses, how are you?" I looked around the office. To my dismay Victória was not there.

"I'm well. Where have you been? We haven't seen you around the house."

I took a seat in a soft leather chair. "I'm sorry, I've been so busy lately. Tell Verónica I will be by before the week is out."

"Perhaps you should tell her yourself. She is going to wonder when I saw you, and that's going to open up a whole dialogue that I don't think you or I want to have."

"You've got a good point. I forgot myself for moment. Is there anything new going on that I should know about?" I was ready to get this meeting under way with or without Victória.

"I hope you don't mind, but I'd really—"

We both looked up when Victória came into the office. There were a few uncomfortable seconds as she came in and took a seat.

"Hello, Victória." I felt awkward because I wanted to hug her and I didn't know how she would react if I did. I certainly didn't want to do it in front of Moses and risk the embarrassment of her pushing me away.

"Padre." She stared at me as if she wanted to say more.

I longed for the day when we were more than just civil to each other. Until that day came, I would take what I could get.

"Carlos, I met with Victória earlier today and we discussed our desire to find Tilo. I told her that you also wanted to find her so we asked you here so we could all be on the same page, working together."

I nodded. "Okay, I'm okay with that."

Moses said, "Victória, did you bring the bill?"

She handed him an envelope. "I was paying some bills when I noticed two charges on my credit card that I couldn't possibly have made. They both were made while I was in the hospital so I called Moses."

"Did someone steal your identity?" I asked.

"No, I don't think so," Moses answered for her. He handed me the envelope, but I missed any correlation I was supposed to get.

Moses said, "It means she's on the move. These charges to the airline look like luggage fees to me. It's too small to be airfare. If I'm right, she's been in Atlanta up until two weeks ago. Victória, can I hold on to these details for a few days while I check them out?"

"Yeah. Should I cancel the card?"

"No," Moses and I said together.

Moses elaborated, "She might not ever use the card again, but if she does, we'll know."

I said, "You should sign up for credit alert. It notifies you every time a purchase is made on your cards. You could set up how, when, and how often you want to be notified. It's easy. I have it on all my accounts."

Moses leaned forward. "That's a good idea, Carlos. I think I might sign me and Verónica up for this as well. Makes sense."

"Moses, don't forget to let Padre hear the message from Tilo?"

"Dag, I almost forgot."

I was getting excited because I felt like we were finally doing something to bring this matter to a close. Moses started dialing what I assumed to be his number on the phone. We all sat in silence as the office greeting came over the speaker. He pressed a few more buttons and finally the message played. We sat in silence until it was finished, but I was chilled to the bone.

"That's Tilo's voice," Victória said.

"I thought so too, and Victória and I compared it to the voice on their answering machine, and I'd swear in a court of law it was the same person," Moses confirmed.

I jumped up from my chair, outraged. "I know this voice too." I was so angry just thinking about the implications.

"You should. Didn't she call you and tell you to come home?" Victória looked at me strangely, but she couldn't possibly understand where I was coming from.

"Carlos, what's going on?" Moses looked at me.

I heard Moses talking to me. So many thoughts were going through my head; however, I couldn't process them all. I was getting angrier by the second; but more important, my chest started pounding. I realized I was losing control as I clutched my chest and fell to the floor. Victória screamed as she fell to her knees beside me. I tried to get my pills but Victória's hands were in the way.

"I need an ambulance at 435 Peachtree Street. Hurry, it may be a heart attack." Moses slammed down the phone. "Victória, do you know CPR?"

"Uh—"

"My pills," I whispered through parched lips.

"What did he say?" Victória shouted.

"Move," Moses said as he took command.

I was grateful he was there.

"My pills," I said again.

He pushed my hands away and found my pills. "How many?" He had the bottle open and poured them in my hand.

I blinked once. The pain in my chest was so tight I couldn't even talk. I was afraid to move.

"I'm going to assume you mean one." Moses took the pill and placed it in my mouth.

I moved it under my tongue. I tried to smile but I was still in too much pain.

"What's happening?" Victória was losing it. She was crying but I couldn't help her. Not at that moment.

Moses pointed to the phone. "Call your sister. I think she knows something. But do us a favor and take the phone outside."

The pill was working, but each episode was worse than the one before and it scared me. As the pain receded, I cried. If I wanted to be around to be in my children's lives, it was time to do something about this. I couldn't keep ignoring the pain.

"You good or do you need another pill?" Moses asked.

"Better." I struggled to get up but he pushed me back to the floor.

He said, "Not so fast. You're going to the hospital to get checked out."

I didn't have any fight in me. I was going to do whatever they told me, if it meant an end to the pain. I settled back on the floor and waited.

# CHAPTER FORTY-TWO

## VERÓNICA RAMSEY

I wasn't in the best frame of mind when I rushed into the hospital. It seemed like much of my life was being spent at Grady Memorial Hospital. It seemed as if my family members were being plucked from my life one at a time. "God, please don't take my father away from me again."

Victória wouldn't give me much information. She was hysterical. Moses wound up giving me a brief recap of what was going on. However, I could not figure out how or why all three of them were together when my father collapsed. I left LM with my in-laws and rushed to the hospital.

Moses and Victória were seated in the waiting room when I rushed in. I was out of breath from running from the parking deck. Moses leaned over and gave me a soft peck on the lips. I was embarrassed by his public display of affection since we'd spent most of our relationship hiding behind closed doors.

"What happened?" I said, looking between the two of them. I hugged my sister and sat down next to Moses. "Padre was having chest pains, and Moses told me to call for an ambulance. He didn't want to come to the hospital but Moses insisted, so I rode over with him."

I said, "That's good. I'm glad you both were with him to make sure he took his pills."

All eyes swiveled to me.

Victória jumped out of her chair and got in my face. "You knew about this and didn't tell me? I can't believe you."

"I wasn't trying to keep it a secret, but I haven't had time to tell you."

"After what happened to Mom? Are you serious?" She walked over to the window, obviously pissed at me.

I walked over to her but she brushed my hand off her shoulder. "Victória, it happened the day I was coming to take you home. Padre wanted to know what I'd told you about him and Ramón. I told him you didn't know anything and he went ballistic." I turned to Moses because Victória was ignoring me. "Moses, you came home right after it happened. Don't you remember?"

"I remember something, but I agree with Victória. What if he couldn't tell us about the pills? We wouldn't have thought to check his pockets and he might've died."

I looked around in disbelief. How did I become the bad guy when I just got there? I felt like they were ganging up on me. "Okay, I admit I should have said something. I wasn't trying to hide it, though. Victória, I haven't seen you since the time we met at our old house, and, Moses, you know what's been going on at the house. Damn, can't I get a break?" I was close to breaking down in tears. Everything that had been happening seemed amplified.

Moses came over to me and wrapped me in his arms as I started crying. "Honey, I'm not mad at you and neither is Victória. We're all acting on our emotions. Please stop crying." He rained tiny kisses along my hairline and forehead trying to relax me. Moses might not have been mad, but I still had to fix things with my sister.

Victória said, "Verónica, you have to stop babying me. I'm not a child. Believe it or not, I am a strong Latino woman and I can take it."

I swallowed the lump in my throat. "I wasn't trying to baby you, and I know how strong you are. In many ways you're stronger than me. But think about this honestly: when have you and I spent ten minutes together to talk? You haven't even been around to see my son but I understand." I pushed away from Moses. Suddenly I was mad when I realized what I'd just said.

"So you're going to turn this around on me?" Victória was livid.

"Yeah, I am." I was pissed too. If my sister wanted a fight, she was about to get it, and I didn't care who saw it.

"Wait, hold up. You two are taking this too far." Moses pulled me back in my seat and stood between us.

Victória tried to get around him but he wouldn't let her. I didn't understand what was going on. I wasn't even mad until she said I was babying her. But wasn't that what older sisters were supposed to do? I was confused by my emotions.

Moses said, "Victória, your sister's hormones are fucking with her so please don't take any of this personally."

I pushed away from Moses. He pissed me off for belittling me in front of my sister.

"Moses, what are you saying?" I was all over the place and they both were looking at me like I'd lost my damn mind.

Moses fixed me with a stern look. "Stop." As our eyes connected, Moses brought me back to my senses. Before I could examine my feelings any closer, a doctor walked into the waiting room. It was a moment I lived through before, and I assumed Victória felt it too because she walked over and took my hand.

"Is there anyone here for Mr. Mendoza?"

I could not read the doctor's face, and I couldn't answer his question. The only thing I could think about was the last time we were in the hospital and the doctor told us our mother had passed away. I closed my eyes as if it would help stop me from hearing bad news. I leaned into my sister.

"Yes, we're his daughters. How is he?" Victória asked.

"He's stable right now. We're going to keep him for a few days to run some more tests."

"Is it his heart?" I knew the answer before I asked the question.

The doctor nodded. "Yes, I'm afraid it is. He told me he has known of his condition for some time but refuses to have the surgery."

"What type of surgery?" Moses asked.

"He needs a bypass. He has severe blockage to the heart and it needs to be removed."

Victória asked, "Did he say why he is refusing the surgery?"

"No, but I was hoping one of you could convince him to change his mind. As you know, the heart is a muscle and your father's heart is tired and overworked. Nitroglycerin relaxes the blood vessels and takes the strain off your heart, but you can only do it so many times for it to remain effective. Unless you get your father to change his mind, the next time this happens he might not be so lucky."

Victória said, "Thank you, Doctor. We will speak with him. Can we see him?" Just as she did when our mother took sick, Victória controlled the situation.

"Actually, I'd prefer it if he was allowed to rest right now. He's heavily sedated."

Victória was getting pissed but she worked to keep her cool. "With all due respect, Doctor . . ."

"Sorry, Broomfield."

"Dr. Broomfield. We recently lost our mother to heart failure. She came in and we never got to see her alive again. May we please see him, just for a minute? I promise we won't disturb him. We just need to tell him . . ." Victória's words trailed off then she started crying.

I knew what she was trying to say. "We need to tell him we love him. Please, he really needs to know." I had to step out of myself on this one. If Padre was attached to a bunch of machines, I really didn't want to see him that way, but I'd never forgive myself if I allowed my discomfort to stand in the way.

"All right, but please don't upset him."

"We won't."


"He is so cute. Moses, he looks just like you," Victória said, watching me feed LM.

"Uh-oh, she thinks I'm cute. Watch out now." Moses did a little dance around our living room while laughing.

"Don't let that go to your head. You're already conceited enough." I laughed at Moses' face as he pretended to be hurt.

"Woman, you wounded me." He sank down on the seat beside me as Victória reached out to hold LM. "Don't pay her no mind. She's just jealous the baby doesn't look like her."

"He does look like me. He has my . . . um . . ." I couldn't even think of a single trait my son showed. He favored me when he was born but he had changed.

Moses said, "Don't feel bad, sweetie. My mom said our family has very dominant genes."

"Yeah, whatever." I got up to put LM down for his nap. I didn't want him to get used to all the attention he'd been getting. When everybody left and went home, I didn't want to be stuck carting him around all day because he wanted to be held.

"Sit down and enjoy your sister. I'll put LM to bed." Moses kissed me on the top of the head and left us alone.

Victória watched as Moses bundled up LM and carried him upstairs. "Things look like they are going well between you and Moses."

"Yeah, I honestly can't complain. He wants to marry me again, the right way this time."

"Verónica, I'm so happy for you. Have you set a date yet?"

"No, not yet. I really want LM to be older before we do it. At least if he was older, I'd feel better about leaving him alone when we go on our honeymoon."

"Y'all gonna do a honeymoon too? Wow, I'm impressed. Does Moses have any brothers?"

I laughed out loud. It made me feel good knowing my sister approved of my choice.

"No, sorry. He's the only one; trust me, he's enough."

"Damn. Girl, when you first told me you loved him, I thought you'd lost your damn mind."

"I know, and you let me know it every chance you got." I was laughing now, but it wasn't so funny when we were going through it. My mood immediately shifted; I felt myself feeling emotional again. "You know, Moses may have been right about these mood swings. One minute I'm happy as a pig in shit and the next minute I feel like bawling my eyes out."

"I'm sure. We've been through some major shit. I'm thankful every day just to be alive," Victória said.

"Why were you and Padre at Moses' office today?" I knew the answer but I needed to be sure.

Victória's face got hard and defensive, but I was determined to find out the truth. "Verónica, Moses told us that you didn't want him going after Tilo. I need his help, though. I have to find her."

"Why? What good would it do to find her? Will it change anything?" I was desperately trying to understand what I was obviously missing.

"No, it won't change anything. Then again, she didn't shoot you and leave you for dead, did she? Now you might be able to pick up the pieces and go on with your life but I can't. Padre feels the same way because Tilo shot Ramón too. All of our lives have been drastically altered, can't you see that?"

"Okay, I can see your point, but why does Moses need to be involved?" I asked.

She sighed before she answered. "He doesn't. If you feel so strongly about it, I'll get someone else to help. I thought he would be the logical person because he knows Tilo, and he's familiar with everything that went down. But on a more serious tip, I thought you'd want to find the person who has changed our lives forever too."

Victória hurt me deeply by insinuating that I didn't care. In my heart I knew Moses wasn't going to let it go. I was beginning to realize that I was being unfair to him by asking him to step away. My biggest fear was pissing off the cartel. It consumed so much of Padre's life. I didn't want the same thing for me and my family.

I said, "What are you going to do if you find her? Get yourself in trouble?"

"I ain't gonna lie to you. If I find the bitch, I'm going to kill her. Plain and simple. I can't go to jail for killing someone who's already dead. Feel me?"

# CHAPTER FORTY-THREE

## TILO ADAMS

"Your bag is over the weight limit."

I wasn't paying attention. I'd finally worked up the nerve to leave Atlanta and the stress was more than I anticipated. I just wanted to get on the plane and go to sleep. I stared at the attendant and wished she'd hurry up. She stared at me as well.

"What?" I didn't have time for this high-yellow heifer to be giving me attitude and shit.

"I told you your suitcase is overweight."

"So?" *Hell, I didn't make the damn suitcase.*

She rolled her eyes. "So you need to either take out three pounds worth of stuff or pay a fifty-dollar penalty."

I wanted to reach over the counter and snatch the ugly-ass, no-neck-having bitch.

"Fifty? I ain't paying no fifty nothing. When did y'all start charging and shit for luggage?"

"Fine." She stepped over to the scale and placed my suitcase on the floor in front of me. She rolled her eyes again and said, "Next."

I lowered my Gucci shades, looking the attendant straight in her eyes. "What do you mean *next?* I still need my ticket."

She looked at me like I was a special person who should be riding on a short bus instead of a plane. "You said you weren't paying the fee so I'm moving on to the next customer. Now if you could kindly remove your bag, I do have other customers to wait on."

Even in my crazed mind, I knew better than to threaten airport personnel. Nevertheless, I was very close to doing it. This woman had plucked my last nerve with her condescending attitude. I grabbed my bag and moved off to the side and thought of my next move. I couldn't believe this was happening, and if the situation were different, I might have waited around for the bitch to get off work and put her ass on a scale or two.

My flight was leaving within the hour. I didn't have a lot of time so I had no choice but to pay the fee. I needed to get in control of my emotions. I felt like I was teetering on the edge of sanity and a swift breeze could carry me over. I stepped back outside to cool off and have a cigarette. I might have paid the fee right away if the bitch wasn't giving me attitude, and if I had enough cash in my wallet. My money was in my carry-on and I didn't want to open it and have a bunch of strangers gawking in my bag. However, my problem was solved when I saw another couple use a credit card to pay their luggage fee at the curb check-in counter. Tossing out my smoke, I approached the check-in.

"Excuse me, sir. Can I check my luggage here?"

"Boarding pass and identification."

*What the fuck has happened to customer service?* Would it have hurt the motherfucker to say good morning? I was nervous as I handed over my fake identification card, but I shouldn't have been because the man only used my identification to type my name in the computer.

He said, "Put your bag on the scale."

*Hello, can I get a little help with it? It is heavy, you dickhead.* Using both hands, I lifted the bag onto the scale. I was not feeling this whole airport experience. If I didn't need to get out of town today, I would have caught the damn train.

"Your bag is overweight."

*Ding, ding, ding—tell 'em what he won, Johnny. Of course my bag is overweight, why do you think I'm waving this credit card at you?* He took my card and placed my bag on the belt. As I walked back into the terminal, it took everything in me not to flip the bird to the bitch behind the counter.

I had to stop several times to ask for directions. In my frazzled state, nothing looked familiar. My thoughts were so jumbled in my head, I could barely read my ticket and I completely forgot the do's and don'ts of the airport security screenings. The line was horrendously long, but I was surprised at how quiet the people were. I hated waiting almost as much as I hated idiots and rudeness, and I'd encountered all of the above. I used the time to put my identification and card away and close my purse. I was beginning to sweat because I wasn't used to being around so many people.

"I'm sorry, what did you say?"

The lady in front of me practically ignored me as she continued to point at her ear. My mind told me she was being disrespectful, and I wished I had a gun so I could show her who the fuck she was dealing with.

"But I can't hear what you're saying." I poked her in the back. *How do you expect me to answer you if you've got your back turned to me and I can't hear what you're saying?*

The guy behind me started talking too, but I refused to turn around. I didn't want to speak with him at all. He was wearing some torn-up shoes and was probably blowing rent money just to take this trip. Nine times out of ten, he was looking for someone to bail him out of whatever drama he had imposed on his life.

The lady said, "I'm not speaking to you. I'm on the phone."

*Well damn, how was I supposed to know she was pointing to an earpiece?* I saw her lips moving and she was looking at me at one point. "Sorry," I mumbled. As I looked around, everyone appeared to be on the phone talking to someone. I started to feel left out because I didn't have anyone I could call and shoot the shit with. Unwanted tears welled in my eyes; the painful reminder almost brought me to my knees. I stumbled and the man with the fucked-up shoes grabbed my arm.

"I got it," I said as I snatched my arm back. Perhaps I spoke a little too loud from the way people stared. The last thing I wanted was to draw attention to myself, but it seemed like everything I did had the opposite effect. I decided to ignore everyone around me and concentrate on getting through to the gate. "Boarding pass and identification?"

I tried to walk past the lady sitting on the chair. I saw her lips moving. I tuned her out thinking she was also speaking on the phone. She reached out and grabbed me as I was walking past. I snatched away but was quickly restrained.

"Get your hands off of me, I didn't do anything." I was furious. This whole airport thing was just too much for my fragile state of mind. The people, the pace, protocol, and procedures were simply too much. I was so focused on what I needed to do in New York that I had forgotten what I needed to do to get there.

"You cannot go past this point without a boarding pass and identification."

I had male guards on each side of me holding my arms. "Okay, I have both of these items in my purse."

I was being pulled over to the side, and I was afraid I would have to go to the back of the line.

"Where are you taking me?" *Do they know who I am?* My thoughts were in hyper drive.

The cute guard said, "We're not taking you any-where. We just needed to get you out of the way until we got your identification. You're supposed to have them in your hand before you approach a TSA agent. Didn't you see the signs?"

"I'm sorry, I haven't flown in a minute and I keep forgetting all this nonsense we have to endure. My boarding pass is in the side pocket, but I'm afraid I put my identification back in my wallet." I smiled, hoping to take all the testosterone back down a notch or two. Instead of allowing me an opportunity to give them the items myself, one of them retrieved my pass while the other handed me my wallet. I showed him the identi-fication while the other one ran my purse through the x-ray machine.

"Where are you traveling to?"

Was this any of his motherfucking business? Better yet, it was on the ticket. Couldn't he read? I didn't get a chance to answer.

The less attractive one said, "Is this your carry-on?"

The one who had taken my purse had returned it and was looking at my other bag all crazy. Since I didn't see anyone else getting this type of personalized atten-tion, I was getting suspicious. I realized I was probably being paranoid because the bonds I stole from the Mendoza family were in that bag but I was incapable of stopping myself. Part of me wanted to deny ownership but—on the off chance everything was on the up and up—I 'fessed up.

"Yeah." I was about to hit the panic button. If the agent even attempted to empty out my bag, I was going to take my chances running. Even though there was nothing illegal about carrying bearer bonds, I had no idea whose blood was on them.

"We need to run your bag through the scanner." The prick didn't even wait to see if I was going to object. He slung the shit on the belt and personally viewed the contents. *Booya!* I felt like I had swished a three-point basket. I could tell the officer was disappointed that he didn't find anything that he could use to detain me. They gave me back my boarding pass and ID.

"You can pick up your bag on the other side once you go through the scan. You won't be needing your identification again but you might want to keep your boarding pass handy. Have a nice day."

"You have a nice day too," I answered. I'd practically shit my pants and needed to go to the bathroom and check for skid marks.

*Jackasses.* I started fussing with myself as I inched my way to the screeners. *Unless you have this secret desire to spend the rest of your life sitting in a six-by-nine cell, I suggest you get your shit together.* People were giving me funny looks. I wanted to yell at them so bad it hurt. Why were people so nosey anyhow? What was going on with me ain't have nothing to do with them. I felt myself mentally detach from my body. I allowed the calm me to march ahead of the angry me, so Ms. Angry wouldn't get me into any more trouble.

I saw the line for screening, but Ms. Angry was about to walk right past it as if she were exempt from it. Another officer stopped her, and I was forced to join her before she started acting a fool.

"What now? Am I supposed to get butt-assed naked now?" I looked around, seeking the support from angry passengers who'd had enough of their antics.

The officer said, "No, that won't be necessary but you do need to remove your shoes, sweater, any electronic devices, any change you may have in your pockets, and a belt if you're wearing one. Place those items in one of these bins. You will be told when to walk through the scanner."

"What, are we in grade school again? What the fuck do you think I could possibly put in my shoes?" I tried to shut my other half down, but Ms. Angry was pissed off. In my head I knew what I was supposed to do but getting my body to do it was the difficult part.

"You'd be surprised." The officer acted like he was used to these types of outbursts and moved on, repeating a similar spiel to others in line.

*What is he going to do if I refuse? This has to be a violation of my rights. I'm not doing it.* We were holding up the line and people behind us started walking around us, shooting us nasty looks as they passed.

"This bitch is nuttier than all outdoors," a passenger said to another.

"Yeah, I just hope she isn't on my flight. I'm not up for any foolishness when we get up in the air."

"I know that's right," chimed a third passenger.

I looked around to see who they were talking about and all eyes were on me. I could only assume I was the nut they were referring to, so I made a conscious effort to ignore the voice raging in my head.

Getting with the program, I took off everything I thought would be a problem: toe ring, watch, bracelet, and earrings. Once I was finished with those items, I reached behind me and undid my bra. I slid the straps down my arms and reached under my shirt and pulled it off. I didn't want the little metal hooks triggering an alarm, which would draw even more attention to me. Satisfied that I had taken off everything that needed to be scanned, I stuffed my bra inside my shoes and put them on the conveyor belt. As I waited on the other side for all of my things, I couldn't help but overhear a rude comment.

"Good thing that scanner doesn't detect crazy," someone said.

If I weren't so busy trying to collect all my things from the conveyor belt, I might have gone off. It probably was a good thing I didn't, because even though I was trying to be low key, I was still drawing attention. I looked over my shoulder and noticed the same officer who had handled my bags was behind me.

"Did I do something else wrong?" It was a struggle not to yell at him and ask that he leave me the fuck alone.

"No, why'd you ask?" He had to be kidding. If he got any closer to me, I could have gotten his imprint off my ass.

"Oh, since you were still hanging around I thought—"

"I get paid to hang around." He chuckled, but I didn't find anything funny. His presence was making me nervous.

"Could you possibly hang somewhere else?" I muttered under my breath. This motherfucker had jokes. Before he could respond I grabbed the last of my things and followed the crowd to the terminals.

# CHAPTER FORTY-FOUR

## MOSES RAMSEY

It was a long day, one I was going to put in the history books and lay it down. I took a long shower. That helped me to relax. By the time I came into the bedroom, I was already yawning and preparing a mental checklist for the things I still needed to do.

Verónica was seated at her vanity table brushing her hair. She was nude from the waist up. Her beauty nearly took my breath away. Her eyes met mine in the mirror and suddenly I was no longer tired. She boldly perused my body as I stiffened under her scrutiny.

I said, "Damn, baby, you look good enough to eat."

She smiled and I thought she was thinking the same things that I was until she slammed her brush down with enough force to snap it in half. "So you're still going after her regardless of how I feel about it?"

"Talk about ruining the mood." I slung my damp towel on the chaise chair and got in bed.

"Moses, this isn't funny."

"Do I look like I'm laughing to you?" She might have had a right to be a little upset, but I was mad too. If she thought I was about to spend the rest of my night arguing, she had another think coming. I was not going to be sucked into a fight with her, because we'd end up tossing and turning all night. My parents were finally gone and I'd been looking forward to spending some time with Verónica.

"Are you going to ignore my question?"

"You already know the answer, so why are you wasting time and energy talking about it?"

"So that's it? Because you say so, I'm supposed to automatically agree?" She stood up with her hands on her hips. If she weren't so angry, she would've looked cute.

"You've made it clear that you don't agree, but on this we are going to have to agree to disagree." I patted my pillow for comfort.

"And what am I supposed to do if Tilo kills you too? How am I going to raise LM by myself? Did you even think about that while you're running around trying to be Dick Tracy?"

My heart lurched. I hadn't thought about how Verónica would raise my son to be a man if I weren't around. If she hadn't pissed me off with the Dick Tracy remark, I might have been more diplomatic with my response. I got up from the bed to retrieve some pajamas. "I am the same man you married, Verónica. Dick Tracy is what I do."

She hurt my feelings, and I wanted to get away from her before I said something that I couldn't take back. That was one of the reasons why I hated arguing. In the heat of the moment, the mouth said things without engaging the brain and, in some cases, the heart. Verónica was crying again. I grabbed a couple of pillows from the bed. I was going to the living room to sleep on the couch. I could have used the guest bedroom, but I promised to never go to bed mad. If I slept on the couch, it would be like I was taking a nap.

I stopped in the doorway. "You think you can close your eyes and Tilo will go away? I don't think so. Right before your father had his attack, he told us he had spoken to her a few days ago. It's only a matter of time before Tilo brings her shit to our house, and I'm determined to keep it out of our home." I shut the door firmly behind me.

# CHAPTER FORTY-FIVE

## TILO ADAMS

I got recruited straight out of high school to be an agent for the FBI because of my high academic scores and my propensity toward gangs and violence. I didn't chose the bureau; it was chosen for me, and they didn't give me much choice about accepting their generous offer. It was outright blackmail to be honest. I wasn't in the position to fight back. It was either join the FBI or go to jail.

I was young and naive so when they told me my options, I started the six-month training class. At the start I was still the angry and rebellious child, but the bureau has a way to make sure you conform to the rules. They stuck my ass down in the kitchen washing dishes for the entire compound. It took about two days and the anger dissipated. I was ready to cooperate. I remembered it like it was yesterday.

*"April, are you sure you want to do this? It could be dangerous," my mother asked when I told her of my decision to start training in Quantico, Virginia. My mother knew nothing of my options, and I had no intention of enlightening her. I didn't have the balls to tell her what I'd been up to and why I didn't have a choice. It would have broken her heart. She thought the sun rose and set on my black ass, and this was an-other way the Feds kept me in line.*

"It's going to be okay, Ma," I said, trying to sound like I really meant it. At that point I was so deep into the game, it was time for me to leave the streets or die. I was selling drugs, accepting bribes, and had even participated in a few murders. The bureau had a notebook full of the shit I'd done. They assured me that they would tell it all if I didn't cooperate with them.

I was nineteen years old and going to college was not an option I wanted to exercise. The bureau offered me an alternative, albeit a dangerous one, but it wasn't much different from my life on the streets.

Twenty weeks of intense training, which included more than 850 hours of classroom instruction. I hadn't signed up for that, but I was too far into it to give up without a fight. Not surprisingly, I excelled at everything criminal. I didn't have to be taught to think like a gangbanger because I was one. The hardest part of my training was learning the thin line between honesty and dishonesty. My mother attended my graduation and it was the last time I saw her.

"Sweetheart, I am so proud of you." Her cries were heard throughout the entire ceremony.

I was expecting her to yell out at any minute that I was her baby. I could hear the other students snickering, but if they had anything else to say, they kept it to themselves. My tolerance for bullshit was small and the bureau taught me some pretty effective methods to discourage ridicule.

"It was easy, Ma. I'm a natural, at least that is what my trainers say." I took off the robe and small cap and handed it to my mother for safekeeping.

"What happens now? What will they have you doing?" She followed close behind me as I walked to my car.

*This was my first day of freedom and I couldn't wait to get away and relax. "I can't talk about it." I could see the hurt on her face, but that's one of the things from training that I'd absolutely adhere to. In this business loose lips did sink ships.*

*"Honey, you're scaring me. How come I can't contact you?"*

*"Mom." I stopped walking and led her over to a bench to sit down. I loved my mom and I couldn't stand to see her hurting. "I would be lying if I said I wasn't scared too. If I can't handle it, I'll be the first to bow out. You know me. I'm going to run at the first sign of trouble. I ain't about to get caught up in some shit I can't handle." I smiled at her as I wiped away the tracks of her tears.*

*Mom said, "Watch your mouth. You may be grown, but I can still whip the black off your narrow ass. Humph, beat you like you stole something."*

*We laughed. I was going to miss this woman sitting beside me. She meant the world to me and it would be rough letting her go, but it was necessary for her sake and mine. I was given a new name and a new life that she would never know of. I never saw myself as a hero. Dying was never in my equation; it was a factor of the job chosen for me. I kissed her cheek and went to join my fellow graduates. From that moment on, they were my family.*

*The one good thing I got out of the training was that my body was fine, fit, and fabulous. I had washboard abs, a tight ass, and firm biceps. My thighs were so tight, I could choke a motherfucker with them without using my hands. I was a bad bitch!*

*I was stationed at Century Parkway in Atlanta, learning the ropes. I wasn't in a big hurry to get out in the field because, despite my training, dodging bullets wasn't my thing. I wanted a big come up that would take me away from the bureau before things got too dangerous for me.*

*I was the youngest agent on staff, and I was concerned about my ability to go in the street and actually interact with Joe Blow public.*

*"Agent Adams!"*

*I was startled when I heard my name called during formation. Since day one, I tried my best to remain low key and under the radar.*

*"Yes, sir," I responded as we were taught during training. My heart was beating about a mile a minute because I didn't know what to expect. I didn't even know if he was actually talking to me because I had yet to make friends with any of the other trainees. Since I was the only one to stand up, I assumed he was talking to me and it made my heart beat faster.*

*"Follow me."*

*"Uh-oh, shit's about to get ugly," I muttered as I followed the officer. I didn't have a problem with following orders, but I wasn't prepared to do anything extra. Damn my oath, I just wasn't the one.*

*We walked through the entire complex before he entered a vacant office and took a seat. I was so nervous I was shaking, but was pissed that we had to walk to the end of the complex before he sat down to chat. The complex was big and there was no way he could have made me believe there weren't any vacant offices between where we had formation and where we were now.*

*"Sir, did I do anything wrong?" I knew for a fact that I hadn't but he was just staring at me and I wanted to break the ice.*

*"No, Adams, relax. We just found a job we believe only you will be able to handle."*

*My first impulse was to ask him who the hell "we" was. I could not imagine why I would have been chosen over all the seasoned veterans who met in the meeting room each morning. Clearly there had to be some sort of mistake. All I wanted to do was collect a motherfucking check and be done with this FBI bullshit. "And what job is that, sir?" I would play their game as long as I could. The moment that shit got dangerous, though, I was out. I did what they told me to do. I completed the training. I was very serious about that shit. Some of the agents took themselves way too seriously. I wasn't one of them. I had nothing to prove to any of them.*

*"The Cali Cartel, I want to bring them down and I need you to do it."*

*"Huh?" I started laughing nervously because he couldn't possibly be serious. Even I knew the Cali Cartel ran governments, not the other way around. This had to be some kind of joke or initiation. I looked around, hoping to spot the spy camera they were using to catch me on tape.*

*"I said I want you to bring down the Cali Cartel."*

*This negro obviously had me confused with someone else. "What? Me? Are you serious?"*

*No response.*

*"What the hell can I do?" My voice rose to a high-pitched whine. If this was a joke, they caught me bitching out on tape. My heart continued to beat at a rapid pace. I felt like the bureau was trying to suck me into a situation I would not be able to walk away from. In fact, it sounded like a death sentence to me. The senior agent ignored me and my outburst.*

*"You won't be dealing with the cartel per se, but you will have direct contact with a young girl whose family is involved with them. She's about your age. We*

*need for you to become her friend, find out everything
you can about her and her family, and bring that information back to us."*

I was not believing this shit. There was no way I
was ready for undercover work—especially with the
notorious Cali Cartel. They had agents entrenched in
all facets of law enforcement, so it would be difficult
to know who to trust while undercover. "Sir, no disrespect intended, but I'm hardly qualified to handle this
type of operation."

"Agent Adams, you're playing yourself short. I
wouldn't have chosen you if I didn't think you were
qualified."

I was torn between arguing with his pompous
ass and requesting a new assignment. "Why me?" I
whined again.

"'Cause you're near the youngest daughter's age. I
think the two of you will get along. It's your job to get
along with her."

"But—"

"There are no buts," he sternly commanded. His
cold demeanor frightened me.

"Yes, sir," I whispered.

"Here." He slung something on the table and I
picked it up. It was a driver's license.

"Who is Tilo Adams?" Fear ran through my heart.

"You are. Get a safe deposit box and put everything
with your old identity in it. Lock it up, Adams. There
is no room for mistakes." His warning was clear: fuck
up and I die.

"Sir, did I die?"

"No, April Adams is not dead, but you are no longer
April Adams. Put her identify away and don't use it.
Ever. You have a job interview this afternoon. Study
your background and get this job. Your target is Vic-

*tória Mendoza. Become her friend. I promise you the rest will work itself out."*

*"How do I do that?" I was scared for real. I felt like I was being set up for a job I wasn't equipped to do.*

*"Make friends with her and see if you can find out anything that will help us out in our investigation." He pushed a small folder over to me.*

*I did not want to pick it up, but it seemed as if I didn't have a choice. I didn't have a good feeling about the case or the legality of changing my identity. "What do I do once I have the information?" I had resigned to face my destiny.*

*"That's the easy part. Hustle your ass back here. This one is on a need-to-know basis. The cartel is powerful, and I'm reasonably sure they have some operatives in our department, so you are not to discuss this case with anyone other than me. Am I clear on this?"*

*He was crystal clear and I was tempted to walk out the door and take my chances on the street.*

*"Don't even think about it, Adams. Fuck this up and I promise I will find a way to make your life miserable."*

*I could tell by the tone of his voice that he was not messing around with me. This was serious and that frightened me even more.*

# CHAPTER FORTY-SIX

## TILO ADAMS

*"Hey, Victória, what's up? Want to hang out after work? Let's have a couple of drinks." I was in the office getting my assignments for the day. I spent most of my time over at the courthouse researching titles, but when I did get to come to the office, I tried getting to know the extremely reserved Victória Mendoza.*

*"I can't. I got to go home."*

*"Husband waiting on you?" I was joking because I already knew her situation.*

*"I wish. My mother is expecting me."*

*"What are you, twelve?" I saw anger flash in her eyes. This was the first time I saw her display any emotion.*

*"No." She started grabbing things off her desk and slinging them into her purse.*

*I knew she was mad when she took her Rolodex and put it in her purse. I started laughing.*

*"What?" She glared at me, clearly pissed.*

*"Do you always take your Rolodex home with you?" I laughed even harder when I saw her mortified expression.*

*She snatched the Rolodex out of her purse, zipped the purse closed, and slung it over her shoulder. "One drink." She marched out of the office with me right on her heels. We walked over to Taco Mac in silence.*

*I said, "So, what's up with the attitude?"*

*"Nothing. I just have a lot on my mind."*

*We ordered drinks, strong drinks.*

*"My bad. I hate being the new kid on the block. Of all the people working in the firm, you seem like the only real person there. I can't stand no fake bitch."*

*Victória's head snapped back and she started laughing. "You read them right. All them bitches can kiss my ass," Victória exclaimed as she started to loosen up.*

*I said, "That bitch Tonya is the first one on my list. She's supposed to be our supervisor, but she's got something negative to say about everybody."*

*"I know that's right. She tricked my ass into being a friend for a hot minute, but I had to cut that loose."*

*"You didn't tell her any of your business, did you? 'Cause that heifer can't hold water in a bucket. I hadn't been there but five minutes and I knew everybody's marital status. What the fuck do I care if them bitches is married or not?"*

*Victória shrugged. "She's a trip. I think she has issues with herself."*

*"Exactly. And the men suck. Every last one of them. Why can't we have at least one piece of eye candy up in that joint?"*

*Victória giggled like a schoolgirl. A small light bulb went off in my head. She was a virgin. I was going to have to find a way to use that information to my advantage. Twenty minutes and two drinks later, I signaled for the check.*

*"You ready to go?" She looked surprised.*

*"I thought you said you only had time for one drink. I'm not trying to get you in trouble or nothing."*

*"I'm a grown-ass woman," she declared and ordered another round. Ironically, Jaheim's song "Another Round" was playing in the background.*

I said, "Look, I don't know about you, but I can't afford too many more of these drinks. I work at Title Guarantee Company and they ain't paying me shit."

"I know that's right."

"It's Friday night and I don't live far. What do you say about us getting a bottle and going to my house?"

She smiled. "Sounds like a plan to me."

We paid the tab and Victória followed me to my new apartment, compliments of the bureau.

"Okay, how the fuck can you afford this apartment?" Victória gasped after I gave her the grand tour.

"It ain't off my salary I'll tell you that. They ought to be ashamed of the wages they pay us."

"Yeah, slave labor, but you still didn't answer the question." She looked nervous all of a sudden.

I felt the chill in the air and she looked like she was about to flee. "Relax, girl, I do taxes on the side during tax season. I pay the rent for the entire year so I don't have to stress." I handed her another drink.

"Miss, you're about to miss your flight." Someone poked me in the arm.

"Huh? What's going on?" I struggled to open my eyes; it felt like someone had tied them down with tiny ropes.

"You are on the flight to New York, aren't you?" Who was this person and why the fuck did they keep poking me?

"Uh, yeah." My eyes finally opened, and I was a little dismayed to see a TSA goon standing in front of me.

"Well, they just made last call," he said. "If you want to get on this flight, I suggest you hurry before they close the doors."

I was shocked. I didn't even remember closing my eyes, and now I was about to miss my flight. I gathered my things and rushed to the gate. "Who would have thought the agent from hell could've been a blessing." I took my seat in first class and promptly went back to sleep. *Damn, bitch, you didn't even say thanks.* "Fuck 'em," I mumbled.

# CHAPTER FORTY-SEVEN

## CARLOS MENDOZA

"How long have I been out? Wait, where am I?"

"Padre, you're in the hospital. You've been here for a few days," Victória said.

I sat up. "A few days? Well, I'm ready to go home. I'm feeling better. Get the doctor."

"Padre, they're not going to let you leave. You're very ill. Unless you have this surgery, you're going to die," Victória said.

I was surprised to see Victória. She was fresh out of the hospital herself and now she was sitting vigil around my bed. And from the looks of things, it appeared as if she'd been here for a while.

"Nonsense. I'll be fine. I just got overexcited. It happens from time to time."

"They don't give medication for excitement. Why do you continue to lie to us?"

I was immediately sorry for lying, but old habits were hard to break. So of course it was natural to say the first thought that came to my head. "I'm sorry. You're right." I felt like our roles were reversed and suddenly I was the child.

Victória grabbed my hand. "How long has this been going on?"

"For a few years now. This is the first time I wound up in the hospital, though." I didn't want to alarm Victória, but I was actually scared myself. I didn't want to die, not yet anyway.

"Padre, this isn't good. You've got me and Verónica worried sick about you. The doctor said you have to have surgery—this time you're going to get it."

"Nonsense, I'll be fine." I tried to sound confident, but I failed to comfort my own self.

"The doctor said your body is strong enough to recover, but your heart is working overtime to sustain it. If you don't have the surgery, there might not be a next time. You cheated me out of my childhood, are you checking out on me as an adult?"

Victória was angry but she had every right to be. If she hadn't said that, I might have continued fighting her until I'd talked my way out of the hospital. I'd spent so much of my life alone, it was time I started thinking about someone other than myself.

I said, "Fine, I'll have the surgery, but you must promise me that you'll find Tilo. She won't stop until you do."

Her eyebrow raised. "Stop what? What more can she do?"

"I don't know . . . I honestly don't know myself." It was important to me that Victória understood, even though I was still trying to wrap my arms around it myself.

"Padre, you're not making any sense. I think I need to call Verónica."

"No, don't call her. Once I speak to you and Moses, you can decide what to tell her after I finish telling you what I have to say."

"Okay. Are you sure I don't need to get the doctor?"

"Really, I'm fine, but I do have something very important to tell you. Could you call Moses and ask him to stop by?"

She made the call then said, "He is on his way."

"Good. Wake me when he gets here, okay?"

"Okay, Padre. I'll be right here if you need me."

I was far from sleepy. I needed time to get my thoughts together. I'd been lying for such a long time, it was difficult to tell the truth. My biggest fear was that my children wouldn't be able to forgive me for a second time. The last thing I wanted to do was to bring up the old memories they had just put to rest, but that was exactly what I needed to do to get on to the future. I believed Moses understood the risks we were facing, and I needed his logical mind to make sure Victória understood what we were up against.

I didn't immediately open my eyes when my door opened. If it was a nurse coming to check on me, they could do it while I was presumably asleep. However, when no one approached the bed, I took a peek. I smiled weakly when I noticed Moses. For some reason I felt comforted just having him near. "Moses, I didn't hear you come in."

"Afternoon, sir. I didn't want to disturb you."

Victória was seated in the chair closest to the window. Her face was strained. I made a mental note to tell Moses to make sure she went home and got some rest. She didn't need to be sitting in the room with me.

"Thank you for coming. Help me sit up some more."

Moses pressed the buttons until I was comfortable. I nodded my head in thanks. He took a seat next to Victória.

I decided to get right to the point. "I have two phones. One for my personal use and one is for business. Since the cartel shut down, my business phone has not rung. That is, until the other day. Do you remember when we were in your office Moses, and I told you I recognized the voice on your answering machine?"

"Yeah." Moses nodded.

"Monte was the only person who had that number, but Tilo called it the other day."

"So Uncle Monte gave the number to Tilo?" Victória asked.

"Possible, but not likely," I answered.

Moses said, "Hmm, that doesn't make sense to me either. To my knowledge, Monte didn't know Tilo like that. I'd be willing to bet money on that."

"Okay, you two seem to know something that I don't. Somebody please enlighten me," Victória stated.

Moses reached for his briefcase. "Since we are just throwing out theories, here's one I'm working on. I did a Google search on Colombian drug wars and the results were really quite disturbing. I was more interested in drugs and their relation to Atlanta."

I was excited. This was exactly the type of connection I needed Moses to make, but he needed to think on a bigger scale. Drugs were just the tip of the iceberg. Moses inched closer to my bed. Victória pulled up her chair beside him. If it weren't for the beeping of the various machines attached to my arms and chest, I would've forgotten I was in the hospital.

"Right, look for a trend in theme or occurrence. This was part of what your mother did, Victória, and later Monte took over the job. When the president of Colombia declared war on drugs, he angered many and hurt a lot of families. The cartel struck back with a brutal blow to Colombia, sending a message to the world that the cartel wouldn't be bullied and that Colombia was unsafe," I explained.

"I remember that. In fact, some of it is mentioned in my research papers. People were afraid to travel in fear of being kidnapped or killed," Moses interjected.

"And large groups of tourists came up missing. Mass graves became a familiar sight, and it hit an already poor country right in the pocket. The United States offered its support because American citizens were targets; and, quite frankly, they still needed the drugs Colombia provided. They didn't want the supply to stop, nor did they want to pay more for the drugs."

Victória cringed. "Wait, are you saying my mother was some sort of monster, responsible for the deaths of thousands of innocent people?"

I said with an even tone, "No, Victória, please keep your voice down. That's not what I'm saying at all, however, for a moment, don't put people or personalities into this. The bottom line is it's a business—big business—and the people who got the most money wanted to make sure it continued. The president of Colombia had the right idea but his own people could not be trusted.

"Your mother would leak stories to the press touting the success of various cleanup efforts. But most—if not all—of what she leaked was a lie. Your mother got out years ago and had nothing to do with the current situations." I needed Victória to be real clear on that because I didn't want to change the way she felt about her mother or me.

"You're not making any sense, and I don't think I want to hear any more. This is getting too crazy." She stood up but Moses pulled her back into her seat. She looked like she was about to give him a big piece of her mind but stopped when a nurse came in to check on me.

"Do we need to leave?" Moses asked. His face was flushed and animated.

"No, you're fine. I'm just checking his vitals and I'll be out of the way," the nurse said.

Conversation didn't immediately resume when the nurse left. I guessed we were all taking a break to absorb what we'd learned and the implications.

"When Monte took over, his approach was more violent. He created such a volatile environment, he had to leave Colombia, but I'm guessing he continued his dirt from here, hence the phone call."

"I don't believe any of this bullshit. Padre, you have all the answers, or speculations, if that's what you're calling them. The people you speak against can't refute what you say because they are all dead or MIA. You're so busy pointing fingers at everyone else, what was your involvement? Huh? Tell us about that shit." She was clearly angry but it was expected. At least she didn't run from the room.

"I was strictly responsible for transportation and transportation-related details. To my knowledge, I do not have anyone's blood on my hands," I said.

"Oh yeah, right. And they paid you all that money you showed us just for transportation? What do I look like, a fucking fool?"

Moses was watching and not saying anything, but his attention picked up at the mention of money. "Money? What money?"

Shit, he didn't know.

"Uh, um . . ." Victória stuttered. Her face got red.

"Fuck," I mumbled. My mind went into a deep freeze as I tried to think of a good save. It was obvious that Verónica had not told her husband about the money. Although I never told them to keep the money a secret, I understood why she would.

"So what did Tilo say?" Victória countered.

I was never so proud of my daughter as I was at that moment. "I think she called me by mistake. She mentioned someone named Rome and told me to sell him back the guns we took from him at double the price."

"I thought you said you only dealt with transportation?"

"I did, I swear to you. Something wasn't right with her. She appeared off, if you know what I mean. That's another reason why I think she called me by mistake."

"Well, who the fuck is Rome?" Victória asked.

"I have no idea. I tried keeping her on the phone, so I started throwing out stuff to her that I'd heard on the news. I asked about the mayors who got killed, and she basically said to keep up the good work. She told me to spread out the violence to keep Obama off her back," I said with a shrug.

Moses wasn't participating in the back-and-forth. I was afraid he was still stuck on the money. He appeared to be in deep thought.

"Call me crazy, but none of this makes sense. Why the fuck would she call you of all people if she didn't know who the fuck you are? I've had enough of this foolishness, I'm leaving." She got up again but this time Moses didn't physically try to stop her.

"I think I know who Rome is," Moses announced.

# CHAPTER FORTY-EIGHT

## ROME WATSON

"Fuck." I slammed down the phone.

"What happened? Who was that?" my partner, Greg, asked. He was a little pussy.

I wished I could get rid of his whining ass, but I needed someone to watch my back who had as much to lose as I did. "We've got to get some more motherfucking guns, that's what." My mind was racing through the list of possibilities.

"Are you fucking kidding me? How the hell are we going to do that?"

I knew he was going to pussy up on me, but he was going to have to grow some balls today because the stakes just got higher.

"Be quiet and let me think."

We were in the evidence room where we'd been assigned to work as punishment of sorts. My supervisor deemed our investigative techniques to be overzealous and ineffective. His words, not mine.

"Your thinking is what got us into trouble in the first place."

"Ain't nobody tell your ass to follow me into the house. You could have stayed your pussy ass on the porch for all I cared." Mouth-all-mighty-tongue-everlasting didn't open his motherfucking mouth. Just as I expected.

I was sick of having this conversation with him. There was nothing wrong with my technique; I just chose the wrong job to show it. Two-thirds of the department was on the take, and they believed that we moved more than bullet casings from the Mendoza house. And since they couldn't prove it, we were stuck in the evidence room, which boggled my mind. If they suspected we stole something from the Mendoza house, why the fuck would they put us in the evidence room?

"Well my pussy ass was taught to back up my partner, so that's what the fuck I did."

"Then shut the hell up so I can think of a way to get out of this shit." Frustrated, I paced the room. Ms. Boss, as Tilo wanted to be called now, was a real bitch over the phone, and I wasn't used to her speaking to me in that manner. She acted like she owned me and slavery was over. Tilo Adams worked for the FBI, but she had close ties within the department. The official position of the department was Tilo had died in the line of duty. I knew otherwise, and I was determined to find her because I believed whatever money was in the Mendoza house, she had it. Why else would she disappear? What surprised me even more was that no one else thought about it.

At first it completely blew my mind. I was surrounded by idiots. Then I started analyzing the people around me and realized our department was as corrupt as the now defunct police department in Colombia. They had their guns taken from them and were walking around with sling shots for protection.

"We're taking the dope and selling it."

"Rome, are you fucking kidding me? You have lost your damn mind. I'm not no damn drug dealer," Greg shouted. He needed to take it down a notch.

"Keep your motherfucking voice down. Can you think of another way to get the money to buy some more guns?"

"What about that bitch from the apartment? Do you think she knows anything?"

I said, "No, I think she got screwed, but it might be a good idea to find out her story."

Greg was thinking for a change. I was surprised.

"I guess I can work on that then." Greg was pouting, not a good look for a grown-ass man.

"We've got to get those guns or we are going to be in some real shit, right in our backyard."

"Rome, your gambling is out of control. It's what got us into this shit in the first place. I didn't sign up for this, and I'm damn sure not going down because of it. You're my boy and shit, but damn. You're pushing it. Motherfuckers looking for us on the street and shit, fellow cops acting all shady. This ain't cool, Rome. Work it out because I ain't going to jail for you or any other motherfucker. Real talk. You got me in this shit and I'm counting on you to get me out."

He grabbed his coffee cup and stormed out of the room, and I was glad he was gone. Greg and I had been friends since the academy, but his bitching was getting on my damn nerves. Yeah, I fucked up, but at least I had a plan. What did he have? We'd seized over $3 million of heroin and cocaine during the cartel raid. Normally, the drugs would've been destroyed. For some reason, though, we still had them in the evidence room. I took some of it and I planned on taking the rest to get out of the hole I had dug for myself. Greg thought things were bad, but he'd flip the fuck out if he knew how deep this shit had become.

# CHAPTER FORTY-NINE

## VERÓNICA RAMSEY

"Hey, girl. This is a surprise." I stepped away from the door to allow my sister to come in.

"Where is my nephew? I want to see him."

"Oh, really? He's in his playpen." I was surprised but tried not to let it show on my face.

A few minutes later, she came back carrying LM. "He's such a good baby. I've never heard him cry."

"That's because you haven't been around him much. He can go when he wants to, but for the most part, he's a pleasant baby. He kind of reminds me of Ramón when he was little." The smile disappeared off both of our faces.

I said, "I miss Ramón so much. He had so much life left to live, it's unfair."

"I know. I think about it all the time." She coddled and cooed with LM. The mood in the room was melancholic. "Verónica, we haven't had time to talk. Tell me what is going on with you."

I was taken off guard. "Huh? I'm good. You know, just taking care of the baby and my husband."

"How's that going, the husband part?"

Why was she asking me about Moses? I thought it was a little personal and didn't want to discuss it with her. "It's going well, why do you ask?"

"Oh, no reason. I was just wondering. We talked about Mike all the time. You never talk about Moses so I thought I'd ask."

"Wow, for real? I hadn't noticed."

Victória got me to thinking. She was right, I didn't speak of him because in the back of my mind, I still felt guilty about the circumstances of our relationship.

"Liar, and the truth ain't in you." She laughed but she was so right.

I went to sit next to my sister because I needed a hug. "Victória, I feel so lost sometimes. I want to be happy. I want to let go and love my husband the way I did when we first met but I can't. I don't feel like I deserve to be happy. So many people died. Hell, you almost died. How am I supposed to go on and pick up the pieces?"

She pulled my head onto her shoulder as I cried. "Sweetie, I mean this from the bottom of my heart. You've got to get past this. You owe it to LM and Moses. Even if you don't see it, your baby can feel it. And on the real tip, you got a good man and you're tearing him apart."

I pushed away from Victória. How could she possibly know how my husband was feeling? "What do you mean?"

"Exactly what I said. Just like you pushed away from me, I see you pushing away from him."

I was afraid to speak and my heart was pounding so hard. "Has he said anything to you?" I practically whispered.

"No, he doesn't have to. It's written all over his face every time your name comes up. You have to remember that even though a lot of shit has gone down with *Madre* and Padre, you, me, and Padre are still family, and Moses already feels like the odd man out. You've got to show him how important he is in your life."

"You have spoken to him!" I was upset and felt like she was keeping a secret from me.

"No, I haven't. I swear."

LM had fallen asleep in her arms, so I picked him up and carried him back to his bed. Leaving the room, I thought I was going to have an opportunity to think but that wasn't the case because Victória was right behind me. "Are you following me?"

"Uh, no. I thought we were having a conversation. What's wrong with you?"

"Nothing. I just thought you were going to stay in the living room. You didn't walk around the house before."

"And you've never left the room in the middle of a conversation before, either. What's up with that?"

I felt defensive and like she was trying to pull something from me that wasn't there. "Well . . . um . . . I've never had a baby to tend to before." I was fidgeting and feeling very uncomfortable. Almost as if I were standing in front of her naked, exposed with a huge wart on my ass.

Victória said, "And you're using the baby as a shield to keep me away. What's really going on?"

"Why are you drilling me?"

"Why are you so defensive? You've always been my best friend and right now I don't feel like I know you at all."

Wow, I felt like she slapped me in the face. Was I losing my mind? I folded on the floor like a balloon without air.

Victória dropped to her knees and wrapped her arms around me. "It's going to be okay. I know it is. God didn't bring us this far to leave us."

I tried to pull away because I was seeing my sister in a different light. She always encouraged me but now it was like she was looking inside my soul and it was a little intimidating.

"I keep trying to escape this depression but every time I turn the corner it's right there in my face again."

"I think it's normal—at least from what I've read—for a new mother to feel this way. But your situation is more complicated because of what we've been through. All I'm saying to you is that if you love the man you married, don't shut him out. Let him know what you're feeling. The last thing you want him to do is shut down because you're shutting him out."

I looked at her. "When did you get to be such an authority on relationships? It isn't like we've had the best role models."

"Maybe that's how I got to be such an expert. I've spent so much time watching and listening."

"Point duly noted. So other than offering advice, what brings you around my neck of the woods?"

We had gotten up from the floor and went back downstairs so we could talk without waking LM.

Victória flopped down on the sofa. "I just left the hospital, but I wanted to see you before I went home to get some sleep."

"Fuck, now I feel like the worst daughter in the world. I've been so busy with my own shit, I didn't even remember to ask you about Padre. How is he? God, I feel so bad."

"He's okay. He agreed to have the surgery."

That made me feel better. "Wonderful. What made him change his mind?"

"I think he realized he couldn't keep putting it off."

"That's wonderful. I'm going to ask Moses to watch LM tomorrow so I can go visit Padre. I feel so bad."

"Don't, he understands. However, he did make me promise that we wouldn't stop looking for Tilo no matter what happens to him."

My anger boiled. "I knew it. None of this shit was about me or Padre. It's always been about Tilo. Why the fuck should I put my family on the line to go after this bitch?"

"Because if you don't, she's going to keep coming back. She's not gonna come after me because she thinks I'm in a coma. But you and Moses aren't, so it's not going to end as long as she knows there is a threat to her safety."

"Oh God, I can't deal with this," I wailed.

Victória touched my hand. "Yes, you can, because you don't have a choice. If you tie Moses' hands, you are both sitting ducks—especially if she ever finds out about the money Padre gave us."

"How is she going to find out about the money? I haven't mentioned it to anyone."

"Why haven't you told your husband?"

I gasped. I couldn't tell if her tone was accusatory or if I was just tripping. Either way, I didn't like it. "How do you know I haven't told him?" I bluffed.

"Because you said you haven't told anyone."

She had me cornered. "Oh, um . . . I, um—"

She laughed. "You're a horrible liar."

I felt like crying all over again. I didn't even have a good excuse for not telling Moses. It wasn't a conscious decision, I just never got around to it.

Victória rolled her eyes. "Don't start up with the waterworks again. Maybe you have your reasons for not telling him. But I'm going to say this and be done with it: our whole life was built on deception. Don't make the same mistake our parents did—whatever the reason."

# CHAPTER FIFTY

## TILO ADAMS

"Finally." I kicked off my shoes and waited for the bellhop to bring up my bags from the lobby. It was a hair-raising trip, but I was finally settled in a suite at the New Yorker. I couldn't have been happier to be out of Atlanta. I felt trapped in the city, afraid to go out of my own room. In New York, though, the most impersonal city in the world, I was free to be me. I leaped off the chaise and grabbed the hotel phone.

"I'd like to order room service please." I was ready to act an ass because they placed me on hold without even asking me if I minded. *How fucking rude.* The wait wasn't long but since patience had never been part of my MO, it was enough to push me into bitch mode again.

"Can you have someone send me up a menu?"

"You should have a copy of the menu in your room," the voice over the phone said.

"Do I sound like I want to fucking look for a menu? Just do your damn job and have someone bring me a friggin' menu, and don't take all damn day doing it." I hung up the phone. Nobody could do bitch better than me. I was in a suite, so they should be used to attitude and an innate sense of entitlement. The doorbell rang before I could continue checking out my rooms.

"About time," I snippily replied when the bellhop brought up my bag. I didn't have many; it was just heavy as hell. He lingered in the doorway for a few seconds. If he thought I was going to give him a handout, he was sadly mistaken. I examined my bag to make sure the bonds were still in the false bottom. The doorbell rang again before I could get them out.

"What?" I shouted as I ripped open the door.

A startled Hispanic woman stood there with a full menu in her hands. She appeared to be scared of her own shadow. She handed me the menu and backed away. It was a good thing because, even though I was pretty certain she wouldn't understand a word I said, I would have cussed her out just because. I tossed the menu on the chair and promptly forgot about it.

"What was I doing?" I looked around the room trying to remember what I was doing before I was interrupted. The room was beautiful but distracting because there were too many things to look at.

"That's right. I was about to take a bath." I started taking my clothes off on my way to the bathroom. A nice long bath would help me to relax. Then, maybe, I could finally go out and get some clothes for my trip. A nice white robe was draped across the oversized tub and I put it on while I waited for the tub to fill with scented water. Just as I was about to get in, my cell phone rang.

"Shit, where's my fucking phone?" It shouldn't have been difficult to find, especially since I'd just gotten in the damn room. But my dumb butt was running around the room naked like a crazy person, and I didn't find it until it had stopped ringing.

"Fuck," I shouted. I stood poised to pitch the damn thing against the wall but stopped at the last minute. *Why the fuck are you throwing the phone?* I checked the last call and dialed it back.

"Hello?" he said after the third ring.

"Greg, what's up?" I switched from bitch mode immediately because he did not play that.

"Yo, I'm done with this shit. Where you at 'cause I need some pussy?"

I did not like his tone. "I'm in New York, boo." I wanted to call him a motherfucker so bad I could taste it, but I knew it would not be a good idea.

"I thought you were going to tell me before you jetted. I'm on my way."

"No. You can't come right now. I need you to keep an eye on Rome for a little bit longer."

"Aw, hell no! I told you I'm done with that shit. The mofo gets on my damn nerves, and I'm not no damn babysitter."

"Greg, sweetheart. We've come too far to fuck up now. Just a little while longer and we'll have the bigger prize."

"Tilo, real talk, I can't do it. If that motherfucker calls me a bitch one more time, I'm gonna bust a cap right in his motherfucking face."

"Think of the prize, boo. You like money. I like money—"

"I like pussy, too, and my pussy is in fucking New York without me. Now, how about that?" He was angry.

I hated to make him mad because his anger could be lethal. I could've used some dick too, but I was thinking long term and he was thinking about a few minutes at best. Good minutes, but not enough to blow several million dollars over.

"Baby, I am starving for some dick. My pussy is acting like I've lost my damn mind, but if you leave now, you're going to leave too much money on the table and you don't want that, do you?" *I will shoot you my damn self if you do that.*

"No, I want it all, but I'm telling you this shit is taking too long. Rome finally said he was taking the dope, and I'm gonna give him subtle hints as to where he should take it, but this shit about taking the money and the guns is a little bit much. You got to make up your mind, which one is more important? 'Cause your greedy ass can't have both."

"Why can't we have both? Think about it, Greg, South America is wide open now and we've got an opportunity to take it." I thought it was important to say *we*; but, in reality, it was all about me. I was tired of taking the back seat in life. I was about to jump in the driver's chair, and anybody in my way, shame on them.

"Because you are relying on a jackass to deliver. Rome is one straw short of a bale. He's a loose cannon, and now that you're putting a foot on his neck, he's acting like he ain't got shit to lose. Now that would be fine if the motherfucker was in this by himself, but you've got me posted next to this motherfucker—all up in the spotlight and shit."

"Calm down, baby. You're just horny."

"You damn right I'm horny. My joint is so hard, it could knock down a wall and shit."

"Aw . . . If I were there, I'd take care of that for you." I allowed water to splash as I jumped into my tub and turned on the jets.

"What did you say you were doing?"

"Taking a bath. A nice, long, hot bath. Oooh I wish you were here."

"Fuck, don't go playing with a nigga, 'cause I'll beat the motherfucking jet to New York—that's how much I want to be fucking right now."

"But if you were here, boo, I wouldn't fuck you. Oh now, fucking is for kids. I would make love to you like a grown-ass woman. I would pull your long, hot body into the tub and wash every amazing inch of you." I could tell by the way he was breathing that he was getting into my soft words. "I would slide between your thighs and take your big dick into my mouth and suck it as bubbles dance around us, masking our aroma. Have you ever had your dick sucked while underwater?"

"Uh . . ."

"After I come up for air, I'll wash your balls. One ball at a time. Savoring your sacks and giving them the attention they deserve. One squeeze and I come up again, kissing you. Fucking you with my mouth. That's the only fucking we'll be doing."

"Damn, baby." His voice got deep.

"What are you doing?" I demanded. My voice was harsh and commanding.

"Rubbing my dick, ma."

"That's my dick and I didn't tell you to touch it. I want to do it."

He drew in a deep breath. I could feel its vibration over the speaker in the phone. You couldn't tell me he wasn't stroking his dick.

"I just miss you, boo. It's been so long." He moaned.

I felt it reverberate in my pussy. I missed him too, but I couldn't allow my pussy to think for me. I had to be stronger than that. *Girl, maybe some good dick is what you need. You ain't had none in so long, your shit is about to dry up and fall off.*

"Shut up," I snapped.

"Huh?" Greg said.

I could feel his mental wheels screeching to a halt. I had to recover quickly.

"I just want you to feel my body pressed against yours. No words." I sounded lame even to myself, but I said the first thing that came to my mind. These voices speaking to me were becoming rather annoying. I was having a difficult time deciphering what was real or what was only in my head.

"I feel you, baby," Greg said, obviously back in the moment and waiting to shoot his load.

In my sexy voice, I said, "I want you to grab my dick and stroke it."

"Ah shit."

"Don't stroke it too fast, baby. My pussy is tight, waiting for your love."

"What are you doing to me?" His breathing was ragged.

"Just loving you. My pussy is clutching your dick like a tight rubber glove, only softer. Can you feel my heat?"

"Yeah, I, uh . . ."

I was getting bored and ready to get off the phone. As I sat in the tub, I was making a mental list of all the things I could be doing if I wasn't on the fucking phone.

"You feel that? Umph this shit is good! Now give it to me hard, baby, just like I like it."

"Oh, shit. Oh shit, ma!" His voice rose an octave as he shouted.

I was relieved he didn't take all fucking night to bust a nut. I waited until his breathing got back to normal before I spoke again. "You good?"

"Yeah, I'm good. What do you want me to do?" He was ready to behave like a well-trained puppy.

"Just keep an eye on Rome for a few more days. He's gonna want to find me. Make sure you talk him out of it. If you can't, put his ass to sleep." Satisfied, I hung up the phone without saying another word.

# CHAPTER FIFTY-ONE

## MOSES RAMSEY

Victória marched unannounced into my office and closed the door. "Good morning."

She looked different today. She had done her hair and put on makeup; it was the first time her wound wasn't noticeable to me.

"Good morning, you look nice."

She blushed and appeared to have forgotten her reasons for busting into my office. "Uh, thanks." She placed some papers on my desk and pushed them toward me.

"You've been very busy." I was so excited I could hardly stay in my chair. All the pieces were starting to come together.

"This is becoming so frightfully easy it's scary," Victória said. She was pacing back and forth in front of my desk. She appeared to be deep in thought.

"What?" I asked, suddenly annoyed.

"I don't know. Tilo has been such a precision player all this time. Why is she so sloppy all of a sudden? What if it's a trap?"

I said, "Trap? That's a bunch of bullshit and you know it. I think the bitch is cracking up if you ask me."

She looked surprised, but that's the way I honestly felt. She was making mistakes. The best criminal minds did it all the time or else they'd never get caught.

"Is she? Or is this part of a plan to lure us in so she can finish the job?"

Frustrated, I sat back in my chair and sighed. Victória and her sister had a way of sucking the joy right out of a room.

"Y'all must practice this shit," I mumbled.

"Excuse me?"

"Nothing. So what am I missing, since you seem to have this all figured out?" I demanded.

Victória sat down across from me all smug, as if she had all the answers and I was just digging around in my ass looking for shit to play with. "I still don't understand the credit card. Why would she use it?"

"I explained this before. She probably didn't think to apply for credit in her own name to match her ID."

"But she has money. That negates the use of credit," she replied.

"Not really, not when you're trying to sneak around and not draw attention to yourself. Credit cards can be rather impersonal, and it is possible to use one without showing identification. Cash, on the other hand, slows people down because they have to count it, enter it into the system, and possibly give change. Giving change often lends to touching, which makes the encounter more personalized."

She frowned. "Touching? I don't understand."

"If you gave someone cash, and they laid your change out on the counter, how would that make you feel?" I sat back in my chair, satisfied with my analogy.

"Gotcha. It would definitely piss me off."

I grabbed her credit card statement off the desk and headed for the door. "You coming?" I asked, holding the door open.

"Where are you going?"

"To the airport to see if your friend pissed some folks off."

She leaped from the chair as if it were on fire. "Oh yeah, you can bet your ass she did."

"Have you been to see your father?" I asked while we drove to the airport. I couldn't keep my eyes off Victória. She didn't look like the typical dike to me and it was throwing me off.

"Yeah, he's going to be okay. He's strong. The doctors say he has to take it easy, but he should make a full recovery."

I said, "That's good. It hurts Verónica's heart that she can't spend the kind of time she wants to at the hospital because of LM."

"Padre knows this. She can't afford to take some hospital germs home to my nephew. He's so cute, you must be proud."

I couldn't help the smile that took over my face. Out of all this madness, my son was the best thing to come out of it. "I am. He has stolen both of our hearts and now that he's sleeping through the night, I think we're going to keep him."

We both busted out laughing as I dipped through the light noon-hour traffic.

"When this is over, what are you going to do with yourself?" It was not what I really wanted to ask her. She was such a beautiful woman. I wanted to know, even if it wasn't any of my business, if she would seek out another woman or give a man a chance. Not for myself, I was completely in love with her sister, but she needed someone to love too.

"This has consumed me, and I need closure before I can even think about moving on." She spread her arms wide as if she was referring to the all-encompassing world.

I understood so I didn't press the issue. "We've never gotten to know each other, and I'm sorry about that, especially since we're now related. I want you to know I loved your brother and I adore your sister."

"Thanks, you didn't have to say it because I could tell, but I appreciate it just the same. My sister and I had a discussion about you a few days ago. I kinda explained to her why it was important that we continue to search for Tilo; and more important, why you should be the one to help us."

She caught me off guard and I temporarily lost control of the car.

"Hold on now, don't kill us," Victória said.

"Dag, how did I get to be the topic of conversation?" I was a little uneasy as to how this conversation was going. I hadn't yet figured Victória out, so it could honestly go in any direction.

"Don't let your butt cheeks clinch up. It was a good conversation. I was telling her about Padre and . . . Oh shit, stop the car!"

"What? What's wrong?" I said as the car shook from side to side. We were traveling in the fast lane of I-285 and she wanted me to stop the fucking car? I eased the car onto the shoulder.

"Get over when you get the chance. I need to think and I can't do it at eighty miles an hour." Victória was clearly agitated but, then again, so was I.

I was also nervous about any connections she could have going through her brain. "You got some kind of death wish or something?"

"No, you said you think you know who Rome is, right? What if he's the same dude who came to my apartment looking for Tilo?"

I pulled the car back into traffic.

"What? You don't think it's plausible?" Victória asked.

"At this point anything is plausible. I think our greatest concern right now is finding Tilo. Once we do, the rest of the puzzle will come together. I'm working on another piece, too, that might prove to be interesting."

"Really, what?"

"Your father mentioned someone named Rome in his phone conversation with Tilo. I'm almost positive he is talking about a guy who went through the academy with Tilo but did not make the bureau. He's working for the Atlanta Police Department, and he was the first officer on the scene the night Tilo shot you."

"Are you serious? How did you find out this information?"

"Dag, sis, did you forget it's what I do?" I said, laughing.

"My bad. My bad."

"When we get back, I'm waiting for a picture of him. When I get it, I want to see if this is the same guy who paid you a visit."

"Hmm, I wouldn't be surprised. We'll see."

I was a little disturbed by her non-reaction to my news. If someone had busted up on me, demanding information and threatening me, it would worry the fuck out of me. I would want to know who he was, what he wanted. I felt like she was trying to hold back on me and this made me a little nervous, but I parked those thoughts with the car at the airport.

# CHAPTER FIFTY-TWO

## VERÓNICA RAMSEY

"Padre, how are you feeling?" I'd been sitting by his bedside for several hours and was happy that he finally woke up. He gave me a big smile that raised goose bumps on my arms because, even though the doctors told me he was doing fine, I was afraid that he wasn't going to wake up.

"I'm fine. I was just taking a little nap." He fumbled with the buttons on the side of his hospital bed and I took the remote from his hands.

"Nap, hell, you've been out for hours. What are you trying to do?"

"It's the drugs they give me, makes me tired. I would like to sit up please." My heart ached as I watched him wince in pain.

"Do you need for me to call the nurse?" I didn't know what else to say.

"No, the sooner I lick these drugs, the sooner I can get out of this place and go home."

"Good, that's what I like to hear." I felt relieved that he felt strong enough to resist the temptation to drug himself out so he could get out of the hospital.

"Is your husband home with the baby?" Instantly my guard was up. I still didn't know exactly how my father felt about Moses. I didn't want to fight with my father, especially since he was recovering from heart surgery.

"No, his mother came down for a few days so LM's with her."

"Ah, more people I have to add to my list to meet," he replied. I definitely caught his attitude and I could tell things were about to take a turn for the ugly.

"Padre, if you have something to say, please say it. I don't want to argue with you about this, but if you feel you have to get it off your chest . . ."

"Why are you getting so defensive? I do need to meet his parents, don't I?"

"You're not throwing me shade?" I was confused.

"Huh? I didn't throw anything."

"Shade, it's slang, Padre. I was asking if you were trying to be sarcastic or something?"

"Oh, okay. No, I wasn't. I was just stating a fact."

There was an awkward silence in the room. I moved closer to the bed and adjusted Padre's blankets.

"Are you cold? I could ask them for another blanket."

"I'm fine, stop fussing over me," he barked at me.

I jumped back, confused. If he wasn't angry with me, why was he fussing? "You are mad. Look, I'm going to go." I turned around and grabbed my jacket and purse as I fought back tears. I didn't know why I was crying because technically my father hadn't been in my life for so long. Why did it feel like I was losing him all over again?

"Verónica, wait. I'm sorry. I hate hospitals and the timing sucks. I've missed so much and there is so much to do."

"There is still so much I don't understand. Are you considered to be a good guy or a bad one?"

"I suppose that would depend on who was telling the story."

His words shocked me. I wasn't sure what type of answer I was expecting, but it certainly wasn't this one.

"What's that supposed to mean?" My heart was beating very fast as my imagination ran away with me.

"I'm not going to lie to you. Not everything I did was good, but to my knowledge, I was never directly involved in anyone getting killed, but I'm sure I could inadvertently be connected to some very bad things."

"What kind of bad things?"

"Honestly, I don't know the wide-spread implications, but I'm sure I could be considered guilty by association with a variety of crimes."

"So what are you telling me? Am I going to wake up one day and see your face splattered all over the news?"

"Verónica, calm down."

"Don't tell me to calm down. You just came back in my life and now you're telling me there is a good chance you might be leaving by default!" I was foot-stomping mad and I didn't care who knew it. I was tired of other people, places, and things controlling my life. I just wanted to lead the normal life I used to live before all this shit started happening.

"I said keep your voice down." Padre gripped his chest, and I was reminded of why we were in the hospital in the first place.

"I'm sorry." I sat back down and tried to get a hold on my raging emotions.

He said, "I'm doing my part to make things right, but it's going to take some time."

If he was trying to make me feel better, it wasn't working. If fact, he was making me even more nervous.

"What does that mean? I feel like you are talking in code or something," I said, exasperated.

"Sweetheart, I will tell you as much as I can, but some things I will keep from you for your protection. Did you see on the news where they arrested this guy at the airport for smuggling guns and money?"

"Yeah, didn't he work at the airport?"

"He not only worked at the airport, he was responsible for exporting guns and drugs south of the border. He was also one of the point people for human smuggling for the cartel."

"How could you possibly know that?" I demanded.

"Unfortunately, it went with the territory. It was part of my job to know these things but I didn't connect Tilo with any of it until a few days ago. It appears that she was also working with Monte."

"Here we go! Can I have at least one conversation with someone that does not involve Tilo? To hear everyone tell it, she's like some omnipresent being who can do all things! I'm sick of hearing this hussy's name." I really didn't mean to cuss to my father, but I was fed up with hearing about Tilo.

The nurse came in the room. I was happy to see her because I was done with this conversation. I had two names on my list of people I hated and he had mentioned both of them in the same sentence.

"Sorry to interrupt, but I need to check Mr. Mendoza's vitals." She brushed past me and began checking his fluids and taking his temperature. "Are you in any pain, Mr. Mendoza?"

"No, I'm fine. I'm ready to go home."

She said, "I know that's right. I suspect if you keep on doing the way you are doing, you might be going home soon."

"What's soon?" Padre asked.

"Mr. Mendoza, you know I can't answer that. I'm sure if you ask your doctor, he'll know better than me."

"So he's doing good?" I asked as I packed up my things.

"He's doing fine, and he's the sweetest patient on the ward." She smiled at both of us as she finished up her duties.

I was ready to go and this was the perfect diversion I needed to get out of the room. "Padre, I need to be going anyway. I'll be back to check on you later, and make sure you have the doctor call me." I could tell Padre wanted to say more to me but I didn't give him the chance. I kissed him on the forehead and rushed out of the room. I felt like I was being forced into a corner and I didn't like the feeling one bit!

Everyone in my life was consumed with one thing: finding Tilo. I was going to have to find a way to deal with their obsessions or it would certainly drive me insane.

# CHAPTER FIFTY-THREE

## VICTÓRIA MENDOZA

I was excited to finally be doing something. After months of inactivity, I was eager to actively look for my ex-lover if only to shoot her ass right in between her eyes. I wanted my face to be the last face she saw on this earth. I wanted this so badly it hurt. As I got out of the car, I had to stop myself from running into the terminal. "So, what is our game plan?"

Moses did this type of shit for a living, so I would have to defer to him when it came to this type of stuff.

"Assuming she bought her ticket online, she probably didn't go to the check-in counter, so let's start with baggage drop-off."

The only time I ever flew in my life was when I was a child coming to the United States, so I knew nothing of an airport. I had no choice but to follow Moses' lead.

"Damn, I wish I had a more recent picture. The one I have I got from her file with the FBI." Moses held the door open for me.

I stopped walking and pulled out my wallet. I had a picture of Tilo that we'd taken in the mall about a month before I got shot. "Here, this one is fairly recent." I was thrilled that I was able to help, and I could not keep from smiling.

"Perfect." Moses took the picture from me and increased his stride. It was hard to tell which one of us wanted to find Tilo the most.

"Hey, slow down. My legs aren't as long as yours are."

"Sorry, force of habit."

I stood behind Moses as we approached the desk.

"Excuse me, miss. I was wondering if you could assist me," Moses said.

"Sure, what can I do for you?" She seemed like a pleasant woman.

"I'm trying to find someone and I wanted to show you a picture to see if you remember her."

I stepped from behind Moses and the expression on the woman's face told me she was on guard. I snatched the picture from his hand. "Look, I know you are super busy. And nine times out of ten, with the amount of people who come through this airport, it is very unlikely that you would remember our friend, but we'd really appreciate it if you'd at least look at the photo please." I put the picture on the counter and entwined my fingers in a prayer position. The woman eyed us before she picked up the picture. Her eyes narrowed. I could tell she was actually thinking about her answer.

"Sorry, I don't remember her. Did she come through today?"

"Ah, actually it was last week."

She looked at me like I'd lost my damn mind. Instead of saying it, though, she pushed the picture back at me. "Sorry."

My hope plummeted, but I wasn't ready to give up. I took the picture and continued down the line with Moses following me. At the last station, I repeated my spiel and we got our first glimmer of hope from a black woman.

"Um . . ." She frowned and pushed the picture away.

"Take your time," Moses said. He gave her back the picture but she dropped it down on the counter.

I wanted to push him away before he ruined the moment, but thankfully—if the lady noticed his intrusion—she didn't tear her eyes from the photo.

"Honey, I don't need any time. I remember this . . ." She looked around as if she was afraid.

"Miss, please, we really need to find her. Her mother has taken ill and we have to let her know." I said the first thing that came to my mind. As the words came out of my mouth, I realized how stupid they sounded. I was surprised she didn't come back and ask me why we didn't call Tilo on the phone instead of running around the airport like the village idiots.

"Her hair is different, but I definitely recognize those eyes."

I was so excited, I almost started jumping up and down at our first lead.

"How is her hair different?" Moses said.

"She is blond and very, very rude." She turned up her nose again.

I knew the bitchy side she was referring to, and I could not help but to smile. "That's my friend. She can be a bitch when she wants to be."

"You ain't never lied," the lady responded as she looked around again to see if she was being watched.

"Is there anything else that you can tell us about her?" Moses asked.

"I didn't help her. She refused to pay the luggage fee."

My heart sank, but I didn't understand how she could have used the card and not paid the fee. Before I could argue with the lady she pointed us in another direction.

"I think she used curbside check-in. We were busy and she came in here trying to be some sort of drama queen."

I shared a look with Moses because I felt like we were definitely on the right track. "Thanks so much," I gushed, barely containing my excitement.

"No problem, I hope you find the —"

"Be nice," Moses warned, but he laughed as well.

I was starting to warm up to him and feel more comfortable. I was also beginning to see why my sister fell in love with him.

"Honey, I'm always nice but when I'm naughty, I'm better."

If Moses noticed that she was flirting with him he didn't acknowledge it, and I gave him another five cool points because of it. The last thing I would have wanted to do was go up against his head for disrespecting my sister, but he passed up on the obvious offer.

We were going to the curbside check-in counter when the lady summoned us back.

"Do you want a more recent picture of her? I'm sure we have her on our security cameras because they followed her through the terminal."

"Yes!" I shouted a little bit louder than necessary. This woman was being so helpful. I loved it, but I was also leery because people rarely go out of their way to be helpful.

She gave me a look, which let me know she wasn't helping us because of me and I was cool with it so I took two steps back. She nodded her head and I fought the urge to go over the counter and smack that ass. Moses shot me another look and I clamped down on my sudden anger.

"She was very feisty and nervous. I'll bet you money if you show her picture at the gate, they will remember her." She spoke with a coworker and went behind a partition. She came back within minutes with a photograph.

"Wow, that was quick," Moses commented.

"We printed it because we knew she was going to be trouble. Your friend is special." She gave the photo to Moses.

I wanted to snatch it from his hands, but once again I suppressed my impulsiveness. "Thanks," I mumbled.

She gave me a dismissive glance, and I walked away before I said something I would later regret. After a few more minutes Moses joined me.

"Tilo must have really showed her ass 'cause that lady wanted her bad." He chuckled.

"Let me see the picture," I eagerly stated. I was eager to see how Tilo changed her look. I was stunned at the beautiful lady looking back at me. My hands were trembling. She was stunning and totally unrecognizable. In my opinion, she chose the perfect disguise. Just looking at her hurt me to my heart. I passed the picture back to Moses.

"Damn, I didn't know she had it in her." He stared at the picture, studying the face.

"Yeah, I always thought she was cute, but I never saw her wearing anything other than jeans and a baseball cap. She has on makeup, for Christ's sake. She didn't even own any makeup when we were living together."

"And she got rid of the dreads. Damn."

He didn't have to say any more. I knew exactly where he was coming from. She was fierce.

"What now?" I asked. Even though everyone told me she was still alive, I was still holding out hope that they were mistaken, but I held positive proof in my hands that the bitch was still breathing. I was furious. I got back in line and waited for the lady who waited on us before to handle her customer.

"What are you doing?" Moses asked.

I ignored him. If it were possible to see fumes coming from inside a person's body, mine would be smoking. I walked up to the counter and placed $200 on it. The woman looked at me in surprise. "I know you can't tell me where my friend went, but could you please issue me a ticket to the same place on the next flight?" I knew there was a good chance she was going to turn me down but it couldn't hurt to ask.

She took the money and folded it up in her hand, sliding it into her pocket. Her fingers got to flying across the keyboard. "Will you be checking any bags with us?" She smiled.

Moses grabbed my arm and tried to get my attention. I shook my head no.

"Victória, what are you doing?"

"What does it look like?" I gently removed his fingers from my arm. I wasn't certain what I was going to do when I got to wherever, but I was sure going to figure it out.

"Will this be round trip or one-way?"

"One-way." I had no idea how long it would take me to find Tilo so I thought it would be best to do it this way. I could also get a return ticket once I found her. In my mind, not finding her was not an option.

"One ticket or two?" the lady asked.

"One," I firmly replied as I grabbed my ID from my wallet.

"Two," Moses announced.

He surprised me. He didn't appear to be the impulsive type, and I wondered how all this would play out with my sister.

"Will that be cash or charge?"

I had my card out but Moses beat me to the punch and gained another five cool points. Later, when he found out how wealthy I was, I would return his money, but for now, I enjoyed his gesture.

"If you're going to catch the next flight, you're going to have to hurry." She took our ID's and presented Moses with the tickets.

"Thanks," he said as he signed for the transaction.

As we walked away from the counter, I started to feel guilty. I was relieved that he was going with me, but I didn't want to cause any problems in his marriage. "Moses, you don't have to go there with me."

"I know, but you may need my help, and I would feel terrible if something happened to you and I didn't do what I could to prevent it."

"Aw, ain't you sweet." I said it jokingly but I really meant it.

"Shush, don't tell anyone."

I followed him through the airport because I didn't have a clue what to do, and we made it to the departure gate without any problem. "What are you going to tell Verónica?"

Moses took a deep breath and I saw the worry line across his forehead. "I will handle that when I get back. For now, I really just want to ask some questions to see if anyone remembers her and see if we can get a lead on where she is now."

"I got to say this, Moses, I never believed finding Tilo would be so easy."

"We haven't found her yet."

"I know, but we're in a much better position than we were yesterday. I can't believe how she changed her look." I turned away from Moses so he wouldn't see the tears in my eyes. However, he was much more perceptive.

"Don't beat yourself up, Victória. She fooled us all, and I understand how personal this is for you. But if we do find her, you're going to have to take your emotions out of it or you may wind up getting us killed."

My heart skidded a few feet as I digested what he was saying to me, but he was absolutely right. Tilo had tried to kill me once before so it stood to reason she would try again, and next time she might even be successful. "I wish the bitch would," I replied as anger replaced my pain.

# CHAPTER FIFTY-FOUR

## ROME WATSON

"Greg, where you at, nigga?" I said into my cell phone. And I already knew where he was.

"I'm at the house."

Greg was obviously sleeping because I could hear him yawning.

"Wake your ass up 'cause we got trouble."

"What now?"

I gave him a few seconds to get himself together. My mind was still spinning with all the implications from this latest bust, but I was doing my best to hold it together. "You straight, your ass awake yet?"

"I'm good. What's going on?"

"I'ma need to see you. I got some things to talk to you about, and I don't want to do it over the phone."

"Why, what's going on? Shit, man, it's raining like hell, so I don't even feel like coming outdoors."

"I knew your punk ass would say some shit like that. Open the fucking door, I'm outside." If he was surprised that I came by his house, he didn't acknowledge it. He left me standing there long enough. I was beginning to believe that he had someone else in the house with him. Just as I was about to dial his house again, he answered the door.

"What was so damn important that you had to bring your ugly ass over to my house?" Greg demanded. He was wearing a pair of sweatpants and a loose-fitting T-shirt that had obviously seen better days.

"I see why your ass didn't wanna go outside. You look like something the damn cat dragged in."

"I didn't ask your ass to come over here, so don't come in my house talking shit."

I didn't know what was up Greg's ass. Here lately you couldn't say shit to him without him getting all mad and shit. "This ain't really a social call. Shit ain't looking too good for the home team."

"What's that shit supposed to mean?" He walked to the dining room table and I followed.

"Haven't you been watching the news?"

He looked at me sideways before he switched on the flat-screen television suspended in the corner. "Nigga, I was asleep," he complained as he came back to the table.

I was getting sick of his surly attitude, but I ignored it because I didn't have time for his foolishness. "That fool I was working with done got his ass busted."

"What fool?" Greg looked like he was still asleep, and I needed his ass to get with the program.

"That motherfucker at the airport I was dealing with," I answered.

"I don't have a clue what you're talking about. Can you start from the beginning instead of the middle of the conversation?"

I shot him a questioning look but he seemed like he was sincere with his request.

"My bad, I might not have told you about this guy. Anyway, I had this guy who works at the airport. He helps me sometimes when I need to get things through that can't go through screening. Most times it's money or a small shipment of drugs, but every now and then I'll have him do something major. Especially if I don't have a lot of time to make things happen."

"Okay. Get to the reason why you had to show your ass at my house so I can take my ass back to sleep."

"Shit, nigga, you the one who asked for the whole damn story when I was trying to give you the *Reader's Digest* version. You know I had to replace the guns that got jacked a few weeks ago, so I had to find another way to get them there."

"Aw shit, don't tell me they jacked the guns again," Greg shouted.

"Not yet, but they are investigating his fool ass because he shot his damn wife. That crazy motherfucker was chasing her up and down the street shooting. He shot and killed her boyfriend and seriously injured his wife. They started investigating his ass and now I don't know what the fuck is going on."

"I seen that shit on television, but I didn't know you knew the cat. But what I want to know is what does all this shit have to do with me?"

"It deals with you because I'm gonna need you to go to the airport and sweet-talk that bitch you used to deal with to find out what is going on. We need somebody with inside connections to make sure they are not watching us," I said.

"Us? What the fuck you mean *us?* I don't know that nigga, so I ain't got a damn thing to do with your shit." He put big emphasis on this.

I wanted to whip out my pistol and shoot his ass. "Nigga, what you don't understand is that if I go down, you go down too. So it would be in your best interest to get with the program."

"Shit, man, I haven't talked to that bitch in years. I don't even know if she still works there or not."

"She still works there. Trust me on that."

"If you know so motherfucking much, why don't you approach her?"

"'Cause I didn't fuck her, and I wasn't the one she fell in love with."

Greg was really starting to try my patience.

He said, "It don't matter if I fucked her or not. She don't want to have nothing to do with my ass, so I seriously doubt if I can get her to put her ass on the line for me."

"I'm not asking you to ask her to put herself on the line. All I want you to do is go to the airport acting like you forgot she worked there and shit. Hell, buy a ticket if you have to, but get her talking about her coworker. From there, see if you can get her to tell you what they talking about in airport security. If she tells you they have turned up the heat at the airport, then we know we got to do things differently. That's all I'm saying."

"Man, you don't know what you're asking me to do. That bitch is crazy, so I'd just as soon pass on this shit and take our chances," Greg said.

"What, you gonna let some bitch punk your ass?" I taunted.

"Fuck you, man. I hope your ass got a plan B 'cause I'm pretty sure this lame-ass one ain't gonna work."

"Whatever, so when are you going to see ol' girl?"

"What? You want me to go now or something?" He acted like he was about to act the fool on me.

"Ain't no sense in waiting." I sat back in the chair and waited for him to blow up, but he surprised me.

"Fine, let me throw on some clothes."

"Put some water on that ass while you're at it. You want to woo the woman, not run her off," I said, laughing.

# CHAPTER FIFTY-FIVE

## GREG CARTER

"Nancy, I didn't know you still worked at the airport." I feigned surprise. The years hadn't been kind to her and she looked every bit of fifty rather than thirty.

"I guess you didn't, you stopped calling my ass years ago."

I suspect bitterness had a hand in her aging because her face had hideous scowl lines that marred any of the beauty I'd once seen in her. She also looked like she had found another lover, one that put on the extra weight she carried on her hips and thighs.

"You still look good, girl." I was lying through my teeth. I also prayed that God didn't choose this moment to come back and cast my black ass straight to hell for telling this lie.

"Yeah, right. What, you think I got 'idiot' stamped on my forehead? Are you going somewhere?"

It was obvious that flattery wasn't going to get me anywhere, but I was still gonna try. "I was until I saw your pretty face again. Now I'd rather delay my trip and spend some time getting to know you again. What time do you get off?" I could tell she was not expecting me to come back at her like I did. She knocked over some luggage tags and some ticket jackets. Her bronze face turned a shade deeper. When she bent over, I could see the crack of her ass. However, with her added girth, this was not a very appealing sight. I loved the ladies, but I refused to sleep with anybody I had to throw flour on just to find the wet spot. Fuck that. "Did I embarrass you?" I chuckled as she attempted to act nonchalant.

"Can't a girl just knock shit over?"

The madder she appeared to be the more I laughed until she didn't have a choice but to laugh with me.

"Nancy, I seriously would like to spend some time getting to know you again. We could go to dinner or maybe go out for a drink or two."

Her eyes lost focus as she gazed into space and for a minute. I thought I had her, but when her eyes returned to my face, they were as cold as ice.

"I don't think so. The last time we were supposed to have dinner your ass didn't show up." She started looking over my head, perhaps to the next person in the growing line of people who needed tickets to destinations unknown.

"I was young and stupid then. I've matured since then."

She shook her head as she sized me up. "I don't think so. You've fooled me once, I'll be damned if I'll allow you to do it to me again."

"Damn, girl, it's just dinner. I didn't ask for your hand in marriage." I started to get an attitude. With the way she was looking, she ought to have considered herself lucky that I would be willing to be seen in public with her fat ass. I tried to talk myself down from getting angry, but it wasn't working. Fuck it, I didn't want to do this shit anyway.

"Fine, forget it. I need a ticket to Baltimore on the next flight." I pulled my wallet out and dropped down my driver's license and credit card on the counter.

She started typing on her screen without meeting my eyes, which pissed me off. Who the hell did she think she was anyway?

"You're not going to give me a date?"

"Nope. Next flight is in three hours. Is that soon enough?" she asked before she swiped my card.

"That's cool."

"One-way or round trip?"

"One-way. Atlanta don't have anything left for me."

"Were you being serious?" she asked with her arm raised in the air.

"Yeah, I was. But no worries. All things happen for a reason." I was sulking. I wasn't used to being turned down, and it didn't matter that I didn't really want to go out on a date with her. She continued the transaction without advising me of the cost.

"One drink, that's all." She handed me my ticket and clocked out.


"So what made you change your mind?" I asked once Nancy and I were seated in Ruby Tuesday on concourse C of the Delta wing. I allowed her to choose the place and the one she picked was near the gate for my flight. I was truly curious about her abrupt change of heart because it wasn't like she owed me anything or had anything to gain by doing so. For a moment I thought she wasn't going to answer. Nancy and I had been inseparable at one point in time, but over the years, our relationship dwindled away to nothing.

"To be honest, I don't know. I thought I was going to hate your ass for the rest of my life."

"Damn, hate?" I wasn't expecting her to say that and I quickly took a sip of my drink just to have something to do with my mouth. I knew that I'd hurt her feelings but never in a million years did I think my disappearing act would result in such a strong emotional response.

"Hey, I was young back then." She shrugged her shoulders and took a drink herself. She started rifling through her purse.

"You still smoking those cigarettes? You know those things are going to kill you," I said, laughing.

"We all got to die someday."

Damn, back in the day she would have gotten all hot and bothered just for my mentioning death and her in the same sentence. I didn't know this person sitting across from me at all.

"True. So tell me what's going on with you? I don't see no ring, so are you married?"

She looked surprised by my question and her eyes shifted to my ring finger. "If I were married, I wouldn't be in this bar with you," she snapped back.

"What's wrong with having a drink with an old friend?"

"You are not my friend."

This was going to be a lot harder than I'd originally anticipated. While I didn't expect to walk back into her life and be greeted with open arms, I didn't expect this verbal sparring match. "Damn, Nancy. Even though things between us didn't work out the way you wanted them to, I've always considered you to be a friend." Part of me just wanted to throw some money down on the table and get the fuck out of there. I didn't need this bullshit.

"Whatever." She played around with the straw in her glass and kept looking at her watch like she had someplace else to be.

"Shit, you clocking your watch like I'm keeping you from something. Please don't let me hold you up any longer." I was done with begging a bitch. It wasn't like I was trying to get some pussy after all these years anyway. However, I said the wrong thing because I immediately sparked a dangerous reaction by my words.

"You know what, fuck you, nigga!" She was stubbing out her smoke and trying to get up at the same time.

"Nancy, hold on. Why are you getting all upset and shit? I was just trying to be respectful of your time. You didn't have to cuss at a brother." I was trying to hold back my laughter because her girth, coupled with her anger, may have contributed to her inability to get up out of the chair.

"No, *you* hold on. I didn't ask your sorry ass to have a drink with me. Did I? No, you asked me, and when shit ain't going the way you think it should, you want to do the same old shit you did back in the day—roll the fuck out." She was no longer trying to get up, but I could tell she was still mad as hell.

I looked around the restaurant to see if anyone was looking at us because sister girl was rather loud. "Why you got me on loud speaker? Take that shit down a notch before you get us thrown up out of here," I hissed at her. She had a right to be a little upset or even downright mad at me, but I was not about to allow her to show her ass on me in public.

"Because your ass threw me out like dirty dishwater once you were done with me." She was fumbling with her cigarette again, trying to get it relit, and I was glad we were in one of the few places in the airport that allowed people to smoke. Hell, she almost made me want to light up my damn self, but I'd kicked the habit years before.

"It wasn't like that and you know it. We just drifted apart," I said.

"You're a liar and the truth ain't in you." Any other time I would have gotten pissed by anyone calling me a liar, but she was so comical I couldn't stop myself from laughing.

"Oh, you think I'm a joke?" Once again she tried to snub out her cigarette and get up at the same time in a confined space. She was butting people in the back of their heads with her big ol' ass, which only made me laugh harder.

I didn't stop laughing until I realized that she was actually going to leave me sitting there without answering any of my questions. "Nancy, wait. I wasn't laughing at you per se. I was laughing at the way you said it." I was sincere when I said it and I guess she must've heard it in my voice because she plopped back down in her chair. I signaled the waitress for another round.

"Just so you know, I don't take too kindly to being laughed at. By you or anybody else for that matter."

"I wasn't laughing at you. Never that. I thought about you often over the years."

"You didn't pick up the phone. Hell, my number ain't changed, just my disposition." She was coming back with the one-liners and it was truly comical to hear.

"I thought about calling but I wasn't ready for you." Once again, I was being honest with her.

"You might have been worth something if you wasn't running up behind that other bitch who had your nose wide open." She was referring to Tilo, so I wasn't about to tell her that she was still in the picture. Tilo was running me even back in the day, much the same as I ran Nancy. But Tilo was like a drug to me and I just couldn't say no to her. She even had me asking Nancy for money and giving it to her. I should have had a problem with asking her but I didn't, and that was one of the reasons we stopped kicking it. That and Tilo's threat to kick my ass to the curb if she even thought I was dishing out her dick to someone else. She didn't mind my getting money from Nancy, but she drew the line at sharing the dick.

"Like I said, I couldn't give you what you wanted."
It made no sense to sit there and lie to her about my
involvement with Tilo. She knew I loved her back then,
and I assumed she wanted to know the deal now.

"I guess that shit didn't work out too well for you, did
it?" She started laughing as if she'd said some kind of
funny.

"Nah, it didn't work out." I wasn't really lying when
I said it didn't work because, physically, Tilo wasn't
around, we rarely saw each other, but she still resided
in my heart.

"So what's in Baltimore?" She cocked her head to the
side as if she genuinely wanted to know.

"I have family there, but actually I'm ready for a
new beginning." We sat in silence for a few moments.
I was trying to think of a way to bring the conversation
around to the real reason I was sitting inside the airport with her in the first place.

"Humph, if I hadn't put in so many years at this airport, I'd leave too. I'm sick of Atlanta. I'm sick of the
traffic, wages, and most of all, the men."

I knew better than to tackle the subject of men, especially since I knew that last part was directed at me.
"You could transfer to another hub if you really wanted
to leave."

"And get the shit end of the totem pole when it came
to my schedule? Oh, hell no, I don't think so. I'm gonna
stick it out here until I can hang it up for good."

"I hear ya. I didn't think about what it would do to
your tenure here." I nodded my head in agreement.
I admired the fact that she had a job she could retire
from, and I was still flipping from spot to spot with very
little stability to my income. That's another reason why
I continued to fuck with Tilo. She was offering a means
to get out of the rat race and live in the lifestyle I'd only

dreamed about. Throw in some good pussy, it's a wrap. "Hey, did you know the dude who shot his ex-wife and her boyfriend?"

"Yeah, I knew him. It's messed up. They got shit all twisted around here." She finished her drink and looked at me expectantly.

I signaled the waitress. So much for the one-drink limit Nancy had imposed. I was grateful the liquor loosened her tongue and lightened her attitude with me. "What's his domestic battle have to do with you and your job? I don't get it."

"You know the drill, because of his clearance, everybody is on alert. See the media didn't tell the whole story. She filed for divorce and he wouldn't agree to it. So she turned things ugly on his job by telling the bosses that he was smuggling contraband through the airport. Now they looking at all of us all crazy when we come through."

"Got it. That's fucked up. Is there any truth to her claims?"

"I'm not sure about that. I knew the guy, but I wasn't all up in his business and shit." Her words were beginning to slur. I didn't know how much longer her spirit of cooperation would last.

"So I still don't understand why this presented complications for you unless you're doing a lot of traveling."

"Damn, nigga, do I have to spell it out for you?"

I wanted to choke the bitch and tell her yeah, but I just looked at her.

"Okay, it has nothing to do with travel. Seniority has its privileges, and one of those privileges is the ability to forego going through TSA screening. On a good day, screening can make the difference of being late for work, so it's definitely something I enjoy. Now this motherfucker done messed it up for all of us, and now we have to go through the line just like everybody else."

"That's fucked up. I can see why that would have you twisted."

"Yeah, like I said before, it's fucked up. Plus, his wife claimed he was smuggling drugs in and out of the country. The bitch gave names and we have to make sure we're not issuing tickets to folks on the list."

"That sucks because you don't even know if the bitch was telling the truth. How the hell did she know what the man was into?"

"Oh, she knew. I don't know what all she said, but obviously there was enough truth to it to convince my boss to adhere to the list. We're supposed to immediately alert security if the people named on the list even attempt to buy tickets. We have pictures posted at each terminal so they can't get by us. I was told if we messed up and issued a ticket to someone on the list, it was grounds for immediate termination and a possible criminal indictment."

"Shit, that's some bullshit right there. If someone calls security on me, I'm gonna turn this bitch out and sue the hell out of everybody in this motherfucker while I'm at it."

"Exactly. That's my point. The bitch must have been convincing."

"Shit, I'd love to see that list," I said, laughing.

"Ah, fuck that. I'm not gonna lose my job over no bullshit. Fuck that." She got up from the table like she'd finally put together why I was there in the first place.

I grew apprehensive because I did not want her showing her drunk ass now 'cause there was no telling what she would say now that she was fired up with a little booze.

"Fuck, I gotta go." She shook her head and backed away from the table as if she was suddenly afraid to turn her back on me.

I waited until she'd left the restaurant before I high-tailed it out of the airport. I was pretty certain I wasn't on the list, but I was equally certain I didn't have a snowball's chance in hell of ever seeing that list.

# CHAPTER FIFTY-SIX

## VERÓNICA RAMSEY

I didn't start to feel apprehension until I rounded the corner to our house. Even though my mother-in-law didn't call me, I was still apprehensive about leaving my baby with her. As I put my key in the lock, I paused to see if I heard the telltale signs of screams to gauge how their visit was going. I was greeted with blessed silence.

"Hey, you okay?" I asked my mother-in-law, who was nodding out on the sofa. I smiled when I noticed the baby monitor on the end table closest to her.

She sat up as I approached. "You back already? I was just taking a catnap."

"Where is Mr. Ramsey?"

"Child, he's stretched out across the bed. He said the house was too quiet and he couldn't keep his eyes open."

"Quiet? Then I guess everything went well?"

"Shoot yeah. My baby got up, drank his bottle, played with us for a little while, and went right back to sleep. He was a perfect angel."

I breathed a sigh of relief as I settled on the sofa next to my mother-in-law. "Perfect. I was scared you were going to call me crying. I'm glad everything went okay."

"Honey, please, I have a way with men. Didn't my son tell you that?" She laughed and I could not help but to join in. Mrs. Ramsey was such a jovial woman, it was hard not to smile just being around her. "How's your dad?"

"He's doing fine. As long as he doesn't develop an infection he should be coming home sometime next week."

"That's good, that's good. I know how worried you must be."

She didn't know the half of it. It was times like this that I missed my mother the most. She was my sounding board for a lot of things, and I missed having her around to talk to when I was confused and needed some guidance. I felt like I could talk to Mrs. Ramsey in the same manner, but I was hesitant to say a lot of things in front of her because a lot of my confusion surrounded her son. I didn't want her to think that I didn't love him or was unhappy in any specific way.

She said, "What's the matter, child? You look like you're carrying the weight of the world around on your shoulders."

I looked at her in surprise because she almost read my mind. Most days it was exactly the way I felt. "Huh? Oh, I'm fine. Just a little tired is all," I replied.

"Why don't you go upstairs and take yourself a nap. I'm here and I'll look after the baby while you get some rest."

"I'm not sleepy. You ever feel like it's too much effort to even comb your hair? I'm that kind of tired. I don't want to do anything."

"Honey, I feel like that every day, but you've just got to go on and press on through it. I think you and Moses need to spend some quality time together without the baby. Maybe a weekend getaway would be a good idea."

"Ah, man, I like the sound of that. I don't think I'd know how to act if I were to go someplace with my husband and not have to worry about feeding or changing the baby. Wow, that would be something else."

"Why don't you plan a little trip then? We can watch the baby for you while you and Moses go somewhere"

"I wish! Do you know that I've never been on a vacation in my entire life? I wouldn't know what to do with myself nor would I know where to go. Besides, Moses is so busy—"

"Nonsense. If there is one thing that child of mine knows how to do it is let go and have fun. He's been all over the world, so I'm sure he could plan a little trip for you two. It could be like a honeymoon for you, and it'll do a world of good for your marriage."

My head sprung up at the mention of our marriage. Was my mother-in-law trying to tell me something? Since Moses and I didn't have the typical courtship, I was unsure of how much of our relationship Moses revealed to his parents. I didn't know if she knew that I was married before or if she knew we were having an affair before my husband's death. I began to feel nervous and uncomfortable. "I think I might take you up on that nap idea. It's not often that I can go to sleep in the middle of the day." I stood up to leave, but Mrs. Ramsey pulled me back down next to her.

"Verónica, what's wrong? At times you seem so distant. I don't want you to feel like I'm prying, I just want to help."

Ever since Moses told his family about me, Mrs. Ramsey seemed to have taken up residence in Atlanta and visited at least once a week. She said it was one of the benefits of retirement and I truly appreciated her for offering love and support to me, but we barely knew each other. I was afraid that once she found out the sordid details of my marriage, she might not love me anymore, and I didn't think my heart could stand it. I wasn't as strong as I used to be.

"Mrs. Ramsey, there's a lot of things you don't know." I pulled away again.

"What did I tell you about calling me Mrs. Ramsey?" she warned.

"Sorry, old habit. But things are complicated right now. Maybe when things get a little better around here, I'll take you up on your offer."

"That's the problem with you young people today. You always assume there will be time to do the things you put off doing today. Life is not promised to you, so there is no better time than the present time. I've learned that over the years."

I wanted so much to open up to her but my head just would not follow my heart. There was too much at risk. I stood up, ready to end our conversation.

"Honey, my son does not keep secrets from me. He tells me everything."

I was astonished by her admission but still leery. I didn't believe Moses told her everything. "I'm sure he does. You two have such a wonderful relationship. I wish I were closer with my mother."

"Yes, he told me about your marriage and your affair. He even told me that he once wasn't sure that my grandchild was his." She chuckled, and it relieved some of the pressure I was feeling about being alone with her and confessing some of my sins.

"Wow, I wasn't sure you knew, and I didn't want to bring it up if he hadn't."

"Heck, he even told me he'd planned to kill you." She started laughing, but I guess she could tell by the look on my face that she'd gone too far.

"He tried to kill me?"

"Oh, shit."

I didn't know Mrs. Ramsey well, but I did know enough to know she rarely cussed. "Wait, I don't understand. Is that some kind of a joke because if it is, it isn't funny." I was ready to kick her and her husband out of my house. I didn't care who she was, she had to go.

"Damn, my husband said my mouth was going to be the death of me, and that I wasn't capable of holding water. I'm so sorry, sweetheart. I should have let Moses be the one to tell you."

"What are you talking about? Why would Moses want to kill me? And more importantly, why did you find it funny?" It took everything in me not to haul off and smack his mother. Moses on the other hand would not get off so lightly. I was going to call that motherfucker and tell him to kiss my ass. Me and my baby would be gone by the time he got home from work.

"Hold on, before you run off half-cocked, let me explain. When Moses first told me what he'd planned, I was as outraged as you are. However, he wasn't thinking clearly. Tilo had messed up his mind, and that is the main reason he is so intent on finding her."

"Here we fucking go again. What the fuck does Tilo have to do with this? You know what's wrong with me? I'm so frigging tired of hearing that woman's name every single day! To hear y'all tell it, she is the devil herself. I don't think so."

"I don't know Tilo from a can of paint, but she is responsible for putting the idea of killing you on Moses' mind. She had him believing that you played him and suckered him into a relationship. She told him the baby wasn't his and that you were lying the entire time."

"She did what? She didn't even know me." I didn't know who I was madder at, Moses or Tilo.

"I know it sounds crazy, but she convinced him to shoot something into your IV at the hospital, and he honestly thought he'd killed you. He regretted it right away. But once he did it, he couldn't take it back. But Tilo tricked him, she didn't give him a drug to kill you, it may have been water in the syringe for all he knows. She did plant enough doubt and hatred in his heart to make him want to do you harm. He told me that when he found out you were alive it was the happiest day of his life, but he was so scared he'd lose you if he ever told you the truth."

I sat back down. This was a lot to dump on a person at one time, and I felt like my head was about to bust with the implications. How could I ever trust my husband again, especially if he allowed a total stranger to convince him to commit murder? Shit, what was he going to do if I did something else to piss him off? Would he kill me in my sleep? And how could any of them rest at night knowing he was capable of murder? This whole family was nuts and I wanted to get as far away from them as I could. It was perfectly clear to me that I didn't even know my husband at all.

"I can't deal with this. Moses was right. I can't live looking over my shoulder and not knowing if and when it's going to be my last day on earth."

"Child, none of us know if this is our last day on earth. That was what I was trying to say to you earlier. God doesn't promise us anything when it comes to that. When He's ready to call us home, He'll call. The love Moses has for you prevailed, so please don't do anything foolish now."

"Foolish, are you kidding me? You just told me that the man I'm married to tried to kill me. That's not like saying I got a booger hanging out of my nose. He wanted me dead, and I take offense to that." Tears were practically blinding me. As I struggled to leave the room, Mrs. Ramsey grabbed me.

"Stop, Verónica, I thought for sure that Moses would have told you by now. That boy picked a fine time to listen to me. I normally don't like secrets in a marriage, but this was an exception to the rule. He really didn't want to kill you. Believe me. It's not in his nature, but he was so upset when he thought LM wasn't his. I told him that if he really loved you, he was going to have to accept your son as part of the package. But when I saw the pictures of LM, I encouraged him to get a DNA test because he looked just like Moses when he was born."

I felt like I'd just been punched in the stomach and busted in the head at the same time. Moses had my son tested without my knowledge or permission? Who the fuck did this motherfucker think he was? I broke free of Mrs. Ramsey's arms and raced to the door. It was high time I had a conversation with my soon-to-be ex-husband, and it would be best not to have this conversation in front of his parents.

"Verónica, where are you going? Oh God, you didn't know about that either? Me and my big mouth. Honey, I am so sorry. Seems like I'm doing more harm than good." Mrs. Ramsey was also crying. She knew she said more than she should have. Whatever the case, it had nothing to do with me.

"I need to have a conversation with your son. In fact, I think it's long overdue."

"You shouldn't be out there driving when you're this emotional. Why don't you wait until you've had a chance to calm down?"

"No, I need to go now. It won't take me long to say what I have to say." I slammed the door behind me as I fished around in my purse for my keys. At a time when things were finally falling into place for us, I learned this. This explained the changes I'd noticed in Moses' behavior. I reached in my purse for my cell phone to call my sister. I was hoping that she would be my voice of reason, especially since she was the most cynical person I knew. She would give me her honest opinion whether I asked for it or not, but she didn't answer her phone. It went straight to voice mail. I tried to sit still for a minute so she wouldn't be able to tell I'd been crying from the sound of my voice.

A little voice in the back of my mind urged me to go back in the house. If Moses had felt strongly enough to want to kill me, what would his mother do to my son, who was incapable of defending himself? I gave her a smoldering look when I walked back through the door. "Are you going to be okay with my son or should I take him with me?"

"Verónica, you are blowing this out of proportion. Moses loves you very much and wouldn't do anything to jeopardize what you have together."

"I wasn't speaking of Moses, I was speaking of you. You saw fit to keep this horrid secret, so now I have to question your motives as well." A look that could only be described as indignation crossed her face, but if anyone should have been indignant, it should've been me.

Her mouth fell open and snapped shut again. She repeated this several times before she was able to get the words out she wanted to say. "I know you're upset and that's completely understandable, but this also sounds much worse than it is. He really does love you; and, yeah, he had a fucked-up way of showing it because he wasn't thinking straight. None of you were."

She made a valid point, and if I allowed myself to sit back and think about it, I'd probably even agree with her, but right now I was filled with a blinding rage. I remembered all of the sleepless nights I suffered through trying to figure out why Moses was so distant toward me. It tore my heart out every time he walked past our son and never picked him up or offered to play with him. The whole time I thought it was me, and it pissed me off to learn that he was the one with the problem.

So many emotions were flowing through me. I was confused as to what I was supposed to be doing. How could I ever forgive and forget his plan to kill me?

"Honey, shut the door. I really botched this whole thing. I can see it in your eyes. You are looking at me like I'm the enemy. If you give us all a chance, you will see for yourself how much we love you."

I wanted to trust her. I needed to trust her because if I didn't, then it would have meant everything was a lie and I refused to believe it, but something in the back of my head was warning me to tread lightly. I searched Mrs. Ramsey's face and I saw her sincerity. She may have been guilty of withholding the truth from me, but I honestly believed she did it out of love. I was no longer afraid to leave my child in her care. I could feel her pain and her sincerity she had for me and my son. "I'm fine, but I would still like to go to my husband's office to speak with him. I cannot allow something this big to go unaddressed. Please do not call him and let him know I'm coming. Will you please do that for me?" If she failed this little test, I would know not to trust any of them again.

"He will be fine. Go handle your business, but try to remember what I said, he does love you." I wasn't sure who she was trying to convince, but I held on to the small hope it was me.

# CHAPTER FIFTY-SEVEN

## TILO ADAMS

I woke from another crazy-ass dream—soaked with sweat—but this time it wasn't Victória standing over me with a gun pointed at my head, it was Moses. His face was fiery, his eyes sharp as laser beams aimed at my heart. When I woke from the dream, I was shaking so badly, I wasn't even able to make it to the bathroom. I peed right in the bed and sank back onto the soiled sheets, too tired to get out of my own piss.

"This shit is getting old." My voice was hoarse; it felt like I'd been screaming for a very long time. Almost like when you go to a sporting event and your favorite team is winning. My body was beaten down and broken. I hadn't had a full night's sleep since the murders, and I wasn't eating. Every time I forced myself to eat something I threw it up in a matter of hours.

"I can't keep doing this to myself. I've got to find a way to deal with this shit and keep it moving, or I might as well roll over on my damn self."

I'd been having this same conversation with myself for months, but nothing was changing. I thought things would get better for me once I left Atlanta behind but that wasn't working. I was also beginning to believe no amount of money was worth this shit. *I'd much rather be broke and happy than wealthy and miserable any day.*

"Get over it, bitch. It ain't like you could give the shit back and things would magically go back to the way they were." More and more I found myself talking aloud to myself, and sadly I was answering. The fact that I changed the face of an entire family and the inability to talk to anyone about it was slowly driving me insane.

"Fuck you. Why didn't you think about this shit before you pulled the fucking trigger? There were other ways to handle it."

"How? How the fuck do you steal money out of someone's hand and get the fuck away? Oh, did I forget to mention they knew who the fuck you were?"

"Uh, we could have—"

"Bitch, please, you can't even get the thought out of your mouth. That's how stupid you sound right now. You and I both know that shit wouldn't work. We had to shut the door on the investigation because the bureau wasn't going to claim involvement. Killing them closed the investigation and you know it. There was no other way, trust and believe that."

I leaned forward and placed my head in my hands, trying to calm the beating drum inside my head. Fragments of conversations would flicker in and out like tiny light bulbs in my head. I needed for the voices and the visions to stop. I knew that what I was feeling wasn't right, but I didn't know what to do about it.

"So what do you want to do about it? Go to some shrink and confess all of our sins? They'll lock our asses up in a New York minute." I started laughing. The irony of the statement was that I was in New York, and this was one city where it was okay to walk around talking to yourself because nobody cared. From what I'd seen on television, the people were so busy getting from place to place, they didn't take time to see one another. This realization fueled me into getting up.

"I can be anyone I want to be in New York. Shit, I'm going fucking shopping." I rose from the wet bed, my panties clinging to me like a second layer of skin. As I walked past the mirror, I avoided eye contact. Despite my new look, I didn't enjoy looking at myself, not anymore. I turned on the shower, tossing my wet clothing in the trash. I had soiled so many clothes, shopping was not a want, it was a necessity because I was down to my last few pairs of panties. I turned on the water as hot as I could stand it and entered the shower, but no matter how hard I scrubbed, I could not undo my past.

I left the shower feeling rejuvenated and eager to cast aside my demons once and for all. My biggest threat was Moses. Although I didn't think he would come for me, I had to be certain.

"Rome, can you talk?" I was using another disposable phone, which I planned to throw away once I received confirmation.

"Yeah, what's up?" His voice was low as if he were trying to keep our conversation on the down low.

I immediately got suspicious and paranoid. It was becoming increasingly difficult to determine which emotion reigned supreme in my head. "Motherfucker, are you tryin' to play me?" I demanded.

"Hold up, what the hell are you talking about? I ain't got time for no bullshit." Rome snapped back with a fire I'd never heard in his voice when he spoke to me.

This little bitch didn't know who he was fucking with, and if he didn't recognize it, I had no problem with writing another chapter to his life—the ending. "Bullshit? I think you'd better check yourself, motherfucker. I'm not the one. Why the fuck were you whispering?" Infused with anger, I hated the fact that cities separated us instead of miles because I would have handled his ass.

"Because I was in a motherfucking elevator and I didn't want everybody listening to my fucking conversation."

Damn, instead of me checking him, he checked my ass. I struggled for something to say after he reminded me that he wasn't sitting on his ass waiting for me to call. "What's the deal with the package you were handling?" I decided not to mention Moses to him. He had reason to suspect my judgment now, and I didn't want to put the nail in my own coffin.

"Uh—"

"What the fuck does that mean? Either you did or you didn't. It's a simple motherfucking question." I was heated again.

"Look, shit is kind of crazy around here. The narcs and Feds are everywhere so I don't really have an answer for you."

"And, what are you telling me?" I tried hard to keep the rage I felt racing through my blood out of my voice.

"I got the stuff, but I'm trying to figure out how to deliver it," he said with a laugh that could only be described as nervous.

"Pussy, take the shit yourself. I'm trying to get ghost and I need my money." I was angry, but since I still needed his help, I was trying to play nice. But when he delivered my goods, I was gonna make sure he never rose his voice at any other motherfucker in life.

"Tilo, I—"

"Bitch, didn't I tell you not to call me that anymore? Fuck, you trying to mess my shit up?" I was enraged and ready to do damage. I flung a vase from the table at the paneled mirror and glass rang out through the air. Tiny shards of glass and ceramic pieces from the vase stuck in my exposed arms. I dropped the phone, covering my face.

"What the fuck is going on?"

Rome had to be shouting because I could make out his voice clearly, even though the phone was still on the floor. Obviously, flinging the vase wasn't the smartest move I'd made all day. Not only was I going to have to spend the next hour or so picking glass and shit from my body, I would have to pay for the horrible mess I'd made of my hotel room. I picked up the phone with hands that wouldn't stop shaking. I felt like a junkie needing a fix, but I didn't know what I should be taking.

"It's nothing," I lied into the phone.

"Nothing, it sounded like the motherfucking cops were kicking in your damn door."

"Why you got to throw salt on my plate, wishing the cops on me and shit?"

"Ain't nobody wishing shit. I'm just telling you how the shit sounded to me." He was huffing and puffing like he was big shit, which only fueled my irritation with him.

"Rome, if you want to get anywhere close to my Colombia connection, you'd better get me my money by the end of the week. I could probably find ten people who would like to make this connect if I wanted to, but I decided to offer it to you first. But it comes with a big price tag and time is of the essence. If you don't sell the shit then you lose big time, because my ass is about to be dead for real and I'm taking my connect with me."

"I'm gonna get the fucking money. Why you got to keep on threatening me and shit? I said I got you."

In my mind, I could see his face. There was nothing like a grown-ass man pouting like a ten-year-old child. It was fucking sickening, but there wasn't anything I could do about it. "It wasn't a threat." I left the rest of the sentence unsaid. He knew.

"All right then," he said as he hung up.

For a second or two I stared at the phone, unable to believe he had hung up on me. It was ballsy on his part because he never knew where I would be coming from. I could've been around the corner from him and he'd never know it.


Shopping normally made me feel good, and shopping with money in my pocket should have restored my soul. However, the voices in my head continued to fuck with me, and I wasn't able to determine which voices were real. I stopped at my favorite store to shop for some underwear. I liked Macy's selection much better than the highly publicized Victoria's Secret. To me the silk felt richer, and I enjoyed wearing underwear that caressed my skin. I held up a panty set and rubbed the crotch over my lips. As I rubbed the pink panties over my mouth, I thought of Victória. My mouth watered as I sniffed the panties.

"You smell so good, baby," I muttered as I continued to sniff them, lost in a pussy-laden fantasy. Good pussy was like a large lobster soaked in butter. After you cracked the shell and pulled out the meat, your tongue was in for a treat. I sniffed again and sighed.

"You know what I want, I'm gonna suck on your fat clit until I get it." I was enjoying my personal vision so much I forgot I was in full view of everyone in the crowded store. I could smell her fresh scent and it was driving me nuts. I rubbed the panties over my chest, causing my nipples to peak against my blue tank top.

"Damn, baby, why you want to tease me? Stop playing." I urgently needed release. I felt like I'd been holding my nut in for years instead of a few months.

"Oh, you want me to take you home? Is that what you want? Victória, why didn't you tell me?" I rushed to the doors of the store with one thought on my mind, busting a humongous nut. It had started to rain as I got outside, but I didn't care. I was on a mission.

"Excuse me, miss?" I felt a slight tug on my arm.

"What the fuck?" I snatched my arm back and dusted it off. The pink panties were still entwined in my other hand, practically dripping with spit and perspiration.

"I'm going to need for you to return to the store," the buff security guard said.

My trance was broken. I looked around and I didn't recognize where I was. "Huh?" I had obviously walked out a different door than the one I came in because I had no clue where I was.

"I need you to return to the store," the guard repeated and grabbed my arm again.

I misunderstood his intentions. "I'm lost, could you help me find my way back to the New Yorker Hotel?" I was in the beginning of a panic attack, and I needed to get back to my room so I could get myself together.

The guard was leading me deeper into the store; it felt like everyone was watching me.

"Hey, what is going on? I thought you were going to give me directions." I couldn't hear Victória anymore, and I wanted to get back to that happy place where she was whispering in my ear. I needed to find that place.

"... shoplifting. Are you going to add resisting arrest, too?"

*Hold the fuck up. This beefy motherfucker finally has my attention. Does he even know who he is fucking with? Hell, I could pay his salary. I don't need to shoplift.* "What did you just say?" I had no idea what this man was talking about, but if he touched me again, he was going to be really sorry.

"I need to see your receipt for your purchase today."

I pulled back, suddenly conscious of where I was and what was going on. "What purchase?" I couldn't remember buying anything, but if he needed a receipt, surely I had one in my purse.

"If you grant me permission to check your purse, we can typically handle this without calling the police."

Police? He had my full attention now. The last thing I needed was having the police all up in my shit. Even though my identification was legit, there were some gaps in my life that I wasn't prepared to account for. I handed over my purse for inspection. After a few seconds the guard passed it back to me.

"What is going on? Is this the way the store handles its shoppers?" I was about to get black on his ass. Especially since he'd searched my purse and didn't find anything stolen.

"No, it's not, but we also don't expect our customers to steal." He was looking down on me, and it was getting on my fucking nerves.

"I don't need to steal shit. I didn't see anything in this bitch that I wanted." I got up, ready to leave, but he stood blocking the door.

"Did you pay for that?"

Once again I had no idea what he was talking about, but I followed his line of vision to my hand that was still clutching the pink panties.

"Motherfucker." The panties. I'd forgotten all about the talking panties.

"Excuse me? Are you all right?" He put the bass in his voice, but I also detected a little compassion.

I had to climb out of this shit in a hurry. "I am so sorry. I never intended to walk out of the store. I mean who goes to the store and steals fucking panties, especially if they have a purse full of money. I didn't even realize I still had them." I tried to hand him the panties but he refused to take them. When I looked, I understood why. The panties were damp and hanging limply from my fingers. They were no longer pretty; they felt soiled.

"Uh-huh. What's your name?"

Why the fuck did he need my name? I started to hyperventilate. I could not go to jail for stealing a fucking pair of panties. "Sir, I am so sorry. Could we please work this out? I have money." I pulled out a hundred dollar bill and gave it to the guard.

He just looked at me like I'd lost my damn mind.

"What? You don't want my money? My money ain't good enough for you?" I was starting to get mad, and it didn't make things any better because he just continued to stare at me. I threw him another hundred. "See, money ain't the issue. I'll take the panties, ring it up, and you can keep the change." I closed my purse and considered the matter closed. I would sit right there for him to bring me my receipt.

"You sucked the hell out those panties." His voice was low, but I heard him clearly and understood what needed to happen before I was allowed to leave.

"Shit, you act like I tried to steal a flat-screen television."

He shrugged his shoulders but otherwise didn't say anything. His eyes said it all.

"Hell, I don't know your dick. How do I know if it's even clean?" I cried.

"Bitch, please. How do I know your mouth is clean?" Obviously he didn't like what I'd said, but, hell, this was 2011, and there was some dangerous shit floating around. This guy wasn't bad looking so he didn't really have to twist my arm to give him a tweet.

"If I suck your dick, will I be allowed to leave?" I didn't mind sucking his dick. Hell, I might even ride it, if it looked right, but I didn't want any bullshit when it was time to go.

"Yeah, we'll be straight." He unzipped his pants with confidence. He knew it was going to happen even though I was still considering my options.

To my knowledge, the door wasn't locked so I could technically make a run for it, but I would have to come out of the heels I was wearing to have any chance of getting away. However, I decided to take the easy way out and suck his dick, but I would not swallow.

"I'm not getting down on my knees."

"You don't have to. I just want you to wet my monkey like you wet those panties."

My pussy twitched when he pulled his dick out of his pants. It was lovely and I couldn't wait to taste it. He walked toward me, his dick jutting out at me like a wand.

"Don't try no funny shit," he warned. He didn't have to worry. His dick looked like a chocolate pipe and I loved chocolate. I licked it as I would a Fudgesicle, but my mind was not on his dick. In my head I was making love to someone else. He, this unnamed guard, got the benefit of my love and he didn't even know it.

# CHAPTER FIFTY-EIGHT

## VICTÓRIA MENDOZA

"I'm not feeling this, Moses. It's too easy. Why would the gate agent even know which hotel Tilo chose to stay at?" We were sitting in the lobby of the New Yorker Hotel hoping that the information given to us by the gate agent at the airport was correct.

"I know, it has been easy, but your girl is losing her damn mind and creating a scene everywhere she goes. The agent said he put her in a cab and told the driver where to take her. So we'll see if she's still here."

I was nervous about seeing Tilo again. "So what is the plan if we see her?"

"Tonight we watch. I spoke to one of the bellhops and he said she left a few hours ago and hasn't returned."

"How does he know she hasn't checked out?" I wanted to get up and walk around. All this waiting and shit was only adding to my anxiety.

"Would you relax, Victória? Didn't you know detective work is a whole lot of hurry up and wait?"

"I'm guess that's why I'm no detective."

"Well, you are tonight, so sit back and act like we're comfortable. We don't want to be like your friend and draw any attention to ourselves." Moses was laid back in his chair with the newspaper like he was in his living room at home.

I sat back and tried to mimic his calm persona. "Are you going to confront her?" I was thinking about best-case scenarios and it wasn't looking good. We didn't have any weapons, so if things turned ugly, it would be like target practice for Tilo on our asses.

"Victória, if we find her, I have to report it. I can't go with my first instinct and shoot her. I wouldn't be able to live with myself. Plus, I don't want to go to jail for the rest of my life."

"Humph, life behind bars wouldn't bother me a bit," I replied.

"Yes, it would. You're allowing your emotions to govern your good sense. We need proof that she's alive so the FBI can handle it. They have to know how much of a threat she is to your family and quite possibly to their organization."

Moses had made some good points, but I wasn't feeling them. I wanted to give Tilo a dose of the same medicine she had given me. Letting the bitch get away with killing my brother didn't sit well, either.

"What if you can't prove that she is alive? What then?" I was frustrating myself thinking of all the what-ifs. And, through it all, the only thing that kept coming back to me was killing Tilo and the rest of the bullshit was irrelevant.

"I'll make them believe. I just have to get the evidence that she exists," Moses proclaimed. His confidence irritated me.

"Have you ever asked yourself why the FBI didn't search for her? They see some blood in her car and boom, she's considered dead. Why wouldn't they look for her body? They just let it go like she didn't exist." If my words disturbed him, I couldn't tell.

"Truth be told, I don't think they wanted to find her. If my theory is correct, they needed her to go away. It was that or own up to their involvement."

"Whatever. The cat's out of the bag and they still haven't done anything about it," I insisted.

"We don't know what the hell they are doing. For all I know, they might be doing an investigation, but I was told that they believed Tilo was an innocent victim."

"That's another thing, why haven't they been around questioning me to find out what really went down?" I never thought about it before, but it seemed logical to me that someone would have come around just to make sure all the loose ends were tied up.

"Damn, my bad. I still have some connections with the bureau so I stopped that from happening because Verónica said you didn't need anyone coming around reminding you what happened."

"Shit, your wife needs to stop babying me. I'm a grown-ass woman and the last time I checked, my mother was dead." My voice louder, and for a moment, I completely forgot why we were sitting in the hotel lobby.

Moses reached over and shook my arm. "Victória, get a grip. You're going to mess up everything."

My mind was racing as it became abundantly clear to me that Moses was going to pose a problem for me. I needed to get rid of him and I knew just how to do it. "What are you going to tell your wife?"

"I, uh . . ."

Moses was in my way. He wanted to hand Tilo over to the very people who facilitated her escape. Fuck that, I needed justice for me and my brother.

My heart practically stopped when I saw Tilo come through the door. Even though she'd changed her outward appearance, I knew it was her. "There she is." I gasped. I felt my heart pounding loudly in my ears. My quarrel with Moses was temporarily forgotten. In less than a minute, I went from not wanting Moses around to being grateful he was with me.

"Where?" Moses asked. His face was rigid with emotions I could identify with.

"Over by the elevator with that man." Seeing her with someone else inflamed me. It took everything in me not to rush toward her and strangle her until she was limp in my arms. She appeared to be enjoying herself and this made me mad. I couldn't remember a single day of joy since she shot me, but this bitch had clearly gone on with her life.

Moses said, "Damn, if I didn't see it with my own eyes, I wouldn't believe it. She's fierce."

I tore my eyes away from Tilo to examine Moses. Lust was written all over his face and once again, I was questioning his relationship with her. Did something sexual happen between them? Is that why he was here, because she jilted him too? "So, are you gonna just sit there and stare?" I asked angrily. "She could get in the elevator at any moment and we wouldn't be any closer to bringing her to justice."

"Right." Moses moved in closer to Tilo and snapped a few pictures. She was in her own little world and didn't notice either of us as she openly groped the man she was with. Jealousy surged through my veins because it was clear she had gone on with her life. While I was stuck in this warped time capsule she'd left me with. Unable to move forward and in constant confusion of our past.

"Ms. Adams," the lady at the front desk called out. She was looking right at Tilo but she didn't respond. "Hello, April Adams." She snapped her fingers and shook her head while coming from behind the desk. Several people were still waiting for assistance and seemed to resent having to wait while the lady sought to get Tilo's attention.

"What the hell is that about?" Moses asked.

"Who is April?" I wasn't paying attention. I was still checking out Tilo. The elevator came and went several times but neither of them bothered to get on it. They were so busy fondling each other, I doubted if they even realized what was going on around them.

The clerk stopped in front of Tilo, tapping her on the shoulder. "Ms. Adams, the manager would like to speak with you a moment before you go to your room."

"Excuse me?"

If looks could kill, the lady would have withered and died on the spot.

"I'm sorry, I was calling you and you didn't answer," the lady defended herself.

"And that gives you the right to put your hands on me?"

The man who was with Tilo attempted to pull her back but she pushed him off.

"What kind of place is this? Let me speak to the manager." She swayed on her feet, confirming my suspicions about her being drunk. Once again, the man with her attempted to grab her arm but she wasn't having it. She snatched it away from him with an evil snarl on her face.

"If he expects to get some tonight, he'd be wise to stay out of whatever is going on," Moses whispered.

I wanted to get closer so I could hear better, but I was afraid Tilo would see me. The woman appeared to use her two-way radio to call the manager.

"The manager is coming. I'm sorry if I upset you, Ms. Adams," she apologized and walked away. She appeared to be upset as she went back behind the desk.

Moses walked over to the sofa and sat with his back facing Tilo. I didn't realize what he was doing until he placed his phone over his shoulder. He was not only taking pictures of Tilo, he was recording the entire encounter.

"Ms. Adams, can I speak with you alone?" the manager asked.

"Alone, for what? Don't you see I'm busy?" She was loud and belligerent.

I'd seen this side of her before, and it normally happened when she was drunk.

"Ms. Adams, it is very important." The manager acted like he needed to borrow someone else's balls because Tilo had him ready to shit in his pants.

"This"—Tilo grabbed the man's dick in a serious grip and continued her statement—"is very important."

I wanted to laugh. The manager turned so red he was almost purple.

"I see. Uh, there is a matter with your room that I need to discuss," the manager said.

This obviously got her attention because she released her firm grip on dude's dick. He visibly relaxed and started stepping back toward the doors.

"She won't be riding that dick tonight," I said, laughing.

"What did I miss?" Moses asked.

"Her man just slunk his happy ass out the damn door."

I wanted to leap up and rub it in her face but I couldn't. Moses and I shared a smile. I assumed he didn't want her getting the dick either. I filed that bit of information away for later thought.

"Ms. Adams, there was considerable damage done in your room, and the neighbors are complaining of noise coming from your room."

"What fucking neighbors? I'm in the presidential suite, and the only person on my floor is on the other end of the hall. Shit, if they could hear me inside my apartment, you have a bigger problem than a little bit of damage."

"I have an itemized bill that must be paid before you can go back to your room. And since you are paying in cash, we will require an additional deposit if you decide to continue to stay with us."

I waited for the explosion but surprisingly it didn't come. Tilo stood there staring at him as if she was weighing her options. A few minutes passed before she held out her hand for the bill. I was so glad they didn't take this conversation out of our earshot because this was better than a movie with the popcorn.

Tilo pulled out her wallet and counted out several thousand dollars and gave it to the manager. "This should handle it."

"I'll be right back with your receipt."

"Have someone bring it to my room with the keys. I've got some unfinished business to handle." She looked around and I had to duck to keep her from spotting me. She must have been looking for her man, but he was long gone. Shrugging her shoulders, she impatiently pressed the button for the elevator and finally disappeared from sight.

"Wow, that bitch is crazy," I said.

"Damn. That was off the chain, and I've got it all on tape. Plus, we learned which room she was staying in and her alias."

"Great, now what?" I was getting frustrated. I wanted to go catch the next elevator up and snatch the life out of the bitch.

"We take the information back and persuade the FBI to arrest her. With your testimony, she will be put away for life."

"Fuck all that, Moses. You don't understand what she did to me and my family. If I let her leave this hotel, it will be like saying I don't give a fuck, and trust me: I give a fuck."

"I'm not saying to let her go free, Victória. I just think we need to go through the proper channels. I've got a wife and kid and I'm not trying to lose them behind Tilo's stank ass." Moses' voice turned hard. For the first time I heard the love he had for his family.

"So what happens if we leave and she checks out? We might not be so lucky in finding her again."

"One of us has to stay here and watch her. You wouldn't have to sit outside her room or anything like that. I could place a bug in her room to alert you of her movements," Moses said.

"How did you go from one of us to me? How you gonna volunteer me like that, especially since you know how badly I want to kill her?"

"Victória, you can't kill her. You just can't. Your sister would kill me if she even thought I would get you involved like that. Promise me you won't kill her."

"Wait, what's going on here? Why do I get the feeling that you're setting me up or something?" The itty-bitty committee in my head was working overtime.

"Huh? No, that's not it at all. I need to go back and I think someone needs to stay here in case Tilo decides to run."

"I got all that but why all of a sudden do you need to go back? That's what I don't get."

"I told you I was going to go get help."

I could tell he was getting agitated but I didn't care. "Why can't you just pick up the phone and call someone? This is the day of technology so anything you can say in person you can pretty much say and do over the Net."

A myriad of expressions crossed his face until he finally settled on one that resembled defeat.

"Verónica sent me a text that said if I didn't get my black ass home, the next time I saw her or my son, it would be in court."

I could tell he was worried and I tried real hard not to laugh, but I knew my sister and she wasn't playing.

"Fine, I'll do it. What do I do if she runs?"

"Promise me you won't kill her. Just follow her and I'll be back as soon as I can."

I crossed my legs. "I promise," I said sweetly, but keeping that promise was the last thing on my mind!

# CHAPTER FIFTY-NINE

## MOSES RAMSEY

I should have been sleeping on the way back from New York but my mind wouldn't let me. I had so many things to do and very little time in which to do them. I didn't like leaving Victória alone with Tilo, but I didn't have any other choice. My plan was to call my buddies at the FBI as soon as my plane touched down, but I needed to fix things at home first.

I was nervous as I climbed the stairs to our home because I didn't know what I was going to walk into. The house was quiet, which was a good sign, but I was still careful. I didn't want to get on the bad side of my wife's Latino temperament.

"Verónica, honey, wake up."

She looked so beautiful, I just wanted to take my clothes off and get in the bed with her.

"Huh, what is it? Is the baby okay?" She sat up, wiping sleep and hair from her eyes.

"It's okay, the baby is fine. I need to talk to you," I said, bracing myself for what I knew was going to be a fight.

"What time is it?" She peered over my shoulder trying to see the clock. She wasn't fully awake and I used this to my advantage.

I purposely positioned my body so she couldn't see the clock before I was able to explain to her where I'd been all night.

"Are you just getting home?" Her voice was accusatory and bitter.

It would have been easy to lie, but there had been too much deception. It was time to come clean. "Yes, but hear me out before you rip out my heart and set it on fire." I laughed, but she didn't find it funny. "We found Tilo. She's in New York going by the name of April Adams. I got it all on my phone." I pushed my phone toward her, but she turned her head like I was speaking of the bag lady down the street and not the person who had killed a member of her family.

I touched her arm but she moved away from me. "I know you didn't want us to look for her, but you have to understand that if we didn't find her, she would keep coming back."

"Who is we?" Verónica asked.

I hung my head. If I was going to tell the truth, I had to tell the whole truth. "Your sister and I. Victória is in New York too, making sure Tilo doesn't get away before I can get back with the FBI to arrest her."

"Have you lost your fucking mind? How could you leave my sister alone in New York with that killer?" She jumped up off the bed and started pulling clothes out of the dresser to put on.

"You told me to come home." I knew I sounded like an idiot.

"Yeah, well I didn't know your ass was in New York, either. What the fuck were you thinking?"

"Verónica, wait, hear me out first."

She paused but I could tell she was about two seconds away from going off on my ass.

"What? I don't believe this shit." She pulled a shirt over her head as she sat back down on the bed, her foot nervously kicking the footboard.

"Honey, Tilo is evil." I wanted to explain to Verónica how persuasive Tilo could be and how dangerous it was to us just to let her go free, but I couldn't. I didn't want to hurt my wife any more than I already had.

"Is that all?" Verónica got back up and continued to get dressed.

I had to stop her. "Honey, I didn't want to tell you this . . . Remember when the baby was born?"

"Before or after you passed out?" she asked sarcastically. Verónica was spewing venom, but I reasoned she had a right to be upset with me.

"Tilo told me you were playing me and the baby wasn't mine. I didn't believe her, but when I saw the baby, I uh . . ." I pressed on even though my inner voice was telling me to shut up.

"You—uh—fucking what?" She had her hands on her hips and her lips were pinched as if she were biting her lip to keep from saying anything else.

"I believed her. She got me hyped up, baby, and I already wasn't thinking straight. She told me I was going to be stuck married to you and another man's son."

"Hold the fuck up, Moses. You knew I was married before we started fucking." She was hotter than all get-out and she was getting loud.

"I know, baby. I was wrong. I can't make you understand how she deceived me. She's a good talker. She has a gift of gab and she had me going, baby." I was pleading with her for understanding.

"Um-hmm. I see. What about all the love you professed to have for me and the baby? Where was all that, Moses?" She was pulling things out of the drawer and folding them.

This was not the way I wanted the conversation to go, but I had to tell her the truth before it came back to bite me.

"I did love you, baby, but I was hurting inside. I waited so long for love and Tilo made me think you were just using me. She told me the only way I could pay you back was to, uh . . ."

"What? Don't stop now dammit! Say it," she snapped.

"Kill you." I expected her to haul off and hit me but she didn't.

A tear rolled down from her eye, but otherwise she was completely calm. However, I didn't relax because I knew the calm always preceded the storm.

"So what happened, Moses? I'm still here." She was really crying now and I was too.

"Shit, I wish I could explain to you how devastated I was. I wish I could make you understand; but, hell, in the light of day, none of it makes sense. Tilo was at me for days, planting doubt in my head, so when the baby came out, I lost it." My heart felt like it was being ripped right out of my chest as I watched Verónica pack her clothes. I knew I was about to lose the best thing that had ever happened to me so I went for broke.

"On the plane ride I told myself I could confess to all this and not lose you and the baby. I have to be the craziest motherfucker on the planet to think I could make you understand why I did the things I did and everything would be okay. Maybe one day you will forgive me, but I want you to know that I love you and my baby. I am so sorry. I am so very sorry. . . ." I couldn't finish. My heart felt like it had shattered into a million pieces and I couldn't pick any of them up. I fell to the floor, no longer able to support my legs.

I heard Verónica moving around the room, but I couldn't look up. I didn't want to see her walk out of my life. This was a vision I didn't want to carry around with me for the rest of my life. "I love you and the baby."

Verónica got down on the floor and hugged me. I was surprised, but I thought she was saying good-bye.

"Your mother told me everything. It's a good thing you didn't come home last night or we might not be having this conversation. I was so angry with you, I wanted to kill you. I asked God to help me and give me a sign to know your heart. I see God has a sense of humor because I believe you, because no one in his right mind would pull a stunt like this, at the crack of dawn, and confess to trying to kill his spouse unless he was touched in the head or sincere in doing the right thing. I'm gonna trust my God and believe you're sincere. I'm done with this. Do what you have to do." She got up from the floor and went into the bathroom.

# CHAPTER SIXTY

## ROME WATSON

"Fuck." That bitch was getting on my last nerve. Getting involved with that crazy bitch was the dumbest thing I'd ever done. I stomped around my apartment thinking of what to do next. Greg wasn't answering his fucking phone, either, so I had no choice but to deliver the money to the airport myself. I sent him an urgent text and told him to meet me at the airport.

"Damn, I wish that fucker would phone in to let me know whether or not the coast is clear. Fuck!" I wasn't worried about getting bagged at the airport because I didn't go there enough to arouse suspicion, but I disliked making the drops myself because there was always a chance something could go wrong. My problem was I didn't know who else was involved in the shakeup with airport security. But my time had run out. The longer I waited, the more likely it was that I'd get caught. I needed to get paid so I could replace the drugs I'd removed from the evidence room.

"Fuck." I grabbed the duffel bag from under the bed and drove to the airport, unsure if Greg would actually meet me there. My head was pounding. I desperately wanted to stop for a drink, but I fought off the urges. Besides, I needed to have my mind right. I was supposed to meet my connect at ten o'clock and I didn't want to be late. I only had to check the bag and the

connect would tag it and make sure it got through security and on to its final destination. When the package
was delivered, I would receive a wire letting me know
where to collect my money.

I was sweating profusely as I parked the car. This
was my first drop and I didn't like it one bit.

"I ain't doing this shit no more. Lord, if you get me
out of this mess, I promise I ain't never gonna mess up
again."

It wasn't really a prayer, but it was the closest I'd
been to speaking to my Higher Power in years. Funny
I would remember Him now after all the shit I'd done,
but it was what it was. This was another thing I would
work on once my shit was clear. I parked the car in the
short-term lot and carried the case with me. It seemed
heavier to me for some reason. I wiped the sweat off my
forehead and tried to mix in with the other travelers. I
dialed Greg again to see if he would finally answer his
phone. I was going to have to do the deed myself.

"Fucking answering machine. I hate them shits." I
tried to mask my frustration as I stood in line to check
my bag. My connect was working the counter and it
made me feel a little better, but it wasn't over so I kept
my guard up. I was ready to bail at the first sign of
trouble.

"Sir, we've opened up another line to serve you better."

"Huh?" I said.

"Another service representative can take you in this
other line." The man from the airlines was pointing to
another line next to my girl.

"No, I'm good. Thanks." I prayed that he would
go away, but he stood looking at me for another few
seconds before he moved on to bug someone else.
Sweat trickled down my balls and I resisted the urge to

scratch. I pulled out my phone and sent a text to Greg. After this I was done with that motherfucker.

Finally, it was my turn. I pulled out the passport I was using for identification and placed my bag on the scale. My girl processed my ticket and took my bag. Relief flooded through my body as she handed me my boarding pass. I scratched my balls, and I didn't care who was watching. As I was turning around to leave, I was grabbed from behind and forced to the ground. My hands were cuffed and I was placed under arrest.

"Rome Watson, you are under arrest for interstate trafficking of drugs and currency."

"Fuck." When I looked over my shoulder, my girl winked at me as she handed my bag to the officer next to her. I'd been fucked, double-dutch style.

# CHAPTER SIXTY-ONE

## GREG CARTER

"It's a good fucking day." I was grinning my ass off as Rome was being led away from the airport in hand-cuffs. I should have felt bad but I didn't. If he hadn't sent me all those fucked-up text messages, I might not have told Nancy to bag his sneaky ass when he got to the airport. Actually, he did it to himself really, I just helped. It would be a cold day in hell before Rome ever saw the light of day as a free man. His ass was going down. I was tying up my loose ends in Atlanta and Rome was my biggest threat.

"Adios, Rome."

He turned when he heard my voice and the look on his face could've been used to promote a movie called *Oh shit, I've been fucked,* 'cause ol' boy was definitely out-dicked by me.

Rome yelled, "You fucking bastard. What did you do?" He was pulling away from the officers, trying to get at me.

"Chill, bro," I said, laughing. It did my heart good to see Rome in handcuffs. It was about time he saw the business end of a jail cell.

"I'm gonna fuck you up when I get my hands on you." He continued to buck as he was led away through the security doors.

"Detective Carter, thanks for your cooperation," another officer said as he handed me the suitcase they took from Rome.

"Did you get his cell phone? I'll need to book this into evidence as well."

"Yeah, sure, we got it."

I waited for the officer to return with Rome's phone. I had a hunch I would find everything else I needed to know from it.

"Thanks again," the officer said as he handed me the phone.

"All in a day's work, my man. All in a day's work," I replied. I felt so good, my dick got hard. I'd been taking shit from Rome for a minute, but, tonight, I shoved it straight up his ass. After giving Nancy $5,000 for her help, me and the duffle bag boarded the plane for New York. It was time I paid another bitch a visit. I was tired of being fucked doggie style with no Vaseline. Rome, just like Tilo, thought they were going to come up on the sweat off my back, but I was about to turn the tables on her too.

Things worked out much better than I'd planned. I'd been searching for a way to get Rome out of the picture, but I never could catch him with his pants down. When he sent me the text saying he was at the airport, I damn near nutted in my pants. I had the bitch where I wanted him. From there it wasn't hard to set up a sting with a bunch of greedy motherfuckers wanting to get their hands greasy. With Rome's arrest I was able to even the score. The drugs from the evidence room would be returned, but the cash, I would be keeping that and I was cleared of any involvement.

Rome fucked himself when he told me to go to the airport and speak to Nancy. If he hadn't, I wouldn't have known about the sting operation that Tilo had orchestrated. My only problem was I didn't know who the trap was intended for—Me or Rome—so I didn't have much of a choice than to take them both down. Tonight taught me a valuable lesson—"never trust a big butt and a smile." Tilo was my poison; however, she'd grossly underestimated me if she thought I would go away so easily.

Rome made his first mistake when he let me know the drugs seized in the cartel raid weren't destroyed. The FBI dictated the disposition of drug seizures, but when I looked into the logs, the disposal date had been altered. The Atlanta Police Department did not have authority to hold the drugs for any reason unless under the directive of the FBI. This directive was duly noted in the computer and logged in the binders used by the evidence room for tracking. Tilo's badge number was used to remove the drugs from the records room and Rome was the issuing officer. The only way Rome would know her number was if she'd given it to him. Putting together the rest of the puzzle wasn't hard from there. Tilo must have been fucking both of us and playing me to the left. Common sense told me to cut my loses and run, but my ego wasn't hearing that shit. I was going to fuck Tilo up and keep it moving.


"April, where you at, ma? Holla at your boy. You're scaring me, boo, get back with me." I was gritting my teeth by the time I ended the plea on Tilo's answering machine. It wasn't the first message I'd left her since I arrived in New York, but I'd hoped it would be my last because I didn't know how many more nice calls I had in me. I was not in the best of moods as I checked into my hotel for the evening. It wasn't how I wanted to spend my first night in New York, but I wasn't surprised.

Tilo never operated on my timetable and over the years I'd come to expect this type of behavior from her, but it didn't mean I liked it. I would have rather spent my time between her thighs instead of beating my meat in a ridiculously overpriced hotel room, but there wasn't anything I could do about it, so it didn't make much sense getting myself all worked up about it. After I settled into my room, I decided to go downstairs to the bar to have a drink.

My flight from Atlanta was delayed for two hours, and we had to sit on the tarmac the entire time. That was the kind of shit that pissed me off about flying. Airlines had no problem at all leaving your ass if you weren't on the plane fifteen minutes before departure, but would park your ass on the corner lot for hours and offer little in the way of an apology. I could understand weather-related delays and mechanical issues, but it blew me away when the delay was due to congestion over LaGuardia. What the fuck did that mean? I thought scheduling landings was a part of the duties of an air traffic controller, but obviously not when it comes to New York. I just didn't get the hype of New York. The streets were overcrowded with traffic, and now they were telling us the air was littered with planes, too. I couldn't wait to finish my business with Tilo and get the fuck out of New York.

# CHAPTER SIXTY-TWO

## VICTÓRIA MENDOZA

I approached the front desk relatively sure that Tilo was drunk and more than likely passed out in her room. Tilo could not handle her liquor and was probably loudly snoring as I spoke. "I would like to get a room please."

"I'll be happy to assist you. How many nights would you like to stay with us?" The smile on the receptionist's face was so different from the grimace it held when she was dealing with my nemesis, Tilo.

"A week, maybe two. I've never been to New York before and I heard there is so much to do. I want to make sure I have enough time to do it all," I said with fake enthusiasm.

"I heard that. I have a room with a king-sized bed on the tenth floor, or would you prefer to be up higher?"

"Actually, I'd rather have a suite if you have one."

"Certainly, let me check on availability." The fever in the lobby had calmed down and I was ready to get a room and relax. I hadn't realized how tired I was until I started thinking about a hot bath. I'd never spent the night in a hotel, and I was going to take advantage of the opportunity being in New York afforded me.

"You're in luck, we have one available. Will you require assistance with your luggage?" As she looked around me, the smile disappeared from her face.

"Not at the moment. The airport has misplaced my bags, but I hope to have them soon. I'm really missing my toothbrush right about now," I said in a joking manner, but she had to know if it were really true, the last thing I would be doing was joking about it.

"Okay, I will need your credit card and identification please. And just so you know, we have a wonderful gift shop that is open for any incidentals you may need. And of course, we do have some courtsey items in your room."

She handed me the key and my information after I signed the receipt.

"Thanks." I exhaled a deep breath as I walked to the elevator. I was relieved to have someplace other than the lobby to hang out.

"Enjoy your stay."

I waved my hand, acknowledging her wishes. As I exited the elevator, I bumped into the same bellman I saw assisting Tilo earlier in the lobby.

"I'm sorry, miss. Are you okay?" the bellman asked as I read his nametag.

"No problem, I wasn't paying attention."

He kept on moving, but I couldn't get him off my mind as I entered my room. He was definitely sexy, but something about his eyes bothered me and I couldn't put my finger on it.

I checked out the bathroom to see what toilet items I needed and wrote a list using the pen and pad from the desk. Knowing Tilo, I was feeling pretty confident that she was in for the evening, but I didn't want to take a chance on losing her. I was going to need assistance. With Moses being out of pocket, I wasn't sure how I was going to get it. I was about to order from room service when I got a call from Moses.

"You must have been reading my mind," I said.

"Oh yeah, how so?"

"I was trying to figure out my next move, and I started thinking about you, that's all."

Moses was still an enigma to me. I wanted to believe that he was on the up and up, but my trust level with people in general had been shattered, so I was still leery.

"What's Tilo up to?"

"She's probably sleeping it off in her room."

"What do you mean probably?"

I didn't like his tone of voice. "Hell, I can't see through walls, shit. So I can only assume she is asleep. Jeez."

"Victória, chill. I didn't understand what you meant."

I was tired and hungry and didn't feel like any shit from him, or anyone else for that matter.

"Yeah, all right. I got myself a room and I'm going to eat something before I go back downstairs, but I seriously doubt she's going anywhere else today."

"Good, I'm glad you're getting some rest. I'm still trying to get someone to listen to me, but I will be back as soon as I can."

I didn't like what he was saying and wondered just how long he expected me to maintain this vigil. If I knew how to get into her hotel room, I was ready to end it tonight, but first I needed a weapon. "Okay, Moses, room service is at the door. Let me know when you're headed back this way." Disgusted, I ended the call before he could say anything else that might piss me off. Part of me realized I was being irrational, but the other part of me didn't give a fuck. Patience was never one of my strong suits, and mine had been stretched past its tolerance level.

As I waited for my sandwich to be delivered from room service, I made up my mind to end this shit one way or the other tomorrow. I finally understood why Verónica wanted to let this go, because it was tearing me up inside. I was thumbing through the yellow pages when someone knocked on the door. It scared me until I realized it was probably room service with my food.

"Coming," I shouted as I went to get my wallet for a tip. As I opened the door I realized it was the same bell-man who I'd bumped into earlier. "Can you put it in the sitting room?" I asked as I allowed the door to close.

"Sure."

I followed him as he unloaded my food from his small cart to the table. "Hey, I remember you. Are you the only one working here?" I said jokingly.

He chuckled. "Sometimes it feels that way but, trust me, there's a boatload of us working here. Oh snap, I remember you too. Weren't you with that dude who was asking all those questions?" He tipped his head from side to side. He caught me off guard because I thought we'd done a good job at being less than visible.

"Yeah, that was my brother-in-law," I said, laughing to hide my embarrassment at being busted.

"You should tell old dude he needs to step up his tip game, especially if he wants some information on our guest. He could have me losing my job over a lousy ten dollars and shit."

"I hope you won't hold it against him, he wasn't try-ing to insult you." I didn't know what else to say to him, but I did get more money out of my wallet to make up for Moses' shortcomings. He was staring at me as I went through my wallet and it was starting to make me feel uncomfortable.

"No offense taken. I was just letting you know just in case you needed something else," he said. He looked out the window, as if he didn't see the elephant that he allowed into the room.

I held out a hundred dollar bill for him to take. But he shook his head no.

"Sorry, lady, I can't break that bill for you."

I wasn't offering him the money expecting change, I was baiting him with a promise of more.

"Oh, I wasn't asking for change. I was trying to make up for my brother-in-law's mistake." I smiled to let him know that I knew what time it was and I was fine with it.

"Cool, appreciate it." He reached forward and took the money from me. "So, what did she do?" he asked after the money disappeared into his pocket.

He was one step ahead of me because I wasn't sure how to answer his question. My gut told me that I could tell him the truth, but my gut had also lied to me before, so I was hesitant to listen to it now. I continued to stare at him for a few more seconds before I answered him. "See that right there?" I pointed to my head so he could see the trace markings of the bullet that grazed my head.

He jumped back in surprise. "Ah, damn! She did that shit? I thought you were going to tell me she fucked your man. I'm sorry, shorty. That's fucked up." He pulled the money back out of his pocket and tried to hand it back to me.

"It's okay, keep it, because I really do need your help."

He lowered his arm but didn't immediately put the money back in his pocket. "I feel for you, boo, but I ain't into none of that gangster shit. I knew that chick wasn't right the moment I laid eyes on her, and that's the only reason why I'm talking to you now." He was clearly nervous and I understood his fear. If I hadn't been so mad at Tilo, I might have been afraid too.

"Do I look gangster to you? That woman killed my brother and shot me and left me for dead. The only thing I want to do is keep an eye on her until my brother-in-law returns with the police to put her ass behind bars where she belongs."

"So what do you want me to do? I believe you and I want to help, but I can't afford to lose this job. I'm paying my way through college, and this job gives me spending money. Plus, I can sneak away and study when I need to."

I couldn't get mad at him for trying to do something with his life. After all, he was no different than I was before Tilo came into my life. "If you help me keep an eye on Tilo until help comes, I could contribute twenty thousand dollars to your college fund." I was scared. I didn't really know this guy from a can of paint, and for all I knew, he could bash me over the head and no one would be the wiser.

"Yeah, right. I may have been born at night but it wasn't last night," he said, laughing. He turned around to leave, taking away the only hope that I had at the moment.

"I'm dead serious." I really needed his help but I wasn't going to beg.

He said, "She has a gun."

"Figures, but I'm not trying to kill her. I just need to make sure she doesn't disappear again. She faked her death, and we're trying to prove that she's still alive so she can stand trial for the murder of my brother." Waiting for him to respond one way or the other seemed like an eternity.

"You're still going to need a gun. That bitch is crazy. I could see about getting you one, but it's going to cost a little more."

For some reason I trusted him. Maybe it was because I didn't have much of a choice, but regardless of the reason, I did. "Fine, I'll have the money tomorrow."

Instead of leaving he took a seat and got comfortable. "I just hope this shit ain't gonna come back and bite me in the ass, because I really can't afford the trouble, you know what I mean?"

"I feel you, but if I let her get away with what she did to my family, she's going to keep on destroying lives and I can't live with that."

"I think she's been here about a week and doesn't go out much, but when she does, it's always a big production. I think she's having a nervous breakdown because she's always talking to herself. Housekeeping hates her. She's creeping us all out, so I hope your brother-in-law gets back soon."

"You and me both." I wanted to say more but it wasn't necessary. I could tell he knew where I was coming from just from the look in his eyes.

Craig wrote his number on a piece of paper and handed it to me. "Call me if you need me and I'll let you know if she moves."

"Thanks, Craig. You won't be sorry for helping me."

"I hope not."

# CHAPTER SIXTY-THREE

## TILO ADAMS

I knew I was teetering on the edge of insanity and little things would send me into tantrums. I remembered going shopping a few nights before, but I couldn't find any of the items I bought. I scoured the entire suite and couldn't find a single bag from the store. All of my underwear were soiled, and I didn't have anything else to wear. I walked out of the bathroom wearing a towel after a brief shower. I lost track of the days and had no idea how long it had been since I ate anything. The only thing I was doing consistently was drinking until I passed out.

I needed to allow housekeeping into my room today because it had started to stink. "What the fuck am I going to put on?" I still had some clothes that I hadn't worn, but the thought of my southern lips kissing the inseam of my jeans wasn't something I wanted to do. I poured my first drink of the day as I contemplated what to do. I damn near dropped my glass on the floor when the door opened.

I panicked. "Greg, what are you doing here?"

He put down the bags he was carrying and looked at me real strange. "Are you fucking kidding?" He was staring at me like I was crazy or something.

"What?" I snapped. I had so many questions to ask, but I was afraid of his answers. I obviously had invited him to come because there was no other logical reason for him to be here. This only made me question what else I'd done that I didn't remember.

"For real, Tilo, I think you need to lay off the booze. I've never seen you act like this before, and you're starting to freak me out." He walked over to the bed and handed me the bags he had brought in. He dumped the underwear on the bed and walked over to the bar and fixed himself a drink.

I stared at the underclothes, afraid to touch them. Evidently I had a few gaps in my memory, but I didn't know how to get them back without admitting to him my confusion. I continued sipping from my glass as if nothing abnormal was happening to me. I was going to follow his lead until I could remember what the fuck we were supposed to be doing.

"Are you going to get dressed?" he demanded. He had a stank attitude and it was starting to piss me off.

"Look, you can check your attitude at the door. I'm not your child."

"I can't fucking tell," he mumbled.

I tried to ignore his comment because I was still trying to understand why he was in New York. Things were so tense in the room, I was waiting for the next shoe to drop. I didn't know whether I should consider Greg to be friend or foe.

"I'm sorry. I'm not myself, but I'm going to get my shit together." I wasn't used to playing this contrite apologetic role, especially with him. I had always been the dominant one in the relationship and overnight it appeared as if this had changed.

Greg's face softened. He put down his glass and came over to me. Pulling me to my feet, he wrapped his arms around me. I felt so comfortable and secure, I started crying.

"Stop crying, baby. I'm here now and I'll make sure nothing else happens to you."

Happen to me? What was he talking about? My mind was spinning and it wasn't from the booze. I forced myself to remember as he stroked my back. I remembered coming back from the store. The people from the hotel were upset because I'd trashed my room. I lifted my head from Greg's shoulder and surveyed the room, but nothing appeared to be out of place except for some suitcases near the door. At the risk of sounding like a complete nut, I inquired about the bags.

"Whose bags are those?"

Greg turned his head and followed my gaze. If he thought I was cuckoo for Cocoa Puffs, it wasn't etched on his face.

"Ours. We can't show up for a cruise without any luggage. What will people think?" He started laughing.

"Yeah, that would draw some curiosity." I chuckled nervously. I didn't remember telling Greg about going on a cruise. "I got to go to the bathroom."

He dropped his arms to his side and I slowly backed away from him. I grabbed some underwear off the bed and my clothes. I stumbled to the toilet and kicked the door shut.

"What the fuck is going on?"

# CHAPTER SIXTY-FOUR

## GREG CARTER

"Fuck," I whispered. I didn't expect to see Tilo on her feet. Before I left, I managed to slip two roofies into her glass, which should have knocked her out for the rest of the night. I picked up her glass and realized why it didn't last. Tilo didn't finish drinking the cocktail I had prepared for her when I showed up at her door unannounced. She was so drunk, she thought she'd invited me and I played along. I'd just about given up on finding her until I went through Rome's phone. When I saw that she'd been texting Rome, I almost lost it. I couldn't believe she would tell him where she was staying and not me, but it also confirmed my fears that she was fucking him too. It was the push that I had been looking for.

Part of me wanted to grab the suitcases and run, but the other part of me knew I had to get rid of Tilo once and for all. Using the little time I had left, I wiped clean all the surfaces I remembered touching. Not that it mattered, because my plan was to leave the country as soon as I'd disposed of Tilo's body. I refreshed our drinks. Since Tilo had made a name for herself with the hotel staff, I didn't want to kill her in the same hotel. I would find somewhere to ditch her after we checked out. For now, I needed her compliance. I opened the door and rolled in the baggage cart I'd hijacked from the hotel lobby and loaded the luggage onto it. She came out of the bathroom as I stowed the last piece.

"We going somewhere?" She looked frightened. If she weren't such a bitch, I might have felt sorry for her, but I didn't. I walked toward her and handed her the drink. "Didn't you tell me you were ready to leave this dump?" I said, laughing. I was winging it and hoped she wouldn't put up a fuss.

"I did?" She drank from her glass, which lowered my anxiety level by a few degrees.

"Uh, yeah. After the way they treated you downstairs, you said you didn't want to spend another dime of your money in this—to use your words—bitch of a dump." She drained her glass and sat back on the bed.

"Yeah, I remember that." She nodded her head, but her eyes still held remnants of doubt.

"I got us a room over in Times Square. We can leave for the boat in a few days."

She started to lie back down on the bed but I couldn't allow that to happen. I put her shoes on. As I pulled her to her feet, I handed her purse to her. She looked at it for a few seconds as if she didn't recognize it but she finally took it. The drug was working faster than I anticipated, but that was probably because she hadn't been eating. She didn't complain as I led her out of the room and into the elevator. When the elevator opened, she had this goofy grin on her face, but she followed me like she knew where she was going.

As we approached the desk, Tilo started for it and I started to panic. "Honey, where are you going?" She was going to mess everything up, and I couldn't afford to let that happen.

"I got to check out." She was rocking on her feet and slurring her words.

My heart was beating double time and I was starting to sweat. "No, you don't. We paid in cash, remember?" I coaxed. I didn't know if she paid in cash or not, I just needed to get her away from the front desk. When I turned back, Tilo was pointing a gun at my head. Instinctively, I reached for mine too. "What the hell are you doing?" I yelled as I tried to think of a plausible reason I could use for her pulling a gun on me.

Her eyes were wide and wild, and I was beginning to believe she was on to me.

"It can't be," she murmured as she swung her head from side to side. Spit flew from the corners of her mouth. It appeared as if she was waging some sort of internal battle.

"Tilo," I hissed. I needed to diffuse this situation or I was going to have to cap the bitch in the lobby and make a run for it before anyone called the police. "Shit," I yelled as the sound of multiple gunshots filled the air. My arm felt like it was on fire. I looked down in disbelief because Tilo's gun wasn't the first one to go off. My finger tightened on the trigger as I was pushed to the floor, I swung my head around to see what was going on as Tilo's bullet caught me in the chest.

Pandemonium had broken loose in the lobby. People were scurrying like roaches when the lights were turned on. Someone kicked the gun from my hand and it slid across the shiny floor. I wanted to go after it, but the pain in my chest wouldn't allow me to.

Tilo was shaking like a leaf and screaming obscenities. Her head was still whipping back and forth like she was trying to escape from an awful dream. "No, why won't you leave me alone?" she shouted. And just as suddenly as her screams started, she stopped. She raised her arm and pointed the gun to her head and pulled the trigger. Her lifeless body dropped to the floor.

# CHAPTER SIXTY-FIVE

## VERÓNICA RAMSEY

"What else do you want from me?"

"Mrs. Ramsey, I know you're tired, but we need to get your story on tape. Can you just repeat for us what you told the officers on the scene?" the officer asked.

I turned to my lawyer, Ricardo, for his advice. I was ready to go home and be with my family. He gave his approval with the nod of his head. I could see my husband, Moses, and Victória outside in the waiting area, and I was eager to join them so we could leave this hotbed of activity behind us.

"I drove to New York to surprise my sister. She'd been having a rough time and we were going to spend some quality time together. However, when I got to the hotel, I saw that woman who killed herself pointing a gun at my sister. I fired a shot to scare the woman, but I accidentally shot the man she was with. Now, can I go?" I was scared about lying to the police, but they were going to have to catch me in the lie before I'd admit to them that I came to New York to kill Tilo.

"Do you have a license to carry a weapon?" the officer asked.

"Yes, I do," I answered confidently. I had my license and the gun belonged to Moses, so I had every right to have it.

"Then we have no further questions at this time. You're free to go."

Relieved, I walked out of the interrogation room a free woman. Greg Carter died of his injuries, but the shot from my gun wasn't the one that killed him. As we left the police station, I felt vindicated. I did what I needed to do to protect my family, and now we were going to go about the business of living.

"Okay, y'all, I'm done with all that drama," I said as I got into the passenger seat. I had some rest I needed to catch up on.

"I'll second that," Victória said as she closed her door.

Moses laughed as he got behind the wheel. "Remind me not to fuck up with either of you ladies. Y'all don't play," he said, laughing.

"Believe that," I said, closing my eyes to the deceptions from the past. Tomorrow would be the beginning, and I was looking forward to it.

"Well, I want to know when the hell did you get to New York? Last I heard, you didn't want to have anything to do with chasing Tilo," Victória said.

"I didn't, but since you two kept running around after her ass, I had to put an end to it somehow. I just want everything back to normal."

"I guess you're right, sis, and thanks for having my back. She could have shot me."

I smiled. "Not on my watch."

"Well, Victória got the bonds, thanks to her friendship with the bellhop. He rolled their luggage out of the way when the bullets got to flying," Moses said.

I could tell he didn't know what to think about this family that he married into, but given time, I was sure he was going to find out.

# ORDER FORM
## URBAN BOOKS, LLC
78 E. Industry Ct
Deer Park, NY 11729

Name: (please print): _____

Address: _____

City/State: _____

Zip: _____

| QTY | TITLES | PRICE |
|-----|--------|-------|
|     |        |       |
|     |        |       |
|     |        |       |
|     |        |       |
|     |        |       |
|     |        |       |
|     |        |       |
|     |        |       |
|     |        |       |
|     |        |       |
|     |        |       |
|     |        |       |

Shipping and handling-add $3.50 for 1st book, then $1.75 for each additional book.

Please send a check payable to:

**Urban Books, LLC**

Please allow 4-6 weeks for delivery

## ORDER FORM
## URBAN BOOKS, LLC
78 E. Industry Ct
Deer Park, NY 11729

Name:(please print):_____

Address:         _____

City/State:      _____

Zip:             _____

| QTY | TITLES | PRICE |
|-----|--------|-------|
| | 16 On The Block | $14.95 |
| | A Girl From Flint | $14.95 |
| | A Pimp's Life | $14.95 |
| | Baltimore Chronicles | $14.95 |
| | Baltimore Chronicles 2 | $14.95 |
| | Betrayal | $14.95 |
| | Black Diamond | $14.95 |
| | Black Diamond 2 | $14.95 |
| | Black Friday | $14.95 |
| | Both Sides Of The Fence | $14.95 |
| | Both Sides Of The Fence 2 | $14.95 |
| | California Connection | $14.95 |

Shipping and handling-add $3.50 for 1$^{st}$ book, then $1.75 for each additional book.

Please send a check payable to:

**Urban Books, LLC**

Please allow 4-6 weeks for delivery

## ORDER FORM
## URBAN BOOKS, LLC
### 78 E. Industry Ct
### Deer Park, NY 11729

Name: (please print): _____

Address: _____

City/State: _____

Zip: _____

| QTY | TITLES | PRICE |
|-----|--------|-------|
| | California Connection 2 | $14.95 |
| | Cheesecake And Teardrops | $14.95 |
| | Congratulations | $14.95 |
| | Crazy In Love | $14.95 |
| | Cyber Case | $14.95 |
| | Denim Diaries | $14.95 |
| | Diary Of A Mad First Lady | $14.95 |
| | Diary Of A Stalker | $14.95 |
| | Diary Of A Street Diva | $14.95 |
| | Diary Of A Young Girl | $14.95 |
| | Dirty Money | $14.95 |
| | Dirty To The Grave | $14.95 |

Shipping and handling-add $3.50 for 1st book, then $1.75 for each additional book.

Please send a check payable to:

**Urban Books, LLC**

Please allow 4-6 weeks for delivery

## ORDER FORM
## URBAN BOOKS, LLC
78 E. Industry Ct
Deer Park, NY 11729

Name: (please print): _____

Address:        _____

City/State:     _____

Zip:            _____

| QTY | TITLES | PRICE |
|-----|--------|-------|
|  | Gunz And Roses | $14.95 |
|  | Happily Ever Now | $14.95 |
|  | Hell Has No Fury | $14.95 |
|  | Hush | $14.95 |
|  | If It Isn't love | $14.95 |
|  | Kiss Kiss Bang Bang | $14.95 |
|  | Last Breath | $14.95 |
|  | Little Black Girl Lost | $14.95 |
|  | Little Black Girl Lost 2 | $14.95 |
|  | Little Black Girl Lost 3 | $14.95 |
|  | Little Black Girl Lost 4 | $14.95 |
|  | Little Black Girl Lost 5 | $14.95 |

Shipping and handling-add $3.50 for 1st book, then $1.75 for each additional book.
Please send a check payable to:
**Urban Books, LLC**
Please allow 4-6 weeks for delivery